Sandra Heaton

Full Circle

a novel

WWW.JKGSPRESS.COM

Full Circle is a work of young adult fiction. All incidents, dialogue, and characters are products of the author's imagination and are not to be construed as real. The settings and persons within them are entirely fictional. They are not intended to depict actual events or to change the entirely fictional nature of the work. In all other respects, any resemblance to persons living or dead is entirely coincidental.

Cover design: Karen Phillips at Phillips Covers
Book design: Maureen Cutajar at Go Published
Editor: Gini Grossenbacher, M.Ed.
Proofreader: Laureen Urey

Publisher's Cataloging-in-Publication Data
Provided by Five Rainbows Cataloging Service
ISBN: 979-8-9891020-2-0
Names: Heaton, Sandra, author.
Title: Full circle / Sandra Heaton.
Description: San Rafael, CA : JGKS Press, 2025.
Identifiers: LCCN 2025917009 (print) | ISBN 979-8-9891020-2-0 (paperback) | ISBN 979-8-9891020-3-7 (ebook)
Subjects: LCSH: Women--Fiction. | Grief--Fiction. | Panic attacks--Fiction. | Healing--Fiction. |
Mental health--Fiction. | BISAC: FICTION / Women. | FICTION / Family Life / General. | FICTION / Death, Grief, Bereavement.
Classification: LCC PS3608.F85 2025 (print) | LCC PS3608.F85 (ebook) | DDC 813/.6--dc23.

*To my husband, Paul, for his unwavering
support, encouragement and patience
on the long journey to publication.*

Cast of Characters

Banks, Dr. Margaret Josephine – Sarah's trauma counselor.

Burrows, Evie – a woman Sarah meets on the bus ride to Lawson, who becomes her guardian. (Steven, Mavis and Joy – Evie's children)

Crane, Chaplain Tom – an old friend of Augusta who supports Sarah through difficult times.

Grant, Lorraine (Gram) – Sarah's Grandmother, Robert Grant's widow and Emmett's mother.

Hanson, Augusta – Lorraine's estranged sister, Sarah's aunt, and Uriah and Marge Hanson's

McCann, Maggie – Sarah's life-long friend, Liam and Marcie McCann's daughter.

McCleary, Ian – longtime attorney to the Grant family.

Morris, Dr. Braydon – Augusta's neurologist.

Morrison, Sarah Blount – the main character portrayed at the age of forty-two and later as teenage Sarah Grant. Daughter of Emmett and Katherine (Langly) Grant

Morton, Mrs. – a school social worker

Rogers, Rev. Mark and his wife Ramona – Gram's minister and his wife who deal with Sarah's difficulties.

Wentworth, Marian – Augusta Hanson's family attorney.

One

Sarah stands on center stage, a perfect position to survey the renovated 150-year-old Barton Messy Theater in Sausalito. Honored as one of many successful former residents, she accepted an invitation to speak during its four-day grand reopening.

Her chest tightens as she gazes at the empty auditorium. Her mind strays to worst-case scenarios—a trip and fall on stage, her notes are the wrong ones, no one attends. She clutches her purse to her chest and adjusts the garment bag over her right shoulder.

"Sarah, you have earned the right to be here. You will do fine. Breathe."

She turns her attention to happier times spent with her parents seated on plush red velvet seats in Row E, Center. She remembered her first concert as a five-year-old. She wore patent leather shoes that dangled over the edge of her chair. Her mother wore a long shimmering formal of satin and silk. Her father dressed in a tuxedo. She embraced the magic of *Swan Lake*, the thrill of Rachmaninov, and the tension created in children's theater productions.

A lump forms in her throat as she recalls the last time they sat in Row E. She had just turned thirteen. She wore diamond studs in each ear, a birthday present from her parents, and her first formal dress, teal satin with pink rosebud trim at the scooped neck, her feet in matching satin heels rested on the floor, so grown up. Her eyes fill with tears.

She redirects her thoughts overhead. Restored paintings of nineteenth-century country life grace the ornate ceiling—fox hunts, picnics, and children at play. Three enormous crystal chandeliers hang over the audience, sparkling and tinkling as air vents work to cool the auditorium.

"May I help you?" A petite blonde woman dressed in jeans, tee shirt, and a pale blue hoodie hurries toward center stage, a two-way radio crackles in her hand. "I'm the stage manager for this event."

Sarah guesses the woman is mid-twenties. "I'm Sarah Blount Morrison, scheduled to speak at ten o'clock."

"How did you get inside so early? Do you have an ID?"

"I have a driver's license, a written invitation to speak, and a name tag, and I came through an unlocked back door." Sarah unzips the outside pocket of her shoulder bag and hands proof of her identity to the stage manager.

"Thank you." She inspects the contents of the envelope and returns them to Sarah. "Follow me, Mrs. Morrison. We have dressing rooms set aside for our speakers."

"I came early to see the renovations. I attended many performances here as a child. The seats were red velvet then, not blue like now. Other than that, it looks about the same."

"We're very proud of the work done here. The ceiling paintings took the longest. Only a few artists do that kind of intense work perched on scaffolding. It made me dizzy just watching them."

"Those paintings inspired many stories each time I saw them." Sarah wonders if some of those tales still exist somewhere. Maybe in Gram's trunk.

"Have you eaten? A buffet is set up in the conference room across from your dressing room. Please help yourself." The stage manager reaches for Sarah's garment bag. "Let me help you with that. There are towels and a small shower in your room. My name is Bernadette Wilson."

At the mention of food, Sarah realizes she hasn't eaten since she fixed a piece of peanut butter toast at four o'clock this morning in a Barstow hotel. She wishes she still owned the Sausalito house. She could stay there. *I never should have allowed Donald to take it in the divorce.* She clenches her jaw.

"Here we are. This is your space." Bernadette opens the door to a pale green room filled with light and mirrors. A large crystal vase of lilacs sits on the dressing counter, along with a carafe of water and some extra toiletries.

"You can see them setting up the buffet from your open door. There should be coffee by now. I'll leave you to settle in. You'll be notified fifteen minutes before you go on stage. There is an intercom on the wall if you need anything."

"Thank you, Bernadette."

"I'll hang your bag in the closet."

As soon as the stage manager closes the dressing room door, Sarah stretches out on an upholstered lounge chair in the corner of the room. According to her phone, it's eight a.m., plenty of time for a nap. She sets the alarm for nine and closes her eyes.

✺✺✺✺✺✺✺✺

An insistent clang disrupts Sarah's nap. "What is that awful noise?" It takes her a minute to identify the sound. She sits up, grabs her phone, turns off the alarm, and checks the time. Nine o'clock. Another day. Another speech.

She directs her attention to a knock on her door. "Hello, Mrs. Morrison?" The voice doesn't sound like Bernadette.

Sarah glances in a mirror and attempts to untangle her hair before she opens the door to a middle-aged woman dressed in a black and white Chanel suit, a cheery, if forced, smile on her perfectly made-up face.

"I'm Mrs. Murdock, the woman who will introduce you this morning." Her eyes take in Sarah's appearance. Her smile disappears. She wheels in a glass-topped cart with a coffee pot, a slice of quiche on a white china plate, and a bowl of strawberries. "I hear you came early. Thought you might need something to eat."

"Thank you. How thoughtful."

"The stage manager will let you know fifteen minutes before you need to be standing in the wings. I'll leave you to get ready." Mrs. Murdock exits with a frown and a sigh.

Sarah chuckles. "Ah, a critic already."

She studies her appearance in the mirror. "Ugh." Dark circles under bloodshot eyes, sallow skin, and deep lines on her forehead reveal the stress she has been under. Her life has begun to unravel. Nightmares from years ago return to haunt her sleep. Some nights, to avoid sleep, she attempts to work on her new book with little success.

Hungry, she devours the quiche and strawberries, gulps a cup of coffee, and heads for the shower. A clock on the wall tells her she has no time to wash her hair.

Wrapped in a towel, she positions herself in front of the mirror. "Oh boy, Sarah, there may not be enough makeup to cover the flaws." She unzips a large rectangular case and removes jars, brushes, eye pencils, eyelashes, an array of lipsticks, eye shadows, and blushes. She uses a headband to push her hair back from her face.

"Here goes." She slathers on a layer of moisturizer, then a dense concoction of rose beige base and a darker shade of contour powder, followed by a light spray of water to set her artwork. Last, eyeliner, eyebrows and eyelashes. She studies her face in the mirror, wipes her hands with cleansing towels, and removes the headband. A bun at the base of her neck is the best she can do with her hair today. She twists her hair and secures it with hair pins. Today is the last day she needs to wear this public mask. Her calendar is empty at last.

The dressing room clock shows nine-thirty. Sarah unzips her garment bag and dresses. A full-length mirror near the door reflects a powerful, confident woman, back erect, shoulders relaxed, head held high, eyes alert. Her stylist was right about the teal-blue sheath and jacket, perfect for her titian hair and fair complexion. At six feet tall, she could be intimidating, an asset she prized.

At nine-forty-five, Bernadette knocks, opens the dressing room door, and stands aside. "Ready? There's a monitor in the wings if you want to check out the audience."

"Sounds intimidating." Sarah follows the young woman.

"Guess it can be. It's up to you."

Sarah can't resist. The monitor reveals a packed audience waiting for advice on how to live and win in life. Her body grows heavy with exhaustion. Can she fake it one more time? Can she stand in front of her fifth audience this week and pretend she knows the answers?

"Mrs. Morrison?" The stage manager startles her back to the present. "It's time."

Mrs. Murdock approaches the podium, then turns to her and mouths, "Ready?"

Sarah nods.

The sound system seems loud tonight. Her stomach knots. Anxiety skitters up her spine and throbs at the base of her neck.

"It is my pleasure to introduce Sarah Blount Morrison, our speaker for this morning. She is well-known to most of you as an expert on personal power for women. She is a life coach with three published books and a fourth in progress. Sarah, we are so pleased to have you here." The director turns to her and applauds.

Shoulders squared, Sarah strides to the podium. The rapid rise of nausea in her throat threatens to undermine her efforts to keep it under control. Her heart races. Her body shakes. Her knees weaken. *Oh, no!* A silent scream fills her with panic. *Not again. Not now.* She attempts to control her panic.

"Uh, uh, umm." Nausea erupts in her mouth. She grasps the podium to regain composure. Her fingers ache from the intensity of her grip. The stage lights become hotter and brighter. She wishes someone would turn them down. She shivers. Perspiration trickles down her back. The room spins and bucks like an out-of-control roller coaster.

There is no turning back now, no control to be had. The sweat on her forehead feels cold to the touch. A sharp pain and tightness grip her chest.

"Call 9-1-1!" someone shouts.

Sarah descends into a soft white haze. Hands catch her and ease her to the floor. The pain in her chest becomes unbearable. She gasps, desperate for a deep breath.

Sirens scream louder, closer, and stop.

Strong arms lift her onto a soft, flat surface. A blanket warms her body. Less exposed, she relaxes then tenses again as straps tighten around her legs and waist. Someone squeezes her hand. "It's okay, ma'am. The straps are for your safety." The soft female voice soothes Sarah's fear of confinement and loss of control.

The gurney tilts and bumps as it slides into the ambulance. Doors slam and the engine roars. The surface under her vibrates, followed by a sudden lurch. As the sirens scream to life, they remind her where she is—helpless, confined to the narrow surface beneath her, surrounded by strangers and machines monitoring, examining, and assessing. An oxygen mask is placed over her nose and mouth. For a moment, she is certain she will suffocate.

A male voice distracts her thoughts. "Can you hear me?"

She turns to face the dark-haired man in a blue uniform. "Where—are—we going?"

"Saint Anne's Hospital. Can you tell me your name, ma'am?"

"Sarah Blount Morrison." He types her answer on a tablet.

"Are you in pain?"

"Not now. I'm much better. No need to fuss." He taps the screen several times.

"That's our job, Mrs. Morrison, to fuss. Were you in pain?"

"Yes, terrible pain." She senses a cold stethoscope on her bare chest.

"Your heartbeat is a little fast."

The familiar squeeze of a pressure cuff wrapped around her left arm threatens to cut off all circulation.

"Where was the pain?"

"Right now, it's in my left arm."

The EMT chuckles. "Right. That will be over soon. What about during your attack?"

"In the center of my chest and my jaw." She closes her eyes.

"Thanks. That's enough for now."

A second male voice behind her head replaces the first. "Steady, now. Breathe slowly in, out. That's it."

Slow, deep breaths and her rescuers' gentle soothing voices calm her.

"Is there anyone we need to call?"

"No." Sarah sighs, closes her eyes, and surrenders to the kind, disembodied utterances of the team working above her and the steady cadence of sirens speeding toward uncertainty.

Two

Sarah awakens to the sound of monitors and the pungent odor of antiseptic. Except for a slight headache, her body and mind float in a white haze, free of pain and worry. Her hand seems heavy. She raises it to find a tube attached to a port taped to the back of her hand. She attempts to force her unfocused mind to make sense of a voice, authoritative and brisk. "Mrs. Morrison—suffering exhaustion and stress. For a while—home—a couple of days—as long as it takes—sedatives. She—panic attacks before?"

Then a female voice, familiar but difficult to place. "Yes, several that I know of. Take—best place—see to it that she does. Stay with her a few days."

Sarah opens her eyes. The lights hurt; it's challenging to focus. The woman's gestures seem familiar. Someone she knew long ago talked with her hands in constant motion. Who was that?

"Thank you, doctor." The woman approaches her bed. She leans close enough to reveal her features.

"Maggie? Is that you?" Sarah's mouth is dry. Her tongue feels numb.

"Can you hear me?" Maggie strokes her hand.

"Mag—geeee? Why am I—here? How—I get here?"

"You performed a bit of drama last night. Quite unexpected."

"Maggie. I thought after so long, our friendship was over. How did you know I was here?"

"Apparently, I am still your emergency contact. The hospital found my name in some old medical records and called me at my beach house last night."

"What happened? I can't remember anything after walking on stage." Sarah's voice is childlike, small, and thin.

"They told me you opened your mouth to speak and collapsed."

The beep from her heart monitor accelerates. "Did I say anything?"

"As far as I know, you didn't say anything." Maggie strokes her forehead. "Calm down, now. Let's stop the screaming of that monitor."

Maggie continues, "Everything will be fine. Your doctor suggests absolute rest. I suggested your family's beach house. Does that sound like a plan to you?"

"Wonderful. Haven't been there in years."

"I'm at my parent's beach house indefinitely, only a five-minute walk away. Doctor wants someone to keep an eye on you. I volunteered. Twenty years ago, you and I parted on bad terms. Can we forgive each other and start over?"

"I would love to start over. I've missed you." Sarah squeezes Maggie's hand and grins. Warmth radiates throughout her body. She has a family again.

"You need to stay a night or two for observation. As soon as your doctor releases you, we can be on our way. I expect you to be ready. Can't carry you, my friend. You'll have to find the strength to get out of bed and into my car."

"Home," Sarah whispers. Tears fill her eyes.

"Right. Sand, sea, waves, salt air. *Mm*, wonderful for your health." Maggie gives her a bear hug before she leaves the room.

Sarah's monitor returns to a steady, hypnotic rhythm.

After two days of medical tests and mental health assessments, a petite, dark-haired nurse enters her room holding a clipboard. "I'm here to sign you out and deliver your aftercare instructions, Mrs. Morrison—no work, no stressful surroundings, no large groups of people. Get lots of exercise, good nutrition, and sea air. Wish I could go with you, Mrs. Morrison. Sounds like heaven." The nurse hands Sarah the clipboard.

"Doesn't it, though?" She glances at the sheaf of papers that will govern her life for the near future.

"Sign the first two sheets to acknowledge you received the instructions, and the last two signatures are your discharge. Doctor will call you at home tomorrow afternoon to check on you."

Sarah signs her discharge papers with a flourish.

Maggie arrives a few minutes later. "Are you ready to go? It's two o'clock. I want to have you at the beach by dinner time."

The exact opposite of Sarah, Maggie's short, stocky frame, curly red hair, and boundless energy fill the hospital room. Her ability to tell the truth no matter the consequences and her no-nonsense attitude gained Sarah's trust years ago. Why has she let twenty years pass without forgiveness and reconnection?

"Ready or not, we're going to the beach, Missy. Brought you some comfortable clothes for the trip." Maggie unzips a brown duffle bag, pulls out a bright red sweat suit, and shakes the pieces out as if displaying them for sale.

"That's my Maggie. Everything done with a flair, even the color of the sweat suit. What would I do without you?"

"*Hmm.* We'll see if you still feel that way in a few days. I have orders from your doctors to make you rest. I plan to be relentless, so beware."

⁕⁕⁕⁕⁕⁕

Most of the three-hour trip to White Sands Beach passes in silence. Sarah dozes, soothed by the hum of the engine. In a dream, she hears her mother's voice. "You sleep now. We'll be at the beach soon. Do you want your blanket?"

She wakes with a start. Confused, she glances at the back seat to answer her mother's question. No one is there. She bites her lower lip. Just a dream. Must be the sedatives.

She drifts off again. "Honey, we're going to the beach." She hears the voice of her grandmother. "You can ride the Ferris wheel and the merry-go-round at the boardwalk. Then, we'll get ice cream and a bag of saltwater taffy."

"Gram?" No. She died in a car accident when I was fourteen. "If only I had stopped you, made you stay, hadn't been so selfish, maybe." Her throat aches. She grasps both elbows and bends at the waist.

"What did you say?" Maggie glances at her. "Are you in pain, nauseous?"

"Nothing. Just a dream." Sarah leans her head against the car window and dozes off again.

This time, her dream takes her to a wetland path. Her precious Great Egret flies overhead, its long, graceful neck folded for flight, its huge wings stretched wide to catch the thermal currents. Often, when she was young and life was too hard to bear, a Great Egret would appear. It might be in flight or fishing in tall wetland grasses. She believed the bird was a sign of God's love, a message from her parents that they still watched over her. She still believed in God, then.

Gravel crunching under the tires wakes her. The clock on the dashboard reads four o'clock, the exact time Maggie predicted they would arrive. Sarah lowers her window. Salty air and crashing waves on the sand below the bluffs revive her. Maggie rolls to a stop in front of the cottage and cuts the engine.

Sarah exits the car and leans against it. Her childhood vacation home seems smaller than she remembers. A white picket fence surrounds a pale blue single-story cottage. At every window, white wooden flower boxes overflow with yellow, purple, and red blossoms. The cottage, at least, had not changed much. The property manager took good care of it.

Memories of summer fill her mind—the family would unload their station wagon, packed with luggage, grocery bags, beach toys, and several boxes of books and games.

Afternoons, Gram and Mom lounged under beach umbrellas with unread books that had piled up for months, waiting for their precious time at the beach. Sarah, her nose white with zinc to protect her from sunburn, happily built sandcastles or enclosures for small creatures she captured in the tide pools.

"Are you going to stand there all day?" Maggie chuckles as she raises her hatchback to remove one of the many suitcases jammed in the trunk.

"Just enjoying some special memories. I remember the day we met. You stood, pail in hand, watching me build my castles."

"We built many a fortress together." Maggie joins Sarah. "Once we built a village with saved popsicle sticks, rocks, and seaweed."

"What a beauty that was. I remember us gathering a collection of our many miniature plastic and rubber figures to populate our town." Sarah laughs.

"At night, your dad built a fire on the beach. We roasted packages of marshmallows; your grandmother told marvelous ghost stories. You and I lay in the sand gazing at the stars while your dad played guitar like a pro." Maggie sighs. "Good times. Seems awfully quiet, now, doesn't it?"

"Yeah. It's good you are back at your parent's house so close to me." Sarah touches Maggie's arm.

"Welcome home." Maggie returns to the trunk, removes two cloth grocery bags, opens the front gate, and ascends four steps to the front porch landing.

Sarah follows and observes her long-time friend. Her curly red hair is streaked with gray, her gait is slow, and she has a noticeable limp. When she last saw her, Maggie and her new husband were racing to board a plane headed for their honeymoon.

Maggie places the bags on the porch, reaches under a wooden planter by the front door, and holds up a key. "Ah, there it is, as promised." She unlocks and opens the front door. "Smells a little musty, but a good airing will fix that. Bring in the grocery bags, will you? I need to sit for a minute." She sinks into an easy chair with a groan. "Not as young and thin anymore."

Sarah carries the grocery bags into the kitchen and fills two glasses of water from the sink. "Here. Rest for a minute." She hands Maggie a glass and sets her own on a side table.

"Time to open the windows." Light and sea air fill the room as Sarah draws back the curtains. She slides open each of the dozen casement windows and the patio door. "Love this view, ocean waves, dunes, tall grasses, and our beach, a short stroll from here."

"Oh, yeah. I was so happy to return to our family cottage permanently when I retired. Been back for six months. Already a new person." Maggie empties her water glass.

Sarah turns to observe the living room. It looks much the same as she remembered. Gram painted the wood paneling white their last summer at the cabin. She loved do-it-yourself projects. She helped for a while, but DIY never thrilled her. So many of the old board games remained on the shelves by the stone fireplace her great-grandfather built when he inherited the property.

"Just thinking about my great-grandfather who braved the trip from St. Louis on a wagon train to start over here. Grateful to have inherited a place to live, he rebuilt this house as a wedding gift for his wife, then sent her a ticket on the new cross-country railway. One brave lady."

"They all were. I doubt I would do the same. Too soft."

"Same here."

Maggie eases out of her chair. "Enough rest. I'm going to unpack the car, then fix us something to eat. You relax."

"I'll be out on the porch swing. Let me know if you need me."

"Will do." Maggie hastens down the front steps, headed to the car.

Sarah leans back and surrenders to the motion of the porch swing and the sound of the waves. She feels peace for the first time in weeks. There was nothing but laughter and love with her family in this house. She and her mother read *The Lion, the Witch and the Wardrobe*, her favorite, together on this swing while Gram sat next to them, busy with her intricate needlework.

Maggie groans as she drags two large suitcases over the uneven surface of the front walk.

"Let me help you with that." Sarah steps to the edge of the porch. "Where did all that luggage come from?"

"Your apartment. Just a few essentials I thought you could use." Maggie grunts as she lifts one of the suitcases up the steps. "You sit. I'll be fine." The second case takes a little longer to haul. "There. The worst part is done." She stops to catch her breath, then rolls both cases over the threshold. "That's as far as I go. The rest of the work is yours."

"Will do it later. Right now, I need to go to the bathroom and rest on the porch swing."

"Good. We have plenty of time to settle in." Maggie returns to the car.

When Sarah joins her, Maggie is seated on the wrought iron bench by the front door, fanning herself. "Whew. Glad that's over."

Sarah hears what sounds like an animal whining inside the cottage.

Maggie says, "Okay, boy. I'm coming." A tornado of fur rushes out the front door, claws clicking across the wooden porch.

"This is Chester, my undisciplined companion. Will take him for dog training soon."

"Chester," Sarah squeals. "Come here, you sweet thing." Maggie's yellow lab skids sideways on the slick surface of the porch. She widens her arms to embrace him. Chester leaps on the porch swing to cover her face with slobbery kisses.

"Oh, dear." Maggie attempts to grab Chester's collar with little success. "I forgot to tell you that Chester and I moved into the guest room for a few days—doctor's orders. I'll take him home if he's a bother. I thought it would be easier to keep an eye on you if I didn't have to go back and forth twice a day to care for him."

"I love dogs. I feel better already. Haven't been kissed with such enthusiasm for years."

"I'll leave you two to get acquainted while I fix lunch." Chester jumps off the porch swing and stretches out at Sarah's feet.

"Okay, boy. I see you have things under control." Maggie enters the cottage and closes the front door. Chester snorts, lowers his head to his paws, and closes his eyes.

Sarah lies full length on the porch swing, pulls a turquoise afghan up to her chin, and focuses on the rhythm of the waves. "I'm exhausted."

Three

Sarah begins her first full day in three weeks without the ever-present Maggie and Chester. Anticipation of freedom and doubt about her ability to be alone swirl in her mind as she tightens the belt of her green flannel robe. The only sound in the cottage is the slap of her slippers against her heels as she heads to the kitchen. Coffee is her priority. She fills the two-cup drip coffee maker on the counter with water, measures two tablespoons of her favorite hazelnut grounds into the filter, hits the *on* button, and grabs a blueberry muffin from the glass container on the counter.

As she waits for the coffee to brew, she sits and revels in the comfort of a heavy fog that clings to the many paned windows of the breakfast nook. It gives her the sense she is wrapped in cotton, safe, protected, hidden from the outside world and its demands, judgments, and cruelty.

She pours a cup of coffee and inhales its rich, hazelnut aroma. There is no conversation this morning, no rambunctious Chester to greet her. She only has her thoughts to keep her company while Maggie and Chester are in Monterey on business.

Sarah returns to her wooden breakfast table worn by years of cleaning, stained from hours of meal preparation, and marred by sewing and quilting projects. Years of poker, hours of board games, and competitive chess tournaments filled the family's quiet nights and stormy days in this room.

She senses the presence of her ancestors, who shared stories and laughter here for five generations. Gram taught her how to cook in this kitchen, from how to boil eggs when she could barely reach the stove to creating meals from favorite family recipes. Patient as ever, Gram modeled the best techniques, proudly served Sarah's sagging cakes and burned scrambled eggs to friends and relatives who vacationed in the summer. She remembers the day Gram served her final failure. "Precious Sarah, you are competent at many things, but cooking is not one of them. You set a beautiful table, which is very important. Maybe potlucks and easy recipes are your future."

Sarah was relieved. She hated cooking. In fact, she hated failing at anything. "Good idea, Gram. Can I go surfing instead?"

Tears fill her eyes. "I miss you, Gram," she whispers. "I wish—" Her throat aches. "Stop!" she shouts. The hospital counselor had admonished her, "Live in the present. Love what you have. What you had is a precious memory. Take time to heal." She struggles with that advice every day. Her battle to move forward seems impossible.

"Time to get moving. Wallowing never fixes a problem." Sarah hurries to her bedroom and dresses in sweatpants, a hoodie, and sturdy shoes. She heads out the back door and down the well-worn path to the beach.

Thick and damp, the fog shrouds all but a few feet of visibility. Other walkers appear through the mist. They nod, say good morning, then disappear as if they never existed. Her life had been like that—loss . . . gain . . . loss.

The rhythm of the waves muffled by the dense air provides a calming effect. Five miles down the coast, the foghorn at Dempsy Point groans a 149-decibel warning of a dangerous shoreline. Strands of slippery kelp, left by high tide, litter the beach, a hazard for those not paying attention.

Cold and wet, Sarah retraces her steps. Clouds thin to reveal wet sand covered in increased seaweed deposits and high waves moving further inland each time they break. She realizes it's high tide and dangerous if you get caught in it. Next time, she needs to check the tide tables before going out in the fog, a lesson she learned at one time and forgot.

Once, when she was six years old, she wandered away from Gram and got stranded in the tide pools. Relentless waves knocked her down on jagged rocks and left her gasping for air. Even now, her heart begins to race from the memory.

Sarah trudges uphill over the dunes. Each step requires enormous effort. Was the outing too ambitious? Her goal, the back porch of her cottage, seems farther away than she expected. Her legs grow heavy. She stumbles, lands on her hands and knees, and raises her head to gauge the distance to her house—two more dunes, the concrete patio, up the steps to the back door and inside. *But first, rest.* She rolls on her back with a sigh. *Breathe.* Wispy cirrus clouds float overhead, so delicate. With the fog gone, she notices her skin redden in the sun. She must find shade before her fair skin burns.

"Come on, Sarah. One last push. Think of it as a race to the finish line." She rises, grits her teeth, takes three deep breaths, and plods forward. Every muscle in her body aches from the strain—she is much weaker than she thought.

Breathless, she reaches the back door, opens it, steps inside the laundry room, and leans over the dryer to catch her breath. She tosses her soaked clothing in the washer, grabs a towel from a laundry basket perched on a stool, and heads to her room for a hot shower.

"Ahh." Hot water eases the tension in her shoulders and neck, erases the chill from her body, and encases her in the steamed glass of the shower stall. "I could stay here forever."

Spray from the shower head begins to cool. The limited capacity water heater that the Ocean Commission requires eliminates long, hot showers to save the planet. Sighing, she turns the handle off, steps out of the cubicle onto a plush green bathmat, and scrunches her toes in its soft fibers. She shrugs into the green flannel robe she left on her bed earlier and revels in its warmth as she ties the belt. She longs to accomplish something while Maggie is gone. Once she returns, it's back to *doctor said to rest*. Tiresome.

First, some hot tea, food, and a nap. Sarah heads for the kitchen and opens the refrigerator. Leftover stew from last night and French bread—*perfect*. Hungry, she downs the warmed stew and several slices of bread and finishes the meal on the porch swing with a double chocolate brownie and a glass of milk.

A possible project churns in her mind. How about going through those boxes in the shed? Funny how that sounds like a good idea. Heavy with exhaustion from the morning walk and hot shower, she changes her mind about the shed. She eases into the soft cushions and snuggles under the lavender-infused afghan Gram made for her years ago. A warm breeze and the rhythm of the waves lull her to sleep.

"We need to talk." Maggie stomps up the front steps, Chester close behind.

Sarah glances at her watch. "Maggie, it's six o'clock. I expected you to return this afternoon. What kept you?" She stands and folds the afghan.

"So sorry I didn't call. Got hung up talking to a contractor." Maggie plops on the wrought iron bench. Chester paces between the two women, wagging his tail and nuzzling each woman in turn.

"No problem. Four hours ago, I lay down on the swing and slept the whole time."

"Are you all right?"

"I feel great." Sarah joins Maggie on the bench.

"That contractor in town has a hole in his schedule for tomorrow. Been trying to get repairs done before winter. Need to do it now. I told him to come at seven a.m., so if you feel you can manage it after dinner, I'd like to move back to my house to supervise his work."

"Absolutely. You've spent more than enough of your time caring for me. If I need anything, I'll call. You're only a five-minute walk away." After the trouble during her walk on the beach this morning, Sarah wonders if she is ready to be alone.

"Okay." Maggie pats her hand and heads inside. "I brought take out from Lou Chou's. I'll heat it up."

"Come on, boy. I'll feed you your favorite dog food." Chester follows Sarah to the back porch, his tail wagging.

After dinner, she helps Maggie load her Jeep. Chester climbs into the passenger seat, focused on the front window, ready for another ride. "I'll come back for the rest."

The two women hug. Maggie hurries to the driver's side, hops in, starts the engine, and speeds out of the driveway.

Sarah waves goodbye until the Jeep rounds the corner of the property and disappears. A sudden sense of loneliness in the quiet surprises her. This morning, she relished the time alone; now, there is no timeline for Maggie's return.

She finds it hard to settle on any activity. In another week, she sees her doctor for clearance to drive. Maggie and a friend drove into Sausalito last week to pick up Sarah's car from the theater parking facility. Maybe she could ease the car out of the weathered clapboard garage and risk a drive into town tomorrow. Tempting. No television to watch. Maybe a book and an early night.

Tomorrow, the shed. It might keep her occupied enough to get used to the empty cottage.

Four

Refreshed by a sound sleep, Sarah anticipates the job ahead as she eats her breakfast oatmeal. There is no fog this morning to block her beach view. Ten years had passed since Gram's attorney moved her belongings from the Sausalito storage facility to the family beach house shed. She planned to deal with the contents, but time, a full schedule, and a need to procrastinate delayed the task.

"I have nothing but time now." Sarah swallows the last of her morning coffee. "May as well tackle the shed."

The shed is padlocked, and she needs to find a key. The junk drawer in the kitchen holds the family's miscellaneous screws, pens, unidentified parts, and broken items in need of repair. Her fascination with the junk drawer kept her busy as a toddler while Mom and Gram prepared meals. The drawer seems an excellent place to start the search.

To her surprise, the labeled key lies on top of the junk pile. She places it in the palm of her hand and closes her fingers around it as she weighs the risks and possibilities of what she might discover behind the shed doors—treasured memories or more heartbreak. She hopes to discover Gram's trunk, the only item she truly cares about. An inventory of the packed items isn't in the documents marked *Lorraine Grant*, which the law office mailed to her. She's more likely to uncover spiders, mice, and more bugs than she cares to think about. She wrinkles her nose.

"Be brave, Sarah. Get dressed." She pulls out a pair of old jeans and a baggy sweatshirt from the back of her bedroom closet, then tugs on a pair of Wellies over her jeans to block little beasties from running up her pants legs. On her way through the laundry room, she notices a can of lubricant on a storage shelf and shoves it into her jacket pocket. Old locks, sea air, and rust could be an issue.

She steps out the back door and hesitates for a moment on the patio. Tucked behind the garage, the shed looms larger than she remembered. She begins to doubt the wisdom of her decision. Her heartbeat increases. Her breathing becomes shallow. She longs to flee to the front porch swing and spend the day with a good book, followed by a long nap. Maggie would approve of that plan, but she isn't here.

"Come on, Sarah. Don't be a wimp." She grits her teeth and strides to the shed.

The lock, rusted from exposure to the salt air, refuses to budge. She saturates the lock and door hinges with lubricant. The lock gives way with great effort. The doors of the shed slant inward, level with the ground. This offers no handhold to force them open.

Sarah grasps the upper edge of one warped door. It scrapes and grinds a few inches. Determined to access the shed, she yanks the wood with both hands and all her strength. A plank tears away from the main door. "Ouch!" A splinter about one inch long protrudes from the soft tissue under her thumb. She attempts to pull it out with her teeth but retrieves only the tip. Impatient to finish what she started, she decides splinter removal can wait.

She sits on a weathered wooden bench across from the shed to stare at her enemy and figure out how to defeat it. "All right, doors, show me your weakness. You're old and falling apart." She chuckles at the irony. Here she is, confined to quarters for falling in public. "Okay. Point taken. We're pretty much equal, but I'll find a way."

Sarah takes a closer look at the shed. "Ahh, I see your weakness now. Your hinges are rusty." Held by a few loose nails, a screwdriver and a hammer could bring them down.

She returns to the junk drawer in the kitchen and rifles through old owner's manuals, take-out menus, and piles of broken tools to find a wooden-handled screwdriver and an iron wedge strong enough to use as a hammer. "Gotcha', doors."

It takes her the better part of an hour to loosen the hinges on one door and create a space large enough to enter the shed. As the door collapses to the ground, she hears the skittering of little unseen creatures the daylight has disturbed.

She flips a switch to her right. Black beetles, silverfish, and multiple crawling creatures skitter across the dusty floor to disappear in and under moldy, decayed cardboard boxes stacked three high and three deep. Sarah covers her nose as the reek of mold and animal feces assaults her senses. With the door dismantled, the shed's contents remain exposed to the air. She groans. She thought this job would be tolerable, but she needs to finish the project if she wants to save any items stacked inside. Too late to procrastinate once again.

Three hours into the job, Sarah realizes there is no treasure, only garbage bags of trash and a towering stack of soggy cardboard. A box of clothing and bed linens designated for charity waits on a table to be laundered. She decides to search inside one more stack of boxes before dinner. As she moves the last box, she notices the edge of Gram's trunk. With great effort, she drags her find out of the shed. She and Gram spent hours reviewing the contents when she was little.

She slides her hand over the dusty lid, loosens the worn leather straps, and tries the brass lock. *Click.* She opens the lid. Metal hinges groan from lack of use and age. Inside, sealed in plastic, lies the obituary from the back page of her parents' funeral program. Two beloved people stare back at her, both young and vital, with the back of her mother's hand facing toward the camera to display her engagement ring. Gram loved this picture and its promise for the future. Sarah tucks it in the pocket of her jacket.

She was thirteen the last time she held the obituary in her hands. Her heart races. Her head spins. She drops to her knees beside the trunk. *Breathe in—breathe out.* Her childhood therapist's mantra repeats in her brain. Her heartbeat slows. She removes the obituary from the trunk. Under it lies a stack of notebooks labeled *Sarah Grant* filled with stories, musings, and her fight to heal. Her fingers slide across her name. Tenderness and compassion for the struggles written on those pages bring her to tears. Sarah closes the trunk and drags it across the lawn to the patio. She removes the notebooks and carries them to her desk in the living room. *Time to rest.*

Five

Sarah brews a cup of Gram's "happy tea," strong black tea, whiskey, lemon, and honey. She adds a slice of lemon cake and slides into a chair at the kitchen table. She places the obituary on the table in front of her. The tea warms her as memories flood her thoughts. They seem as vivid as the day they happened.

Two days after her thirteenth birthday, Gram came to stay with her in Sausalito while Mom and Dad attended a three-day conference in New York City. She promised to behave for Gram. They promised to bring her something special when they returned. They blew her a kiss as they got into a taxi.

Sarah and Gram had a wonderful time that day. They went shopping. Gram bought a paisley silk scarf. Sarah chose a set of enamel bracelets painted with floral designs. High Tea at the elegant Fairmont Hotel served delectable pastries, bonbons, and custards. They rode the cable car to Ghirardelli Square for an afternoon chocolate sundae and had clam chowder in bread bowls for dinner at Fisherman's Wharf. She had no time to miss her parents.

The next day was quite different. The doorbell chimed. Life was about to change.

"Get that, will you, Sarah? I'm fixing lunch," Gram called.

"Sure." She peered through the beveled glass of the front door. Distorted figures on the other side spoke to each other in voices too low for her to understand. "Gram, there are two large men at the door. Should I still open it?"

Gram, a towel in her hands, hurried to the door. "Good thinking. Probably a couple of missionaries." Gram opened the door. "Yes, may I help you?"

"Are you Mrs. Lorraine Grant?" Strangers wearing black suits and solemn faces stood on the porch. They carried briefcases and wore badges with their names and, in small print, Bandore Airlines.

"Yes, I'm Lorraine Grant. Why are you here?" Gram swayed and reached for the door frame.

"May we come in? I'm afraid we have some bad news."

The conversation in the living room made no sense to Sarah.

"Missed connection—different flight. An unexpected storm—a crash. No survivors."

Sarah could not comprehend the meaning. Gram's face paled. Her eyes welled with tears. "No, no, no. It can't be." Gram rocked back and forth.

⚜

For days, Sarah rushed to the front door every time a car drove up to the house, convinced her parents were finally home.

A week later, she rode in the back seat of a black limousine with Gram. She ran her hands over the soft leather, leaned her head against the window, and closed her eyes. She did not remember much about that day except the cloying, sickly sweet fragrance of lilies that filled the church and two closed caskets side by side. So many speeches. So many tears.

People dressed in black arrived at the house afterward with food and sad faces. They murmured words of consolation and hugged her so tight she could barely breathe.

"Poor, poor dear." A tall, buxom woman thrust Sarah's face between her breasts and swayed side to side. She exuded an overwhelming floral fragrance. Sarah had to fight to keep her toes on the floor. She wondered who this woman was and how to escape her grasp.

"So young to lose your parents. Oh my. *Tsk, tsk.*" A gray-haired man bent to her level and touched her cheek. His breath smelled of fish and alcohol. His watery blue eyes searched her own. He seemed to be waiting for some response. "You must be heartbroken. My parents died when I was young, also. Terrible thing."

Exasperated, Sarah twisted away from him, tired of all the people and their incessant need to touch her without her permission. What was their problem? *Rude. Creepy.*

"They're not lost," she shouted, her fists clenched. Conversation stopped. Everyone in the room stared at her. "They're just late."

Gram hurried to her granddaughter's side. "Is there a problem here?"

"So sorry, Lorraine. Apparently, I overstepped with Sarah." The gray-haired man touched Gram's hand and disappeared into the crowd.

"When will Mom and Dad be back? They never miss a party. These people are all wrong." Frantic for Gram's confirmation that all was well, Sarah fought to control her panic. She found it hard to breathe.

"I wish that were true, precious girl." Gram sighed, held her close, kissed the top of her head, and turned to greet more guests.

In time, Sarah realized her words of denial were useless. No one seemed to believe her. She was certain she was right, so she trudged upstairs to sit in her bedroom window seat and focused on the street below.

Six

It took Sarah a couple of weeks to understand that her life had changed forever. Gram remained with her. The move to Gram's house would happen during summer break. She attended her normal load of classes but did no homework. After-school activities and social time with friends ceased.

At home, she withdrew to her room and refused to eat. Friends called and texted, but she never returned their messages. Soon, they stopped trying. Gram bought journals, hoping that Sarah might write thoughts and feelings about her loss. She stored them in a box under her bed.

One afternoon, Sarah, bored with material she already knew, cut classes and headed to a nearby park to enjoy the rare sunny day and feed the birds. When the sun set, she wandered through the shops around the park, then found an arcade filled with other teenagers, where she played for several hours and returned home long after dark.

A police car parked in front of her house told her she might be in trouble. Gram had panicked again. Who cared? Tired of the constant adult monitoring of her behavior, she longed to escape. What if she kept going, avoided the house, and changed her name and appearance? Where would she go? Good question.

Sarah, shoulders back and chin raised, strode up the walk and opened the front door, ready to meet her fate. She hesitated in the entryway for a moment to overhear the conversation in the living room.

"I'm at my wit's end." Gram's high-pitched voice quivered.

Sarah closed the door and peered around the corner to see who was in the room. Perched on the edge of her leather easy chair, Gram leaned forward, hands palms up, as if pleading with her visitors.

A dark-haired lady in a gray pantsuit sat on the couch across from Gram. The lady held a clipboard. "The school called us concerned about Sarah's attendance and failing grades." She held her pen over her notebook, poised to write as Gram answered her questions.

The lady spied her in the hallway. "Oh, you must be Sarah. So glad to see you're safe." The woman's honeyed tone nauseated her. She'd heard it before from adults faking concern. She moved to the archway and stood in full view.

Gram's head whipped around. "Where have you been?" Her voice was stern. "Are you okay?" She stood and held her at arm's length, inspected her from head to toe, and attempted to hug her.

Sarah stiffened. "Who are these people?" She jerked her hand toward the two visitors.

The police officer stood and hooked his thumbs in his belt. "We are here at the request of your principal to investigate your home situation. My name is Officer Harris, and this is Mrs. Morton from Child Protective Services. She has spoken with your grandmother. Now, she needs to hear from you."

"Leave us alone," Sarah snapped. "I just needed to go for a walk. Can't I go for a walk anymore without someone going crazy?" Her eyes narrowed, and her jaw ached from the pressure of her clenched teeth. "I'm as fine as I can be for an orphan." She stalked out of the room, ran up the stairs, slammed her door, and turned the lock. She longed to be a normal person, not a research subject to be poked, prodded, questioned, and analyzed. She lay on her bed, curled her body in a fetal position, pounded her pillow, and growled in frustration.

A week later, concerned about her granddaughter's behavior, Gram sold her home in San Francisco and moved to Sausalito. "There's no need for you to move out of your home, change schools, or leave friends, Sarah." They sat at the breakfast table, intent on watching the hummingbird feeder outside the bay window. "At least that won't change."

"That's something, I guess," Sarah mumbled as she picked at a plate of bacon and scrambled eggs. "Will Mrs. Morton and the police be back to spy on us?"

"They're not spying on us. They're just doing their job." Gram lifted her chin to gain eye contact. "All they knew was that I was taking care of you and not doing a great job of it, apparently, with you cutting school and neglecting your class work."

"Mom and Dad and I had plans, dreams. What's going to happen to them now?" She stared at her uneaten breakfast. "We had plans to go to Japan for my fourteenth birthday to see the gardens. They promised to get the tickets when they came back from the conference. That won't happen now. Mrs. Morton might decide to send me to a foster home with my behavior problems. With a black mark on my record, I'll never get into Stanford like Mom wanted."

Gram slid her chair closer to Sarah and squeezed her granddaughter's hand. "Those plans and dreams can still happen, only in a different way." She lifted her chin and peered into her eyes. "We can work on the future together. I won't allow you to be placed in a foster home. I'm your next of kin. That counts for a lot. We need to work together to turn things around."

"If only . . ."

"I know, dear. I miss them, too."

A tear fell on the placemat, then another, and another. Gram and Sarah held each other as their sobs and groans of buried sorrow spilled over until they were both exhausted.

Gram agreed to drive Sarah to and from school for six weeks and check in with her teachers and the principal on her progress.

"Why do you have to come to school? It's embarrassing?" She whined, complained, and sighed until she realized her attempts to get her way were useless. Despite her parents' wishes, Gram had always let her have her way, spoiled her, and let her do and have what she wanted.

"That's what grandparents do: spoil their grandchildren," Gram would say when Mom and Dad protested. Sarah loved that about Gram. She missed that relationship. Instead, Gram had turned into a parent.

Sarah was grounded, had no phone, no TV in her room, and no weekends with friends until her grades improved. Life began a slow, steady return to calm and routine.

Mrs. Morton returned for a six-week follow-up visit in the same gray pantsuit, her face makeup free, her hair slicked back in a bun knotted at the back of her neck. She reminded Sarah of movie characters who ran orphanages or women's prisons.

Gram and Sarah sat on the edge of the couch, their backs straight and hands folded in their laps. Mrs. Morton's eyes seemed to bore inside Sarah's as if to read her mind; she fought the urge to run. She wondered if the woman ever changed her appearance. Did she ever smile?

Mrs. Morton placed her briefcase on her lap, opened the flap, and withdrew some papers. "Mrs. Grant, I'm happy to report that Sarah's school is pleased to see her regular attendance. The stability you created for her has had a positive effect."

"So happy to hear it." Gram's response was stilted, her lips pinched in a smile.

"Sarah may need some counseling to help her with trauma. The school will support you in any way you need. We all realize that both of you have much to deal with now."

"Thank you for your understanding." This time, there was no expression on Gram's face. A vein in her neck bulged; her jaw clenched.

"I will phone once a week to see how things are progressing. Here is the report." Mrs. Morton handed Gram a manila folder with "Case Number 1799" written on the tab. "You'll find all the details of our investigation in the folder."

Sarah hated that she had been reduced to a number. She hated the school. She hated Mrs. Morton's endless robotic speech. She hated her situation. Her fingers ached from the intense grip needed to avoid lashing out.

"Do either of you have any questions or concerns?"

Gram and Sarah glanced at each other with raised eyebrows, then looked at Mrs. Morton and shook their heads.

Gram took a deep breath. "Would you care for some coffee?"

"No, thank you. I must run. More appointments today." Mrs. Morton closed her briefcase and headed toward the front door. "I will mail any future reports to you after each phone call."

"We appreciate your concern." Gram sighed and followed Mrs. Morton.

Sarah watched them go; their words were garbled as they said their goodbyes.

She shrugged her shoulders, strolled into the kitchen, and opened several cupboards in search of something appetizing. With all this food, there should be something good to eat. She opened the refrigerator. "Yes! There's cake. I forgot there's cake."

She grabbed the leftover chocolate cake and headed for the kitchen table. With her hand full of the first cake slice, she gobbled it down as if she hadn't eaten for days. Her fingers and mouth were sticky from the rich frosting; she grabbed a second slice.

"Leave some for me." Gram sat down and took a piece. "This is the perfect medicine for any problem." Soon, frosting and cake crumbs covered Gram's fingers and lips.

"So, what did you think of the meeting?" Gram wiped her mouth and fingers with a napkin.

"Now what? We've both been good girls. Do we get a prize or something?"

"The prize, my dear granddaughter, is you get to stay in your house, I get to stay with you until the end of the semester, and we may never have to see Mrs. Morton again."

"Did you notice that I am a number on a file tab and not a person?"

"I did. Sometimes, it pays to accept the system to get what you want. It's not easy, but—"

"Yeah. I hate it."

"Me, too. Let's have more cake." Gram placed another slice on Sarah's napkin.

"I see people on the news fighting the system."

"Sometimes it's necessary, and those people usually have others fighting with them. In this case, we have nothing to gain and no real reason to shake things up. This system exists to protect children, though it may have flaws. Patience is the best choice."

"If you say so, Gram."

"I do say so, but as long as there is chocolate, all is well." Gram chuckled and popped a piece of cake in her mouth.

They finished the cake, laughing and chatting like two delighted children.

"Oh, I can't eat anymore." Sarah placed her hands on her stomach and groaned.

"I agree. Come help me unpack the rest of my boxes. They seem endless."

"Oh yeah, for sure. Can't wait to see the old trunk. Haven't been through that since I was little."

All the boxes were stacked on the upstairs landing. "Where's the trunk? I can't see it." Sarah peered around and over the boxes without success.

"They put it in the truck last, so it came in first. We have the incentive to wade through at least one stack of boxes to reach the prize." Gram and Sarah moved several boxes and began unpacking. "Take any clothing to your parent's bedroom. Just put it on the bed. I'll sort it later."

"Where're you gonna sleep tonight if the bed in Mom and Dad's room is covered with clothes?"

Gram stopped and turned toward her. "No. I won't use their room. I can't right now. I'll stay where I am, in the guest bedroom."

Sarah nodded. She couldn't go into her parent's room either. Too many memories of them remained on the walls, in the closet, and on the dresser. There was no need yet to go through their belongings. She had her room, and Gram had the guest room.

After several hours of work, the landing was strewn with piles of packing materials and stacks of items organized according to their destination. Gram stood with her hands on her lower back and leaned backward. "Oh, that feels good. I need to take a break. We've been at this for three hours. The trunk is back there somewhere. We'll find it. Let's make popcorn and watch a movie on TV. There's a rerun of *Old Yeller* tonight. I'll pop the corn."

"I'm in. Should we clean up first?"

"Nah, I vote we break another rule and leave the mess for later. After all, we already ate almost half a cake with our hands. How much worse can it get?"

They sprinted down the stairs, Gram to the kitchen, and Sarah to the family room.

"I've seen *Old Yeller* at least half a dozen times and still cry every time." Gram carried a large bowl of popcorn to the couch and settled next to Sarah. "Saw it the first time with your dad when he was a little boy. He begged to see it over and over, and then, when you were small, he wanted to share it with you."

"*Old Yeller* was the first chapter book Dad bought me. He and Mom used to read it to me before bed; then, I read it again on my own. I miss them so much," Sarah whispered.

"Me, too. You were so precious to them. They tried to have you, their little April baby, for five years." Sarah laid her head on Gram's lap. "You were a handful, so smart, so active. Once your tiny legs were strong enough, you dashed out of their sight at every opportunity." Gram grinned.

Sarah's eyes grew heavy.

"You were always hungry to learn and explore your world. You were a joy, my dear, and . . ." Gram's soothing voice faded.

Sarah's eyes closed.

Seven

When Sarah woke, she lay on the family room couch covered with a blanket. The house was dark except for a light in the downstairs bathroom. She strained to hear familiar sounds of life. A digital clock on the television blinked 04:00. *Where was Gram?* Panicked, she tossed the blanket aside and dashed upstairs. "Gram. Where are you? Don't leave me. What will happen to me if you leave? I'll have no family left. How does anyone live without a family?"

Gram rushed into the hall. "I'm right here. I won't leave you. It's okay." She knelt, arms open to receive her panicked granddaughter. "You're okay. It's okay. Take a deep breath." Gram rocked her and hummed a lullaby in her ear. The two of them, arms around each other, returned to Sarah's room. "Stay with me," Sarah said.

"Of course." Gram lay next to her granddaughter, rubbed her back, and continued to hum the lullaby Sarah's mother used to sing.

Gram made an appointment the next day with a counselor known for her successful work with grieving children. She had to convince herself and Sarah that the sessions might be helpful. "Let's give it a try. The sessions could convince the school and Mrs. Morton that you should stay here in Sausalito with me as your guardian."

Sarah had nothing to say on the twenty-minute ride to the counselor's office. She rode with arms crossed and body slumped as low as possible in her seat. "This better be good," she growled.

"It'll be fine. You'll see." Gram turned into the parking garage adjacent to a three-story office building. "Here we are." She parked and hurried to the entrance lobby. Sarah slid out of the passenger seat and strolled several steps behind.

"Margaret Josephine Banks. *Hmm.*" Gram ran her fingers over the long list of tenants. "Let's see. *Uh-huh*, there she is. Third floor, room 325. Come on, Sarah. Give it a try. If you dislike her, we'll find someone else."

"Right." She decided to reduce her communication to one-word responses today. She had no intention of cooperating with this foolishness Gram and the counselor had concocted behind her back and no intention of talking, liking, or bonding with this lady.

Room 325 was behind double doors at the end of a long hallway. The waiting room resembled a children's daycare center. In a room to the left, a media area was set up with computers, video games, and a small arcade. On the right, an area was filled with blocks, interlocking bricks, coloring books, a small playhouse, and books arranged on multi-colored shelves. The space hummed with the sounds of young children and attentive parents.

"May I help you?" chirped the plump white-haired lady behind the reception counter, the perfect complement to the jolly-painted cartoon characters dancing across the front of the reception desk.

Sarah scoffed at symbols better suited to young children—more reason to resist.

"We have an appointment at 10:00 for Sarah Grant?" Gram drummed her fingers on the reception counter.

The lady handed Gram a clipboard. "Please fill these papers out and return them to me when you're finished. I'll let Doctor know you are here."

"Let me out of here, now," Sarah mumbled as she crossed her arms and rolled her eyes.

"Yes, well, uh. Please be seated if you'd prefer." The receptionist raised her eyebrows and then returned to her computer screen.

Sarah slumped in an overstuffed armchair, crossed her arms, and kept her eyes riveted to the flowered carpet beneath her feet.

"Sarah Grant?" A tall, slender woman surveyed the waiting room, directed her attention to her, and smiled. "You must be Sarah." Wearing a calf-length gauze skirt, the woman seemed to float across the room. For a moment, Sarah thought of a fairy tale princess. Her long, wavy blonde hair added the perfect touch to this saccharine office. All she needed was a wand.

The counselor's office was more comfortable than magical. The woman's desk reminded Sarah of the heavy oak desk in her father's office. The sight of it softened her mood with memories of the good times she spent playing on his office floor or, when she was older, reading her school essays for his reaction to her ideas. An entire wall of windows filled the room with light.

"Please make yourselves comfortable." Dr. Banks motioned to a dark brown leather couch. "May I get you some tea or coffee? I also have lemonade if that suits either of you better." Her voice was throaty, deep, and soft.

"We're fine, thank you." Gram sat on the edge of the couch, hands clasped, shoulders erect. Sarah dropped full force on the couch, slid to the edge, and rested her feet on the coffee table in front of them.

Dr. Banks sat in a wingback chair facing the couch, crossed her legs, and consulted the clipboard with Gram's papers attached.

"Let's see. Both parents were doctors. Your mother studied the criminal mind at Johns Hopkins, and your father was a professor of behavioral science at Stanford. Very impressive. So, it makes sense that you read by age three, were curious about everything, successful in school, and a talented writer." Dr. Banks paused and leaned forward, both forearms resting on her thighs. "Tell me about school and your writing."

"What?" She resented having to return to the present.

"Tell me about school and your writing."

Sarah had nothing to say. She felt empty and did not want to feel. She wanted to stay in her thoughts, and this stranger wished to bring her back to the present, where her pain lived. She stared at Dr. Banks. Who would blink first? She determined it would be the nosy lady across from her. She needed to win. She needed this woman to leave her alone and tell Gram there would be no further need for appointments.

Sarah heard Gram and Dr. Banks speaking. They seemed so far away that she could not understand what they said.

Dr. Banks touched Sarah's hand. "Our session is over for today. I will see you next week. Please bring your journals with you. I want to see them."

Sarah strode out of the room while Gram stayed behind. The open office door allowed her to listen to the conversation.

"Don't worry, Mrs. Grant. Her behavior is normal for a teenager. I do want to see those journals. Next week, Sarah and I will talk alone, but I want you nearby in case we need you."

"Thank you, Dr. Banks. She used to be such a happy child."

"Losing parents so young and so suddenly changes life dramatically. Are you getting help from someone? The loss of a child is a horrible shock as well."

"My minister is working with me. It is hard to keep your faith when something so senseless happens. He's doing his best, but I'm not sure about a loving God yet."

"I agree, but faith can pull you through eventually. I'm so, so sorry for your loss." Dr. Banks opened her arms. "I'm a hugger. Is that all right with you?"

"You bet. I can use all the hugs I can get."

Sarah raced out of the office with tears in her eyes and exited the building. She sat on a bench near the entrance and swiped through her phone. For the first time, she realized Gram was grieving, maybe more than she was. She saw herself as a thoughtless, selfish human being undeserving of Gram's love. And—Gram might leave her, too.

"There you are. Are you alright?" Gram sat beside her and attempted to put her arm around her shoulder. Sarah did not look at Gram.

"Are we going now?" She turned off her phone.

"How about some lunch first?" Gram moved toward the parking garage. Sarah sauntered behind her.

Sarah was even more sullen during her next session with Dr. Banks. Instead of handing the doctor her journals, she dropped them on the coffee table, rattling the candy dish in the center.

"Thank you for bringing these." Dr. Banks leafed through the first one, then the second and third.

"These journals are empty."

"Obviously." Sarah clenched her jaw, crossed her arms, and stared at the floor.

"Look at me." The counselor's tone was stern.

She glared at the woman sitting across from her. Her head throbbed. She spat, "I don't care what you want! I don't have to do what anyone says, lady—especially you." She grabbed one of the notebooks and threw it across the room. It sailed end over end, pages rustling, until it reached its mark. *Bam!*

A lamp hit the hardwood floor. Its oval base broke from the impact. The light bulb exploded, and the lampshade rolled in circles on the hardwood floor. A second notebook slammed into a mirror hung near the waiting room door. It crashed to the floor. Shards scattered in every direction.

The door to the waiting room flew open, "What's going on in here?"

Sarah whipped around and hurled a third notebook toward her grandmother's face. Gram ducked as the notebook flew past her ear.

"Stop this." Gram's body filled the doorway, hands on her hips, a frown on her face.

The shock of Gram's stern voice and sudden appearance drained Sarah of any ability to continue her rampage. Her breathing became shallow. She sank into the overstuffed couch and tried with all the strength she had left to stop the tears about to escape. *Done for. The last straw. Gram would leave her now. What a stupid thing to do.*

Dr. Banks held up her hand. "Almost finished. Sarah will be with you soon."

Gram hesitated, returned to the waiting room, and shut the door.

"Are you finished, Sarah? Do you feel better? You could have hurt someone with that tantrum."

Her eyes darted around the room. "Did I do all that?"

"Yes, you have quite the pitching arm. Your aim was remarkable." Dr. Banks sat beside her. "Take a deep breath, now. You're all right. This can't happen again. You frightened all of us, including the clients in the waiting room. You need to apologize; I expect it to be a written apology. Do you understand?"

A uniformed officer entered the room. "Everything all right in here, Dr. Banks? Your receptionist called security." He turned to Sarah. "This young lady needs to leave. Should I call the police?"

"Thanks for coming, Stan. This time, I'll give her a warning. If it happens again, well—"

"Okay. As long as you're all right." The officer glared at Sarah and left.

"Where is Gram? Did she leave? She was angry with me, I could tell. She can't leave me, too."

"Your grandmother loves you. She's worried about you."

Sarah began to cry, then sobbed so deeply that she had trouble catching her breath. "My parents loved me too . . . and they left. They will never come back. What if Gram leaves me, too?"

Dr. Banks touched her arm. "It hurts to lose someone you love, doesn't it?"

"Why did God take them away from me? Gram says God is love. How is that love?"

"I wish I had an answer for you on that question. Right now, you have your grandmother and me. I bet you have friends who care about you."

"I guess."

"I imagine you do. Let's begin the work needed to get you better. I want you to try something with me. Take a deep breath, hold it for three counts, and then let it out. Take another one and do the same, then take one more and see if you don't feel a little better. Okay, breathe in. Hold one, two, three. Breathe out, one, two, three. Now, two more."

Exhausted, Sarah leaned against the back of the couch.

"You're all right," Dr. Banks patted her arm. "Can your grandmother come in now?" She nodded.

Gram said, "Oh, my, I'm so sorry. Look at your office. This isn't like Sarah at all. Of course, I'll pay for the damage."

"All is well. I have insurance. Anger is one of the stages of grief that Sarah and I will work through together with your help."

Dr. Banks handed a folder to Gram. "Here are some worksheets and resources for you, Mrs. Grant. Have her complete the first two before our next meeting. My receptionist has a list of excellent books about grief that you may find helpful. I will prescribe her a mild sedative for the next couple of days, and then all she needs is kindness and patience. She will write in her journals when she is ready."

"Sarah, Mrs. Mallory, my receptionist, will take you to the bathroom where you can wash your face and then stay with you in the waiting room while I talk to your grandmother."

Mrs. Mallory offered her chocolate cookies and milk as they waited.

"No thanks." Sarah's attention focused on the counselor's closed door. She paced the room, and her heart pounded. She wondered what they were up to behind the door.

"I need to go to the bathroom." She hurried out of the room before Mrs. Mallory could respond. She locked the door and sat on the toilet, her head between her legs. No one could see her, judge her, or tell her what to do in this private space.

"Sarah, are you okay in there?" Mrs. Mallory inquired. "Your grandmother is waiting for you in reception."

"Coming." She opened the bathroom door and found Gram and Dr. Banks chatting like old friends.

"So glad you can help us. I've been so worried about Sarah."

"See you next week." Dr. Banks and Gram shook hands.

"Let's go." Gram put her arm around Sarah's shoulder.

On the ride home, Gram and Sarah stared straight ahead for several minutes before Sarah broke the silence. "Why did I do that to Dr. Banks's office? Mom and Dad would be so upset that I broke stuff and spoke that way to an adult. I failed them." Her shame sat in her belly and tightened her throat as she struggled to hold back her tears. "I'm not the perfect child they adored. What will I do . . . if you leave me, too?" She found it hard to breathe. Gram pulled to the side of the road. Sarah struggled to catch her breath.

"What is it?" Gram leaned toward the stricken girl. "Stop! Please stop. You'll make yourself sick."

Sarah couldn't stop. She gasped and shook and sobbed, aware of nothing but the hysteria that rolled over her. She felt arms around her. "My precious girl. It's going to be okay. You're going to be okay. Oh, Lord, please help us." Gram held her tight and stroked her hair.

"I'm so sorry. I said terrible things. That was not me. You know it was not me. Please don't leave me. I'll be good." Her voice was small and thin.

"I won't leave you. Let's stick together and help each other heal from the shock of losing your mom and dad. Right now, let's head home. I think we could both use some sleep."

Sarah lay her head in Gram's lap. *Breathe in—breathe out.*

Eight

"Happy Birthday to you. Happy Birthday to you. Happy Birthday, dear Sarah. Happy Birthday to you." Gram's cheerful voice woke her.

She rolled over, lifted her sleep mask, and peered at Gram. "Go away."

Gram stood next to Sarah's bed holding a tray in her hands. "I made breakfast in bed for you, all your favorites." Gram set the tray on the bedside table and perched on the edge of the bed, a giant mug of steaming coffee between her hands.

"Ooh, peanut butter and banana pancakes with whipped cream and pineapple." Sarah picked up her fork and took a bite. "*Mm*, heaven."

"What would you like to do today, my precious granddaughter?"

"Dr. Banks suggested we take a trip to Golden Gate Park to do some of the things Mom and Dad and I used to do together, sort of like spending my fourteenth birthday with them. She thought that might be good for me since we've made so much progress in the last eight months."

"Okay. Let's give it a go. Get dressed, and I'll meet you at the car." Gram grabbed the breakfast tray and strode out of the room.

Sarah threw her covers back and jumped out of bed. Today would be her first time in San Francisco since her parents' death. As she dressed, she had second thoughts about the adventure. What if she couldn't do this? Would all her progress be wiped out if she failed? Was it too soon? Beads of sweat formed on her forehead. She straightened her shoulders and recited the mantra Dr. Banks taught her. "Breathe in—breathe out." With each repetition, her shoulders relaxed. She drew a comb through her tousled hair. "You got this, baby."

She bounced down the first few steps, finished with a slide down the banister, and opened the front door. Gram waited for her in the car. Sarah stood on the front porch, glanced at her grandmother, locked the front door, slid into the passenger seat, and fastened her seatbelt. "Ready?"

"Ready." Gram turned on the ignition and backed out of the driveway. She glanced at Sarah, then turned her attention to the road. The trip from Sausalito to San Francisco took them across the Golden Gate Bridge. The dense fog gave Sarah the feeling they were floating on a cloud broken by monoliths of orange steel that supported the span.

When she was younger, the ride across the bridge stirred her imagination. She created tales of magical lands floating beyond gates of solid gold where dragons flew over fairy castles, and knights saved terrified villagers and won the hearts of beautiful maidens. Her parents paid close attention as she shared her stories with them.

"Good one, sweetheart." Mom clapped her hands.

Dad smiled. "One day, you could be famous, and I will brag endlessly about how I was present for every tale you spun."

She resolved that she would make her father's predictions come true.

Sarah's heartbeat quickened as she and Gram left the bridge, turned left on Veterans Boulevard, and entered the Presidio. Its manicured grounds and well-preserved buildings with red-tiled roofs and Spanish architecture harkened back to a time when California belonged to Spain.

"Gram, did you know the Presidio was built in 1776 as Spain's northernmost outpost of colonial power in the New World? It's one of the oldest outposts in the country."

"I did know that. We're almost in sight of our destination. Going to be a beautiful day."

Sarah took a deep breath to calm herself. Wisps of fog floated above a canopy of Monterey cypress, pine, and eucalyptus trees; coastal redwoods and giant sequoias enhanced a clear view of Golden Gate Park. Neighborhoods of stately old homes and businesses, some in obvious need of repair or a coat of paint, faced the park as they had for decades. The park itself was much the same as it had always been, with its forests of trees and shrubs that provided a taste of nature amid bustling city life.

Gram turned left on John F. Kennedy Drive past the boat house at Stowe Lake.

"We spent many Sundays on Stowe Lake. Dad rented paddleboats, and Mom bought sandwiches and Hershey bars to take along. Mom and Dad worked the pedals until my legs were long enough to reach them and take over. It was hard work, but I felt so grown up."

"Sounds like fun. Your grandpa and I so enjoyed paddleboat rides when your father was little. One day, you can introduce your children to the family tradition."

Parking near the California Academy of Sciences challenged the most patient visitors. Rows of cars with license plates from all over the country lined the slanted parking slots. Gram spied a vacant spot. "Your first birthday gift, a parking place. Are you ready to begin our adventure?"

"You bet." Sarah led the way along a path bordered by red and pink rhododendrons in full bloom. "Mom and Dad loved to go to the aquarium. We spent hours there. So peaceful." She sighed. Her pace slowed as the familiar academy buildings came into view. She hesitated at the foot of the steps to the California Academy of Sciences. Maybe this trip was a bad idea. Dr. Banks could be wrong about her progress. Her body grew heavy. She placed one foot on the first step. Her chest tightened. If she continued and had a panic attack inside the building in front of all the visitors, that might set her back instead of forward in her healing. She withdrew her foot from the step. She'd lost her courage.

"You okay, sweetheart?" Gram placed her hand on Sarah's waist.

"Let's sit a minute." Sarah pointed to an iron bench across the street. "I'm not sure about this. There might be too many painful memories."

They sat on the bench shoulder to shoulder. "Tell me about what you remember." Gram took Sarah's hand in hers.

"We spent hours staring at giant blue tubes filled with species of sea life from all over the world. The Philippine coral reefs were my favorite. Hundreds of neon blue, bright yellow, and hot pink fish drifted among varied corals, purple anemones, and orange spotted starfish. Do you think it will be the same inside?"

"Are you ready to see for yourself?" Gram rose from the bench and offered her hand.

"I think so." Sarah put her hand in Gram's, and they headed toward the academy entrance.

Sarah stared in awe at the enormous T-rex skeleton that dominated the entrance hall. "Whoa! He is headed right towards us."

Gram studied the skeleton. "Would hate to encounter that creature. The aquarium is to the left, as I recall."

"Right. Come on." Sarah grasped Gram's hand and led the way.

The aquarium was as astonishing as Sarah remembered. In contrast to the darkened exhibit hall, the twenty-five-foot Philippine Coral Reef tank glowed deep blue, shot through with threads of sunlight from overhead.

Spectators crowded the elevated observation platform facing the tank as divers connected to the surface by thin, flexible tubes fed the marine life. Schools of many-colored fish circled, gulped the tiny grains, and then darted away to continue their journey through the colorful coral forest. Giant clams nestled near the bottom of the reefs dazzled with brilliant hues. The display was as captivating as Sarah remembered. What would it be like to find herself inside, touch the fish, swim beside them, and join in their choreographed dance? Her body swayed.

"Sarah, you're leaning too far over the railing." Sarah winced as Gram grabbed her arm.

"Where did your mind go? I called to you several times."

"Dreaming about dancing with the fish."

"It looked as if you were headed that way—time to eat. The Japanese Tea Garden is close. It's a perfect day to enjoy the gardens."

"No." Sarah refused to move. "Not today. I can't. Mom, Dad, and I drank tea there whenever we visited the park. We discussed plans to go to Japan for my fourteenth birthday. We should be in Japan right now." Her jaw tensed. She stamped her foot on the cobblestone walk. Heat flushed through her body. "It's not fair. They should be here," Sarah yelled. She plopped on a wrought iron bench and hugged her body with both arms.

"Oh, my sweet girl." Gram eased on the bench next to Sarah and held her close. They cried together. "Yes, they should be here, and yes, you should be in Japan, but—let's go home." Gram broke their embrace. "Enough for today. We'll pick up burgers and fries on the way."

"And a chocolate milkshake?" Sarah struggled to get up. Her legs seemed weak.

Gram, her eyes red and swollen, wiped her cheeks and helped her granddaughter stand. "You bet, sweetheart. Whatever we need, we will get."

Gram and Sarah sat silently around the kitchen table an hour and a half later, munching on their burgers and fries. Sarah signaled the end of her chocolate milkshake with a long, noisy draw on her straw. She giggled, "Mom used to hate that noise. 'Sarah, stop that, it's annoying to hear.' Then she would draw her lips in a thin line, shake her head, and sigh. I would do one more slurp to get her flustered."

"Your father used to enjoy bugging me that way, too. He wouldn't stop 'til I left the room exasperated." Gram chuckled at the memory.

"What else do you remember of Mom and Dad? I don't know all that much about them."

"They were both intelligent and witty. Emmett called home so excited when he met your mother at a conference. He told us he would not be home for a few more days and said, 'Mom, do you believe in love at first sight? It's very unscientific, but I think I found it.' And he had."

"They always told me they knew they would get married the first time they saw each other. Is that how people know?" Sarah asked.

"Sometimes, though I believe it's better to get to know each other and become friends." Gram cleared her throat.

"Mom and Dad were best friends. They had so much fun together."

"Your grandpa and I loved your mom on sight. She made our boy happy. I remember they laughed a lot. The four of us, your mom, dad, grandpa, and I, enjoyed many memorable times together."

"I have an idea. Do you feel up to going through my old trunk? Lots of memories of them in there." Gram touched Sarah's hand as she leaned closer to her granddaughter. "Let's clean up and go upstairs. I need to remember them, too."

Sarah hesitated after their morning and her breakdown at the California Academy of Sciences. Maybe some other time would be better, but Gram seemed anxious to open the trunk. She probably needed to remember her time with Mom and Dad, too. Sarah scolded herself for being so selfish. Gram was grieving as much as she was right now. Maybe sharing Gram's happy times with Mom and Dad would be helpful. Her heart rate increased. She wanted to refuse. She wanted to run. She doubted the contents of the trunk would ease her pain.

Sarah followed her grandmother to the upstairs landing. The last few steps brought her within eye level of the goal. Gram moved boxes out of the way.

"Let's look inside. Some of your things are in here, too." Gram held the key to the trunk in her hand. She frowned. "Are you okay? You look a little pale."

"I'm good. Let's see what's inside." As Sarah reached the landing, nausea caused her to lean against the railing for a moment. Gram, focused on the trunk, didn't appear to notice her distress.

Nine

The steamer trunk had leather straps, a brass lock, and a rounded lid, the kind made at the turn of the twentieth century. Stiffened metal hinges groaned as Gram lifted the lid. "This hasn't been opened for years. I'm glad we're doing this together."

On top, sealed in plastic, lay her parents' obituary. It included a picture of them, their arms around each other, still young and vital, joy evident in their broad smiles. Sarah sank to her knees, and her hands shook as she studied the image.

"That was their engagement picture. They managed to find jobs as professors of psychology and behavioral studies at UCSF. Their long-distance romance ended, and their marriage began." Gram handed the article to Sarah, who sat cross-legged on the floor, tracing the sealed edges of short lives encased forever.

"There isn't much about them here, at least nothing about who they were or how they lived."

"That's the way they wanted it. The basics." Gram removed an album Sarah had never seen before.

"Here is a picture of Emmett on the day he received his doctorate in psychology from Stanford." An eight-by-eleven photograph filled the whole page. Gram and Gramps stood on either side of

Sarah's black-robed father with broad grins. She read *DR. ROBERT GRANT* beneath the photograph.

A photo of a young woman in a white coat, a stethoscope draped around her neck, filled the opposite page. She was flanked by her equally proud parents. Sarah remembered them from family pictures grouped on the mantel of the fireplace. She had never met her mother's parents because they died a month before her birth. *Katherine Langly, M.D., Johns Hopkins University*, appeared on a business card attached to the bottom of the page.

"Eventually, your mother specialized in psychiatric research on the study of criminal minds. She wanted to know why people turned to crime and what could be done to change their behavior. I saved her published papers for you to read someday. She was well-respected in her field."

Uncertain how to respond, Sarah closed the album. "What else is in there, Gram?"

Gram pulled out a stack of notebooks. "Look at these old collections of stories you wrote. This book has your first pieces before you learned to write."

Sarah opened the notebook. "This is unreadable. Why did you save this?"

"It reminds me of when you wrote stories in your inventive scrawl, then read them to all of us. We listened and applauded every rambling word. You must have been three or four years old then."

"That must be why you gave me the notebooks after Mom and Dad died. I haven't been able to write anything since. I seem to have no stories or thoughts in me anymore."

"Oh, I think you do, my dear. You had a talent once. I believe it's still in you. It will come. Dr. Banks says you will be able to write when you're ready."

"Look. There is something stuck here in a side pocket." Sara pulled out what looked like an old photograph folded in half. "Who are these two little girls, Gram? It says, 'Lorraine and Augusta, sisters forever' on the back."

Gram's smile disappeared. A vein on the side of her neck began to pulse, something that happened when she was upset. "Never mind about that. Don't ask so many questions. You don't need to know the story. We don't talk about Augusta."

"Who's *we*?" Her mother never mentioned other family. "Why?"

"The family." Gram took the picture from Sarah and tossed it in the discard pile.

"Did you have a sister? Is she still alive?" Sarah longed to know the story behind Gram's refusal to talk about Augusta.

"Yes, and I don't know." Gram closed the trunk and stood. "Let's do something else."

Sarah remained on the floor, her eyes fixed on the carpet. Regret twisted in her stomach. "I'm sorry. I didn't mean to upset you."

"I know. You didn't upset me; the memories did."

Sarah realized that Gram had grieved losses in the past and in the present. They both needed each other to heal.

Ten

"Hey, Mags." Sarah waved at the computer image of her best friend. It was more like being with her in person than with the tiny smartphone image. She got to use her dad's walnut-paneled office, where she had spent so much time. The wood, aged to light honey, glowed in the sunlight from a wall of casement windows that looked out on a stone patio with a two-tiered fountain in the center.

"Sarah! Surfs up." Maggie's freckled face and wiry red hair filled the screen. "You comin' down this summer? Been tryin' out a new board. Saved my old one for you just in case."

"Great. Wax it up. I'm on my way. We're leaving Sunday after church. Glad school's out. They've been watchin' me every day in case I flip out again. Makes me want to do something weird just to mess with them." Sarah rolled her eyes.

"You need some ocean, my friend. Haven't seen you since the funeral. You okay?" Maggie scanned Sarah's face.

"My shrink gave me time off for good behavior if I promised to enjoy surf and sun."

"Excellent." Maggie clapped her hands together.

"You bet. It's been lonely bein' a social outcast. Hope I can get

Gram to move to the beach so that I can go to high school with you."

"Might get Mom and Dad on the job to convince her."

"Great idea. See ya." Sarah waved goodbye

"Hugs await, my friend. Signing off. Love ya." Maggie blew her a kiss.

"Love ya, too."

Sarah stared at the dark screen. She slumped her shoulders and slid low in her chair. She sighed at the sudden quiet of the room. Memories of Maggie and her family filled the silence.

Sarah's and Maggie's parents became instant friends. As next-door neighbors, they spent every summer together. Sarah and Maggie built sandcastles when they were five, learned how to surf when they were eight, and giggled over cute boys and first crushes when they were old enough to notice boys. Maggie was the first person Sarah called when her parents died. If she could convince Gram to move to the beach, she was sure her life would be good again.

❧❧❧❧❧❧❧

Sarah and Gram planned to go to the beach house on Sunday morning, but church seemed to go on forever. They sat in a pew close to the elevated lectern in full view of anyone who climbed the steps to speak. The congregation was forced to gaze upward rather than nap, consult their phones, or pass notes, and they appeared to pay rapt attention to the message. Built in the early 1900s of wood shipped to San Francisco from Washington and Oregon lumber mills, the church had escaped damage in the 1906 earthquake. Its original stained-glass windows reflected the changing light of the rising sun as it highlighted apostles, Bible legends, and Jesus on the cross. A rose window above the altar had been added at the end of World War II as a tribute to the young churchmen who died.

Reverend Rogers was a pleasant, caring man, but his sermons were long-winded. Sarah went to church to please Gram and mirror the respect her parents gave to Gram's beliefs. For her parents,

Sundays were reserved for family, rest, and spectacular views of nature. "How can you deny that such wonder, order, and beauty originated from a higher power?" Sarah's father had stood, arms akimbo, when he introduced her to Yosemite for the first time, or they climbed to the top of Mount Tamalpais for a picnic and the view, or boarded the Maid of the Mist at Niagara Falls to experience the power of its roaring water.

Gram interrupted Sarah's daydream. "Let's go home. We have a lot to do if we want to reach the beach before dark."

Sarah hurried down the church steps to the parking lot, slid into the passenger seat, and fastened her seatbelt before Gram could catch up. "In a hurry, are we?" Gram chuckled.

⁂

When they arrived home, Sarah unlatched her seatbelt and hopped out of the car before Gram set the car brakes. After unlocking the front door, she sped up the stairs and collected two suitcases, a computer, and notebooks. She tossed her favorite down comforter and a packed duffle bag down the stairs as Gram started to climb up.

"Hey, careful." Gram pressed her body against the wall.

"Sorry," Sarah yelled as she rolled the rest of her belongings along the upper landing.

"I'll get my luggage and meet you at the car. Careful. Don't fall down the stairs. Here are the car keys." Gram edged around her granddaughter's luggage and headed to her room.

Thirty minutes later, Sarah had loaded her belongings in the trunk of Gram's CRV and was headed back inside for more. As she appeared on the front porch, she carried another load.

"Come on, Sarah. How much more do you need to take?" Gram closed the packed trunk. "There's barely enough room for my suitcases. You need to rearrange some of your things in the back seat. You'd think we were moving to the beach."

It took more than the expected two hours to get from Sausalito to White Sands Beach. The trip stretched to over four hours between heavy traffic, road construction, and a break for dinner. By the time they arrived, the sun had nearly disappeared below the horizon. Someone, probably Maggie's parents, had turned on the front porch lights and a couple of inside lamps. The house seemed to greet them with open arms.

Sarah dashed up the front porch steps, leaned against the railing, and savored the sound of the waves. A silver path of moonlight stretched across the ocean toward the last rays of the setting sun. "Home." She relaxed. The house, the beach, the ocean, the touchstones of her life, hadn't changed much. Here, she might be able to start over, find peace, and discover some answers to her nightmares and panic attacks.

Eleven

Summer at the beach house gave Sarah and Gram the sense of being a family again. Sarah spent every day at the beach with Maggie, renewing friendships, surfing, and learning to play the guitar. After dark, the girls often joined Gram and Maggie's parents for dinner, cooking around a bonfire on the beach or on the backyard barbecue. On Saturdays, Sarah and a group of friends walked the two miles to the boardwalk where they ate hot dogs, enjoyed carnival rides, and tried their luck at game booths. She wanted more than anything to live at the beach house around friends, not in Sausalito, where she was an outcast, a specimen to observe, and a subject of gossip.

In the first week of August, Sarah presented the plan she and Maggie had devised during their smartphone conversation in Sausalito. "Gram, coming here for the summer was such a good idea. Wouldn't it be great to live here all the time? I could go to high school with Maggie and all my friends."

"I know that sounds ideal to you, but we have a life in Sausalito—a house, a church family, your counselor, friends. We could enroll you in another high school, maybe the Arts Academy. You could start over there. Your counseling with Dr. Banks is going so well. She would be hard to replace here, if not impossible. Your grades and attendance have returned to normal, and your nightmares have stopped." Gram cleared the empty dishes and placed them in the sink, her back to Sarah. "And our house. What about that? We would have to sell it or rent it out."

"If Dr. Banks says it's okay, would you think about moving here just for high school?"

"Let me think about it. There's a lot to consider."

After Gram said she would think about moving, Sarah stopped listening. Her mind wandered to all her belongings. Maybe she could give some of them away. Her bedroom at the beach house was smaller than the one in Sausalito. Would her double bed and dresser fit? The room needed painting, maybe green or yellow.

"So, you see, many important issues may stand in the way of a move." Silence ensued. "Sarah?"

"What, what? Oh, yeah. Okay." Sarah realized she had no idea what issues Gram was talking about. She hoped her grandmother wouldn't ask her any questions about them.

❧❧❧❧❧❧❧

"We need to talk." Gram joined Sarah on the porch swing. "It's the end of the first week of August. I need to go back to Sausalito on business. Do you want to come and look at other high schools? We need to get you registered. How about the Arts Academy? You're fourteen, fifteen next April. You need to have some say in where you want to go to school this year."

"I SAID I wanted to go to high school here at the beach with my friends. I don't want to leave here. I don't want to go home. Maggie's family would take me in, I bet. You could come for visits. You promised you would investigate moving here." Her fists tightened and released, then tightened again. Her struggle ended in frustration and tears.

"Sit down. You are too old to get away with a tantrum." Gram's tone was harsh, demanding, and uncharacteristic.

Sarah's hysteria ended abruptly.

"I do remember our conversation now that you mention it. I don't recall a promise, but I can check on the possibility of moving here. I will need to talk to your lawyer about the trust and the houses and ask Dr. Banks if she can recommend a counselor here. What you want could be very complicated. Do you trust me to make the right decision even if it is not the one you want?"

Sarah slouched in her chair. "It will be the one YOU want, as always."

"Now, Sarah. That's not fair. I sold a home that I loved, put a very nice life on hold to raise you, and did my grieving for your parents at the same time. It might be fair to say that my life decisions centered around what you needed. I love you with all my heart and have done all this willingly, but it's way off the mark to accuse me of being self-centered and selfish."

"Sorry. I want this so much."

"I know you do. I've planned for you to stay at the McCann's while I'm gone. That way, you and Maggie can spend more time together before we leave. Our house will be empty, but not available for parties. Understood?"

"Yes, Ma'am." Sarah rose from her chair and hugged her grandmother. "Sorry to be so awful to you. How can you put up with me?"

"I love you, dear one. That's how."

Twelve

The next morning, Maggie and her parents came to get Sarah and say goodbye to Gram, who said, "I should be back in about a week."

"Don't worry about a thing, Lorraine." Mrs. McCann hugged Gram. "Have a safe journey."

"Love all of you." Gram started the car and leaned out of the window to wave good-bye. The McCanns and Sarah watched Gram's CRV until it disappeared around the bend.

Late that night, Mrs. McCann appeared in the bedroom doorway, hands on her hips. "GIRLS, quiet down. It's almost eleven. Do I need to sit with you until you go to sleep?"

"No, ma'am." Both girls replied in unison.

"I'm going to leave the door open until I hear quiet."

The doorbell rang. Mrs. McCann called to Maggie's father, "Liam, see who is at the door. I'm with the girls. Be careful. It's very late."

"Okay. Will do. Who would drop by at this hour?"

They heard Liam's voice, then more than one other male voice.

"Don't make a sound, girls, until we know who is here," Mrs. McCann said.

Maggie's dad appeared at the bedroom door a few minutes later. He whispered something to his wife. Her eyes grew wide. She immediately shut the bedroom door. The girls heard unfamiliar male voices in the living room.

"What's happening?" Maggie whispered. Both girls were wide awake, seated on the edge of their beds.

"Let's go see." Sarah put on her robe and opened the bedroom door wide enough to hear some words but not enough to make sense of the conversation.

Maggie stood close, her hand on Sarah's shoulder. "What's going on?"

"Don't know." Sarah moved into the hall.

Maggie's mother moaned. "Oh no." Her dad lowered his voice as he continued speaking with their visitors.

Sarah froze. She remembered another visitation when men delivered the news of her parents' death. Gram had said, "Oh no," in the same tone. She leaned against the wall.

Maggie moved in front of Sarah, her head tilted. "What's wrong? Did you change your mind? Aren't you curious about what's going on?"

Sarah waved a hand in the air to dismiss her thoughts and the weakness in her knees. "It's nothing, just a silly memory."

"What silly memory?" Maggie touched her arm. "You're shaking. Tell me."

"It's just—two men came to Gram's house to tell us Mom and Dad died. Gram said, 'Oh, no' in the same way as your mom."

Maggie squeezed her arm. "I'm sure that's not what this is about right now."

"How can you be so sure?"

"One way to find out. Take a deep breath and continue down the hall," Maggie took Sarah's hand as they moved forward.

The girls reached the end of the hall and peeked around the corner into the living room. There were two men dressed in khaki uniforms with large, brimmed hats in their hands, belts sporting guns, tasers, and handcuffs. Voices crackled in short spurts from unseen short-wave radios.

"They're wearing badges, but I can't see any insignia from here. Are we in trouble?" Sarah tried to imagine why these men were in the McCann living room. *Maybe a crime happened in the area. That's it. They're warning us to be careful.*

"Uh, will one of you be able to come to Sausalito to identify the body? We usually ask next of kin, but since she is so young—" The red-faced officer clutched the brim of his hat with both hands.

"Of course." Mrs. McCann put a hand on her chest and tilted her head to one side. "This is unbelievable. That poor child. First her parents and now her grandmother."

A gray-haired man with a cross on the lapel of his uniform stepped forward. "Life can be awfully—"

Sarah's knees gave way, and she lost consciousness.

❦❦❦❦❦❦❦

Sarah opened her eyes. A horrible smell jolted her senses. "What is that?" she wrinkled her nose.

"Smelling salts." One of the uniformed men held a vial under her nose.

"What happened? Why am I on the floor?"

"This is Mrs. Grant's granddaughter." Mr. McCann's baritone voice sounded far away, even though he knelt so close to Sarah that she could smell his spicy aftershave. He carried Sarah to the couch, laid her down, and rubbed her arm briskly to increase circulation. "There you go." His tanned face, broad grin, and curly red hair came into her focus. He had been like a father to her since her father died. A sense of calm eased her fear.

Two additional men appeared behind Liam McCann, the one with the cross on his lapel and another in a long-sleeved navy shirt emblazoned with the letters EMT. The man wearing the cross said, "I called an ambulance for Sarah as a precaution. It could be a while this time of night. Captain Sharpe, here, is a trained EMT. I am a trained chaplain. We are here to help you through this in any way we can."

The heavy gray-haired officer interrupted. "My name is Captain Branson, and I am with the local CHP office. We don't usually notify this late at night, but Mrs. Grant was headed in this direction when the accident happened."

"That doesn't make sense. She left here this morning." Mrs. McCann's shrill voice interrupted the conversation. "She should have arrived at her home in Sausalito a few hours ago."

Sarah swung her legs over the edge of the couch and grasped the cushions with both hands. *They made a mistake. The victim was someone else.*

Chaplain Branson handed a purse to Mrs. McCann. "We found her wallet, went to the address on her license, and discovered the note Mrs. Grant left on the front door directing the mail to your place. We figured you might be expecting her."

Sarah recognized the tan leather Gucci bag with the floral silk scarf tied to one strap. "That's Gram's." Her shoulders sagged.

"We wondered why we hadn't heard from her. She always calls when she arrives." Mrs. McCann said. She perched on the edge of the couch and held Sarah's hand between hers.

"What on earth happened?" Mr. McCann drew Maggie, now in tears, closer to him.

"We will know when the accident report is completed. Captain Sharpe and I were not at the accident site. Can't tell you much except Mrs. Grant and her car were transported to Sausalito. The police will contact you in the morning with details about what's next."

Captain Branson removed a notepad from his jacket. "Need to ask a few questions if you feel up to it. You might want the girls to leave the room while we do this."

"Of course." Mrs. McCann stood. "Sarah, honey, can you stand up?"

She swayed as she stood. "I want to stay. I want to know what's going on." Mrs. McCann steadied her. "Captain Branson, do you mind if the girls stay with all of us?"

"Depends. How old are they?"

"They're both fourteen, Captain, and it might be better for them to know what is going on than to imagine it."

"Good point. You know the girls better than I do. If it's okay with you, it's okay with me."

Maggie and Sarah huddled together on the couch.

"Sarah seems better. Doesn't look like we need that ambulance, Captain Sharpe." She glanced at Mr. McCann as he spoke. "We'll contact our doctor in the morning if there are any problems."

"Yep. She's better off at home right now."

Sarah heard the squawk of Captain Sharpe's radio. "Cancel that ambulance for White Sands Beach."

"Copy that." A female voice responded.

Captain Branson said, "I'll tell you what. I can come back tomorrow to get my answers and bring any information about the accident. Think y'all need some rest and time alone. Would that work?"

Mr. McCann shook hands with Captain Branson. "Thank you. We appreciate your kindness."

"Yes." Mrs. McCann joined her husband. "Thanks so much. Sarah does need to sleep and be with family." She went into the kitchen and returned with a container of brownies. "Please accept these. You need them as much as we do. Can't be easy delivering bad news."

"Thank you, ma'am. That's very generous." He turned to his colleagues. "Let's go and leave these people alone."

The officers put their hats back on, and Captain Branson held the door open as they left.

No one slept that night. They ended up on the couch in front of a roaring fire, huddled together under wool blankets. Their shared memories of Lorraine Grant filled the hours until the pale blue light of dawn shone through the bay windows.

"I'll make some coffee and hot cocoa." Mrs. McCann wrapped one of the blankets around her shoulders and headed for the kitchen.

"We should eat. No telling what this day will bring." She opened the refrigerator. "I'll make some scrambled eggs and toast."

Everyone filled their mugs and gathered around the table. Plates of cheesy scrambled eggs and sourdough toast appeared, served with sweet butter, honey, and jam.

"*Mm.* Looks good. I am hungrier than I thought." Mr. McCann slathered his toast with butter, then raspberry jam, and filled his fork with eggs. "Oh, this is good, girls. Mom has outdone herself this time."

Sarah swirled her fork through the eggs. Her attention lay on the road outside the house. This was the second time in her life she had waited for a loved one to return. She feared the outcome would be the same this time.

"Girls, if you're finished, please clear the table and dress. The dogs need feeding."

"Okay." Maggie jumped up from the table. "Come on, Sarah. Let's go."

"What?" She jumped at the sound of Maggie's voice. "Where?" She had heard but not understood.

"To feed the dogs, silly." Maggie pulled at her arm. "Come on."

"Sure." Was she in a dream? Her actions seemed slow, sluggish. She followed Maggie down the back steps to the dog run and helped fill the dog food dishes.

"The tide's coming in. Let's watch a bit, Sarah." Maggie and Sarah perched on a rock and sat in silence, their shoulders touching until the sun rose above the horizon.

"We better get back, Sarah. Mom will wonder where we are."

When the girls returned, they noticed suitcases near the door.

"Are we going somewhere?" Sarah counted the luggage. Four people, four suitcases.

"We've been busy since you left. Sit down, both of you." Mr. McCann's voice seemed deeper than usual.

Sarah stared at the suitcases. "What's with the suitcases?"

Mr. McCann spoke first. "Captain Branson called while you were gone to ask his questions, and we are all going to Sausalito. Our next-door neighbor will take care of the dogs."

Mrs. McCann added, "We have a lot to do there. Reverend and Mrs. Rogers will meet us at your Gram's house."

"How long will we be gone?" Sarah's voice wavered as she fought for control of her fear. She searched the faces around her for some sign of reassurance that soon life would return to normal.

Mr. McCann said, "We can't answer that."

"Right now, we need to be on our way." Mrs. McCann squeezed her hand. "Girls, check to see that I packed what you will need for at least a week."

Everyone except Sarah stood. Maggie hurried to the bedroom, Mr. McCann began to pack the car, and Mrs. McCann headed for the sink to wash the breakfast dishes. Sarah couldn't move. If she rushed out the door to the car, her life could change again—too big a risk.

The loaded trunk hatch slammed shut. The McCanns were seated and ready to go. "Come on, Sarah, we need to go *now*." Mr. McCann ran his hands through his hair.

Sarah slammed the front door, climbed in the back seat, and huddled in the corner against the window. She wanted to catch what she feared would be the last glimpses of her beach home—no telling where she would end up now that Gram was gone. As the engine's vibration and the gravel's crunch under the tires took them onto the road that led to the highway, Maggie edged toward Sarah and held her hand.

No one spoke until they caught sight of the Golden Gate Bridge. It didn't seem as magical as it had always been. No fog this time of day. No story ideas swirled in her mind. Her neck and jaw ached. She felt a chill and buttoned her sweater.

"We're almost there. Mrs. Rogers, the wife of Gram's pastor, will be at the house when we arrive," Mrs. McCann chirped. "Won't it be great to see the house again, Sarah?"

Mr. McCann turned right on Poplar Street, past the Catholic church on the corner, and into Gram's driveway.

Ramona Rogers, a stocky woman in a teal warm-up suit, rose from her seat on the front porch and descended the steps to greet them. She opened her ample arms to embrace the weary travelers. "Liam and Marcie, I hate to rush you, but you need to see Lorraine's attorney in an hour. He said it's urgent. Take the suitcases inside. I have some lunch ready for you. I can get the girls settled while you go to the meeting. Mark will come here after dinner to help you with the final arrangements." She opened the front door and ushered the group inside.

Sarah's childhood home looked the same as she remembered, but it seemed cold and unfriendly without Gram and her parents.

"It is so kind of you to help us this way." Marcie McCann joined Ramona in the kitchen. "I'll take care of Maggie and Sarah, then come back to help."

"Good idea. There's not much more to do. Sarah's bedroom is ready for her. I added another bed for Maggie."

"Come on, girls. Let's get you settled. Mrs. McCann ushered the girls down a hall decorated with several generations of family photographs, framed drawings of Sarah's artwork, and travel mementos through the years.

Sarah's bedroom, except for the second bed, appeared unchanged—she viewed the Bay Bridge from her window, the blown glass miniature animals and Madame Alexander dolls perched on her bookshelves, and her hand-painted jewelry box on a crocheted dresser scarf. Her room looked the same, but it wouldn't be without her family.

Again, adults, Mr. McCleary and the McCanns, huddled together to discuss her future. She pounded her fist on the dresser. "I should be with them, Maggie. It's not right that they talk about me behind my back." She clenched her fists.

In the middle of unpacking, Maggie turned to face Sarah and plopped on the bed. "Maybe they need to talk about things that would upset you."

Sarah burst into tears. "Secrets. I hate secrets."

Thirteen

When Maggie's parents returned around dinner time with Reverend Rogers, Ramona stepped onto the porch and kissed her husband.

"Let's sit out here and talk about our situation. Leave the girls inside for now." Mark Rogers grunted as he sank into the comfortable cushions of a wrought iron chair. The other adults positioned their chairs around him.

"I'll get some refreshments." Mrs. Rogers stepped back into the living room.

Sarah and Maggie watched her every move from an overstuffed couch with a view of the scene outside.

"Girls, we'll have dinner in a while. Milk and cookies are in the kitchen." Ramona loaded a tray with iced tea, four glasses, and a plate of cookies. She backed out of the house, placed the tray on a side table, and closed the front door behind her.

"How did it go, Mark?" Ramona joined the group and leaned in to hear the conversation.

Sarah heard Ramona's question but couldn't hear the answers. She and Maggie kneeled on the couch and stared out the window. They attempted to read lips to catch words with no success. The frowning adults sat talking on the porch for a long time, their hands animated, their heads bobbing and shaking.

Sarah watched the clock as she paced the living room. An hour passed before the adults entered the house for dinner.

"Sure smells good, Ramona." Mark Rogers was loud and jovial. A shopping bag from Majors Wine Shop swung from his right hand. "Thought this occasion called for a glass or two."

A chorus of "Amen!" followed him as he rummaged through a drawer in the kitchen.

"What happened?" Sarah screeched, her patience at the breaking point.

"Let me help you with dinner." Marcie McCann hurried to put on an apron.

"There you go." Reverend Rogers carried four glasses of red wine and two tumblers of purple juice on a silver tray into the living room and set it down on the glass coffee table. "Will dinner spoil if it's delayed, my dear?"

"Not a bit. Sarah needs to know what happened."

"Take a glass and get comfortable. Marcie and Liam have news for Sarah."

Mr. McCann downed a full glass of red wine and cleared his throat. "The most important thing we discussed was where you will live."

Sarah's heart began to pound.

"Liam and I told Mr. McCleary, Gram's attorney, that we have been like family for years and are more than happy to have you live with us." Mrs. McCann sighed. "Go ahead, Liam. I can't."

Sarah moved to the edge of her seat.

Mark Rogers refilled Liam McCann's glass.

"Apparently, Child Protective Services does not allow fostering until all living blood relatives have been notified and allowed to offer a home." He glanced at Mark Rogers. "Please take over."

Rogers said, "Sarah, records show your grandmother has a sister, Augusta. There will have to be a search for your aunt. Until they find her, you can stay with the McCanns."

"We'll stay at the house for a few days after Lorraine's funeral, Mark. We want to be close to Sarah's attorney and any news of the search." Liam grasped his wife's hand.

"Good idea. Let's eat dinner before it's ruined." Reverend Rogers rose and led the group to the dining room.

Three days later, Lorraine Grant's services were held in Sausalito. The whole ritual felt like a repeat of her parents' funeral, except there was only one coffin. The same cloying fragrance of lilies filled the sanctuary. A catered meal in the church hall replayed more memories. Gram's friends and fellow parishioners, most dressed in black, repeated some of the same tired condolences. All Sarah wanted was to escape. This time, she had no bedroom to hide in. She fled to the bathroom. No one would bother her there. She sat on the toilet with her hands over her face and cried for the first time since Gram's accident.

⁂

Sarah and the McCanns stayed at the house for the news from Sarah's attorney about legal decisions. In two days, the phone rang. Mr. McCann answered, "Yes, hello. We've been waiting for your call."

Sarah dashed into the kitchen. "Is that Mr. McCleary?" She grabbed Mr. McCann's arm.

"Here's Sarah." He handed her the receiver.

"Well, someone is excited to hear from me. How ya doin', young lady?"

"Do you have news?" Sarah paced the floor. "Tell me."

"I do have news. Will be there this afternoon. Let me talk to Liam again."

She groaned and relinquished the phone.

Liam listened for a moment. "Marcie and Ramona plan to be back here for lunch, Ian. Two o'clock should be fine." He hesitated. "Yes, I'll call Reverend Rogers. See you soon."

"Two o'clock. Are you kidding? Ahh!" Sarah threw her hands in the air, circled the kitchen, and stalked out the front door, slamming it hard enough to rattle figurines on the coffee table. She circled the house several times, mumbling. "Unfair to make me wait so long. I'm tired of this. Adults. *Phish!*"

Ian McCleary arrived at two o'clock. Maggie and Sarah sat shoulder to shoulder on an upholstered bench across from Reverend and Mrs. Rogers, who perched on the edge of a brown leather loveseat. The McCanns and Ian McCleary took the matching leather couch under the picture window that looked out on the street. No one spoke. All eyes focused on Sarah's attorney.

Mr. McCleary retrieved several files from his briefcase and cleared his throat.

"Investigators from Child Protective Services and police found records of an Augusta Hanson living in Lawson, California. She is Lorraine's estranged older sister. She is a blood relative and, as such, is the only current legal placement for Sarah."

"Oh, dear, I was afraid of this." Mrs. Roger's hand rested on her chest.

The men groaned. Mrs. McCann grabbed her husband's hand as tears rolled down her cheeks. Maggie and Sarah glared at Ian McCleary.

"No, I want to live with the McCanns at the beach. Did you tell them that?" Sarah leaped off the couch and took a step toward Mr. McCleary.

"I did tell them that, and so did the McCanns. Sarah, I wish things could be different, but this is the law in California. I'm afraid you have no choice but to pack your things and move in with your Aunt Augusta. She assured her local social worker that she is willing to have you live with her as she is a Christian woman and your grandmother's older sister."

"Please sit down, Sarah." Mrs. McCann wiped her eyes and blew her nose. "We'll keep in touch by phone, text, email, and write to you. I'll ask Augusta if you can spend some of your summers and holidays with us."

"There are some other details you need to know. I've hired a property manager to maintain this house and the one at White Sands

Beach. The family trust would not allow either house to be sold or money taken from the estate until you turn twenty-one."

Sarah examined the faces in the room. Each one, including Maggie's, stared at her, eyes glossy with tears. They reminded her of the people who came to the house after her parents' funeral.

Fourteen

ugusta sent a Greyhound bus ticket for Sarah's trip to her
farm. The bus smelled of sweaty bodies and a toilet overdue
for service. At seven in the morning, most passengers were
sleeping or bleary-eyed. Many were half-dressed or lolling in positions that exposed more skin than Sarah wanted to see. She found
an empty window seat near the back of the bus, put her belongings
in the overhead bin, and slid in.

Her long legs had no room to stretch out. She was trapped on
a bus to nowhere, alone, on her way to live with a stranger, the aunt
who had such a horrible past that the family never mentioned her.
Sarah pictured Cruella from *One Hundred and One Dalmatians* or
the witch in *Hansel and Gretel*. She shivered.

Sarah worried she might not see Maggie and her family ever again.
The happiest place for her was at the beach, always had been. She and
Maggie had found Lawson on a map. It was a tiny speck in the middle
of nowhere. The nearest town, Broadmore, appeared slightly larger.

She tried to be brave, but tears came despite her efforts to con-
tain them.

"Here you are, dear." Someone in the seat across the aisle offered
her a packet of tissues. "Is there anything I can do to help?" A middle-

aged woman leaned closer. Her pure white hair and gentle, loving eyes reminded her of Gram. "Where are you going today?"

Sarah blew her nose, dabbed her tears, and turned toward the woman. "I'm going to live with my Aunt Augusta just outside Lawson."

"Would that be Augusta Hanson?" the woman frowned. "She's a neighbor of mine."

"Do you know her?"

The woman's demeanor softened. "I live about a mile from her farm." Sarah thought she caught a trace of pity in her eyes. "I know who she is, but people around here don't see much of her. You must come and have tea after you settle in. My name is Evie Burrows. Go north on the main wetlands trail, and you will find me." Evie's soft, veined hand patted Sarah's arm. "I am serious about the invitation."

Small talk filled the rest of the trip. Evie shared that she preferred to ride the bus on long trips to visit her relatives in the Midwest. Sarah talked about school and her writing. She felt less alone. At least she knew one friendly person in her new home. The bus ground to a halt, brakes squealing and puffing.

"Lawson." The bus driver heaved his bulk out of the driver's seat. "Ten-minute break. I won't wait for stragglers. Two people are getting off here. Pick up your bags outside the bus." He waved a dismissive hand at his passengers, stomped down the steps, unloaded the luggage, and disappeared around a corner of the station.

A weathered sign above the rundown building read *Lawson*. No other inhabitable structures remained. Rotted wood lay under the skeleton of a barn behind the bus stop. Its roof and sides had caved in long ago. Weeds grew tall in what might have been a garden at one time. Trellises sagged from the weight of vines long dead from lack of water and care.

Sarah searched the area for any sign that a woman waited to greet her. A lone dark-haired woman dressed in jeans and a suede jacket leaned against a red SUV.

"There she is." Evie waved, picked up her luggage, and headed toward the woman.

Sarah hoped the attractive lady was Augusta.

Evie said, "My friend is here to pick me up, but I don't see your aunt anywhere. Maybe she's inside the station. Come on, Sarah. Meet Marjorie. We won't leave until we know your aunt is here."

Sarah shouldered her backpack and clutched her purse like a life preserver. *What would she do if Augusta didn't show?* She rose slowly, straightened her blouse, and followed Evie.

"Marjorie, this is Sarah. Her grandmother died recently. She is here to live with Augusta Hanson."

"Oh?" Marjorie frowned, then smiled in greeting. "My, what a surprise. Didn't know she had any relatives." Marjorie stood a head taller than Sarah, a rare event for a six-foot female. "Sorry about your grandmother."

"Thank you. Augusta is my grandmother's sister and my only relative, so here I am. I've never met her."

Sarah tried to smile. Gram always said a smile went a long way in her favor. Right now, she needed the favor of these women standing next to her.

It was nearly an hour before Evie and Marjorie decided Augusta would not show.

"Typical," Evie muttered to her friend.

"Poor girl." The two women exchanged glances that Sarah did not understand. "Come on, dear. There isn't any bus or taxi service out here, and no one operates the desk inside the terminal. We'll give you a ride to Augusta's place. She'll be there. She rarely goes anywhere else."

"Is it very far? Could I walk?" Sarah's eyes darted between the women.

"In this heat with no street signs?" Marjorie chuckled. "It's too far. There are few houses and no water sources in the area. You're in the country now."

"Your aunt's farm is on our way, Sarah, and Marjorie's SUV is air-conditioned." Evie picked up one of Sarah's suitcases. "We can't leave you here."

"Thanks. It is hot." Sarah carried the rest of her bags to the only vehicle in sight, a red SUV.

Thirty minutes passed before Marjorie's SUV bounced up the rutted, dusty driveway to Augusta's house. Everything was bland—the house, the empty fields, and the woman who stood on the porch with her hands on her hips. A shapeless, wrinkled dress hung from her bony shoulders to the tops of her work boots. "Who are you, and what are you doin' here?" she growled.

"Why, Augusta, it's been years, but I'm sure you remember me. It's Evie, your neighbor. We brought Sarah, your niece, with us from the bus station. How nice you will have her for company. She's a lovely girl."

The woman on the porch scowled. "Oh, I forgot. Don't need a kid around, but they're payin' me to take her, and she's my sister's grandchild, not that my sister ever kept in touch."

"Well, I'm sure it will be fine." Evie took Sarah's hands. "Remember you can visit me any time. I am a mile south of here along the main road."

"She'll be too busy for socializing." Augusta turned and went inside.

Evie waved goodbye as she joined Marjorie in the SUV. Before she closed the door, Sarah overheard Marjorie remark, "Slave labor, I'll wager."

Uncertain, Sarah ascended to the front porch, set her suitcases down, and knocked. Augusta, eyes narrowed, opened the door. "What are you waiting for, someone to carry your bags?" She stepped aside.

Sarah gathered her luggage and stepped through the front door. The dark interior smelled dank and stale. A little light shone through a picture window in the front room; its rays exposed the dust in the air.

"This way." Augusta strode down a dark hallway and opened the door with such vigor that it banged against the wall. "This is where you sleep. Get unpacked." She left and slammed the door.

Sarah stood motionless. Her suitcases, still in her hands, felt heavier than she remembered. She took her first deep breath since she encountered Augusta. Brown paneled walls, a brown four-drawer dresser with a stained mirror, and a single bed with a brown blanket tucked around a thin mattress comprised Sarah's bedroom. There was a transom over the door and one narrow window on the opposite wall, placed too high to see out of unless she stood on a chair, but there was no chair.

Next to the bed, a small niche with a tension rod held five wire hangers ready for her wardrobe. The shock of her new surroundings and her aunt's lack of kindness, so different from what she was used to in her former life, began to lift. Anxiety took its place. Her body seemed too weak to stand.

She placed her bags at the foot of her bed. The sweat on her forehead was cold to the touch. Frightened, she sat on the bed, cradled her head in her hands, and breathed deeply as she fought for control. Her heart pounded in her chest. She wondered how she could survive if Augusta were as cruel as she seemed. Gram always told her there was good in everyone, but Sarah saw no good here. She ached to return to her former life.

Finally, she was able to cry.

❧ Fifteen

For a city girl, Sarah's isolated and dreary new home was a shock. Augusta valued simple things—plain food, drab clothes, and a house without decoration.

On her second day at the farm, Augusta stored Sarah's laptop and phone on the top shelf of her office closet. "You won't need these. I don't have internet in this house, and I don't see any reason to start paying for it. If you need a laptop for school, use the ones in their library."

"I can pay for the internet connection." Sarah watched her life and freedom slip away as Augusta stripped her of both. Her throat tightened as she strained to save what was left of her past. "My friends gave me the phone to keep in touch, and I need the laptop for homework. Every school uses laptops for lessons."

Augusta padlocked her closet door and locked the key in her safe.

Sarah's head throbbed. "I have some of my own money. Another phone could benefit you, and the internet would connect you to the outside world."

"Don't need your money. Don't need your phone. Don't want to know what's going on in the world. It's never anything good. I like my privacy, and your friends don't need to know what's going on here.

Leave my office and stop your whining. Do something useful." Augusta shoved Sarah out of the office and locked the door behind her.

A chill shot up Sarah's spine. She wondered what Augusta considered useful and what happened in this house that needed to be so secret.

The third day, Augusta examined Sarah's closet. "Your clothing is not appropriate. The skirts are too short, the necklines are too low, and the designer tags belong in the city, not here on the farm. And look at this jewelry and accessories. You'll have no place to wear all this, anyway." Augusta removed Sarah's clothes from the closet and packed all but a few of her outfits in cardboard boxes. "These will go in the attic with the rest of the boxes you shipped."

"Those are mine. I can wear them to school or when I visit Maggie."

"You won't be going anywhere in these clothes." Augusta carried a box out the door.

Sarah grabbed what she could from her jewelry case and stashed the items under her mattress before Augusta returned.

Augusta reentered the room red-faced and out of breath. This time, she stacked two boxes in her arms. "These are city clothes. You need work clothes and modest outfits for school. I won't have someone from my house dressing like a tramp." Augusta retrieved any items that Sarah grabbed from the hangers.

"A tramp? How dare you call me that. Who do you think you are?" She stepped toward Augusta, her arms flailing.

"I am the person who saved you from foster care. Be grateful." Augusta smirked.

"The McCanns wanted to take me in, and I wanted to go." Sarah sat on the edge of the bed, too exhausted to keep fighting.

"After lunch, we'll go shopping for items that are more functional for your new school and life on the farm."

"I'm not hungry." Sarah's "new life" promised to be a nightmare.

"Fine. I'll expect you in the front yard in thirty minutes." Augusta left the room, her arms loaded with the last box of clothing.

Thirty minutes later, Sarah joined Augusta in the front yard. Augusta's Ford pickup chugged and sputtered out of a dilapidated shed. The slanted left rear fender shuddered with the vibration of the engine. The truck had been patched so many times it was impossible to discern its original color. The square shape of the cab suggested it dated as far back as the early 1940s or late thirties. The brakes squealed to a stop in front of the house. The exhaust blew from the tailpipe with a bang.

Augusta leaned out of the driver's side window. "Get in," she ordered. "You'll need to yank on the door to open it, and the windows don't roll up. Not what you're used to, I'll wager. *Hmph*."

Sarah approached the truck as if she expected it to collapse any minute. She yanked the door handle several times with increasing effort. Finally, the door squealed open enough for her to get in. The cab smelled moldy. Particles of dust swirled off the seat and the dashboard as she sat and tugged at the door, which was as reluctant to close as it was to open.

As they bounced and swerved along the road into town, it was obvious the shock absorbers were gone, and the wheel alignment needed adjusting. When Augusta turned into a parking space on Main Street and shut off the engine, Sarah sighed with relief. She kicked open the passenger door and jumped to the ground.

They strode past a few small shops with simple clothes displayed in cramped windows. The merchandise seemed nice enough, though it was out of date. She lagged behind for a closer look. Augusta hurried her along. "No window shopping. We don't have time for that."

In two short blocks, clothing shops were replaced by hardware stores and auto repair shops. Discount food outlets advertised specials on overstocked items from local grocery stores and canned foods without labels. "Where are we going?" Sarah asked. "I don't see any clothing shops in this section of town."

"That's where you're wrong, my dear." Augusta squared her shoulders and lifted her chin. "Here we are." She opened the shop door and stepped in. "Let's go, miss fancy pants." She headed to the back of the shop. "I will choose the clothes that you need. We won't be long."

Sarah gasped. The sign over the front door read: USED CLOTHING PURCHASED AND SOLD. Grime on the display window made it difficult to tell what was for sale. To complete the picture, the outside of the building desperately needed paint. A few shingles from a decaying roof lay on the ground.

As she entered the shop, a mixture of body odor, stale perfume, and neglect assaulted her senses. Mounds of discarded merchandise lay atop a dozen or more counters, some items folded, some strewn on the floor or tossed on the pile. Mismatched shoes and worn boots, some caked with dirt and scuffed from their labor, lay where customers sat to try them on.

Sarah nearly tripped on some boots piled in an adjacent aisle. More formal wear, coats, and jackets hung askew from wire hangers jammed on the few rods available along the west wall. Unpainted plywood shelves filled with toys, tattered books, games, puzzles, and kitchenware covered the walls to her right. At the back of the store, curtains hung from heavy rods over what served as dressing rooms.

"I'll be right with you." A gentle voice chirped behind a mountain of clothes stacked on the checkout counter.

"May I help you?" A woman's head, covered in white curls, popped above the clothes. The cash register slammed shut. "There, I'm finished." The woman folded her hands in front of her. Petite and wearing a plain calico dress, she looked every bit like someone's great-grandmother. Etched on her face were the lines of a woman who smiled more often than she frowned.

Sarah thought of Gram and chocolate chip cookies.

"Oh, aren't you a lovely young lady? I haven't seen you before. Are you new in town or just passing through? Do you need help bringing in your donations? Oh, dear. Too many questions." The woman waved her hand in front of her face and grinned.

Sarah relaxed. "I just moved here to live with my aunt. I don't have donations. My aunt is here to buy. I'm Sarah."

"Pleased to meet you. My name is Isabelle. Welcome to town. Where is your aunt?"

Isabelle stood on her tiptoes to search the store.

"Ready to check out." Augusta's gruff voice managed to change a pleasant moment into a harsh one. She charged into view, a basket overflowing with clothes. "These will do just fine. No time for idle chatter." Augusta glared at Sarah and Isabelle, who stood eyes wide, mouths open and silent.

Isabelle recovered first. "Would you like Sarah to try anything on?"

"No time. I know her sizes."

"Very well. Let me move this stack of clothes aside." Isabelle frowned as she rang up the clothing. "Are you sure you want these things?" She held up a pair of overalls and some work boots. "I can show you some clothing more suited to a young lady."

"This young lady will need what I have chosen." Augusta glared at the woman.

Isabelle stiffened and widened her eyes. "As you wish, ma'am." Her hands shook as she rang up the purchases.

Sarah, cheeks burning, stared at the rough wooden floor. Augusta snatched the loaded bags and tossed a few bills at the startled woman behind the counter. "Come on, girl. We need to get home." Augusta strode out of the shop as if someone were chasing her.

Sarah peered at Isabelle. "Nice meeting you."

"I enjoyed meeting you." Her eyes were soft and filled with compassion. "You take care now."

"Sarah!" Augusta's angry voice shot through the open shop door.

She hurried outside. A few curious shoppers stopped to stare as she scurried along the sidewalk, head down to avoid eye contact. What must they think of the drama she and Augusta created on such a beautiful day? Did it ruin their peaceful morning, too? She raced toward Augusta's rundown truck. Maybe she could slouch low in the passenger seat to avoid recognition.

"Hallo, Augusta." A middle-aged woman dressed in jeans, a fringed suede jacket, and cowboy boots, waved from the other side of the street.

Augusta did not respond. She turned away from the woman, loaded the truck bed with packages, and slid into the driver's seat.

"Oh, God. Make me invisible." Sarah hid on the other side of the truck and tugged at the stubborn passenger door. It gave way enough for her to squeeze in. She hunched in the seat to avoid being seen through the open window.

Augusta turned the key in the ignition. The engine sputtered and stopped with a thud. Sarah peeked through Augusta's window to see if anyone noticed. Several men at the auto repair shop across the street stopped to stare. One of them waved to the others as he stepped off the curb. Could things get worse today? If that man decided to help with the car, a crowd would gather to watch. There would be no hiding for her then.

"Damn truck," Augusta muttered. She turned the key again, this time with more force and determination. The engine groaned to life. A curious crowd gathered as the vehicle edged out of the parking spot. Augusta ground the gears as she forced the gearshift into drive. She gunned the gas pedal. The truck backfired and rattled out of town, a vehicle as broken as Sarah's life.

⁂

They rode home in silence. Anxiety tightened every muscle in Sarah's body. The fear of what might happen next throbbed behind her eyes and at the base of her neck.

Squealing breaks yanked Sarah out of her thoughts. They parked in front of the farmhouse. "I'm anxious to show you what a decent young lady should wear." Augusta exited the truck, grabbed the shopping bags from the truck bed, and stomped up the front steps to enter the house.

Sarah's body refused to move. Cold and dizzy, she needed to take a deep breath. Tears ached in her throat. She could only endure this prison if she managed to disengage and become numb. "Do not let her see you cry. Do not let her win." She kicked open the passenger door, strode up the steps, and joined her aunt.

Augusta had spread the clothes on Sarah's bed. "There you are. Took you long enough. Come see what I've done." The smile on her face reminded Sarah of a child opening gifts at Christmas, except the eyes, pinched and dilated, held a tinge of cruelty. Augusta arranged all the outfits on the bed; her purchases deepened Sarah's frustration. She stiffened at the sight of clothes with no style, color, or character.

"Let me show you how I organized your outfits." As she talked, Augusta placed her hand on Sarah's back and pushed her close to the bed. She cringed, stiffened, and squirmed to escape her aunt's bony fingers. Augusta removed her hand with a shrug as she resumed her presentation.

"When you start school in two weeks, you have one pair of black penny loafers, two dark blue calf-length skirts, one white and one beige shirt with Peter Pan collars, and sweaters to match." Augusta punctuated her description with a self-satisfied nod. She moved to the next display. "For work around the house, a pair of overalls, two navy tee shirts, and black lace-up work boots." The overalls and tee shirts, faded from wear, and the boots, scuffed at the toes, must have come from a reject pile saved for the garbage. Sarah figured her aunt picked those up for free, a real find.

"And finally," Augusta picked up what appeared to be her prize garment. "This lovely blue calico dress, almost new, for special occasions, along with black ballet flats."

Sarah stared at her. The clothes, the woman, and the horrible day seemed unreal as if she were in a dream detached from the present. She was unaware of any thoughts, feelings, or reactions.

Her body and mind seemed heavy, solid, and numb. *She had succeeded.* The last time she experienced this level of detachment was in Dr. Banks's office when she grieved her parents' deaths. This time, she mourned the death of her former life. This time, Gram could not help her. She needed to survive on her own.

Writing became Sarah's salvation. Every night, she hid beneath her sheets and spun tales of magical adventures. Her characters and their deeds swirled around her private space and transported her to distant places where anything could happen. On other nights, the glow of her flashlight created ominous shadows where monsters crouched, waiting to inflict their evil deeds on unsuspecting victims. In these stories, Sarah became the defender of justice, the one true heroine, wielding her fearsome weapons with great skill and authority to save the distressed and the helpless.

Sixteen

Mom and Gram, both optimists, would end a tough day with their favorite cliché, "Things will be better in the morning. A good night's sleep cures the worst day." Sarah hoped they were right as she turned on her side and fell asleep.

In the morning, she woke in the same house with the same Aunt Augusta. The awful clothes from the secondhand store hung on wire hangers in the nook that served as a bedroom closet. Nothing had changed. Mom and Gram were wrong.

Dawn lightened the rectangles near the ceiling that served as windows. A rooster announced the start of a new day. Sarah heard the kitchen door slam behind Augusta as she left the house to feed her stray cats and dogs.

"Shut up. One of these days, you'll end up chicken soup." Several piercing squawks followed by a thud announced Augusta's morning ritual. She would assault the farm's aging rooster with any object she could find. Sarah couldn't understand why he stayed.

Sarah threw off the covers and sat up in bed, shivering. Augusta would shout at her if she lingered. She had been allowed to keep her warm robe and slippers for early morning trips down the hall to the bathroom. She wrapped the green fleece around her, slid her icy feet into the fur-lined slippers, and then headed to the dresser for clean underwear.

Another shock awaited as she opened the top drawer. Someone had replaced her expensive, delicate lingerie with packages of white cotton briefs and plain, functional bras. More of her past life was gone. With tears in her eyes, she ran to her bed and lifted the mattress where she stashed the items saved from Augusta's packing yesterday. She slid her hand into the torn section near the foot of the box springs where she had managed to hide a packet of mementos, some favorite jewelry, and the notebooks Gram bought for her therapy sessions.

She sank to her knees, propped up the mattress with her forehead, and searched the hole for her stash. It was not there. Did Augusta have that, too? She dove farther into the opening. "There it is," she whispered. The packet had shifted, but it remained in its hiding place. She pushed it farther away from the opening between mattress coils, closer to the wall.

Gram and Mom were wrong. Things don't always look better in the morning. The numbness of yesterday turned to anger. *Action instead of silence.* She had to stand up for herself and protect what was important. Stop her aunt from controlling her. "You can't take everything from me, Auntie. I won't let you take everything."

❦❦❦❦❦❦❦

Two days later, Sarah found Augusta in her bedroom. The covers on the bed were pulled back and the mattress leaned on its side against the wall. Her aunt searched the tears in the mattress and springs for forbidden contraband.

"What are you doing in here?" Sarah hurried to Augusta's side. "This is my room. It's private." Her face warmed.

"What makes you think your room is private?" Augusta reached farther under the mattress. "I intend to keep an eye on you." She ran her hand along the covered surface of the box springs.

Sarah grabbed the edge of the mattress and dropped it back where it belonged.

"You insolent brat." Augusta jumped out of Sarah's way, widened her stance, and jammed her fists on her hips. "I can see you've been allowed to have your way too often."

"I had good, kind parents and a loving grandmother who respected me."

"Spoiled you is what they did." Augusta returned to the bed and lifted the mattress. "That won't happen here." She continued her search.

"You don't know anything about me or my family. You deserted us. You didn't belong." Sarah lifted her chin, fixed her narrowed eyes on Augusta, and slammed the mattress down with both hands.

Augusta's face reddened. Her mouth twisted into a grotesque grin. Her pupils widened. She stepped so close that Sarah could smell her whisky breath. "This is my house. I can be wherever I want." She shook a finger in her face. "You're lucky to have a roof over your head."

"A prison, you mean." Sarah shoved Augusta's finger aside. Augusta slapped her hard across the face, strode out of the room, and slammed the door.

Sarah raised her hand to her throbbing cheek as she fell sideways onto the bed. She wiggled her jaw to check for damage and waited for her eyes to refocus.

Neither her parents nor her grandmother would have entered her room without permission, much less hit her across the face. She struggled to decide what to do next. Mom often said that if you don't know what to do, stop and take the first step that comes to mind.

Sarah waited and reached under her mattress for one of her grandmother's notebooks. She ran her hand over the cover. Tears rolled off her chin and blurred her name written in ink on the front. She searched through the backpack she dropped when she entered, found a pen, and sat cross-legged on her bed. Sorrow, anger, loneliness, and betrayal poured onto page after page until she fell asleep, exhausted and empty.

That night, she tiptoed down the hall to Augusta's bedroom. A dim night light in the bathroom lit her path in an otherwise dark house. She listened for snoring. Her aunt was fast asleep. Sarah returned to her room and clicked the switch on a tiny lamp near her bed. She must hide her treasures, but not in the house where Augusta could find them. After moving the lamp from the dresser to the floor, she wrapped her treasures in notebook pages and transferred them to her backpack. She tucked two notebooks in the stuffing of her pillow, then turned off the light. Uncertain of each room's layout, she moved cautiously to the kitchen, out the back door, and down the steps. There was no moon. She hid the packages in a toolbox behind the stairs until morning when she could find a better hiding place.

Sarah dozed off and on as she waited for dawn. She needed to beat the rooster's crow to move her belongings before Augusta woke. If she got caught, Augusta would snatch what was left of her belongings. There would be no other time to avoid her constant vigilance. At first light, Sarah was out the back door. She crouched under the steps before she made any move. She hoped the loose bricks she found yesterday in the crumbling ivy-covered wall would hide her jewelry and mementos.

The sky turned a pale blue. She had to move. She dashed across the lawn, knelt on the ground by the wall, and squeezed behind the dusty ivy that clung to the wall. She ran her fingers over the bricks, found the loose ones, and hid her precious items in the space. They fit perfectly.

Sarah rearranged the ivy to cover any sign of her hiding place. She clutched her notebooks and sped along the brick wall to the barn, where she stashed them under rusty tools decayed from disuse.

As Sarah left the barn, the rooster screeched its alarm. Adrenalin alerted her to danger. She sped across the lawn, hugged the garden wall, and headed for the front porch. Sarah peeked through the living room window. She heard Augusta stomp through the house as she grumbled and swore at the rooster. The back door slammed.

Augusta locked the front screen but not the door. Sarah jiggled the screen handle. Nothing happened. She yanked the handle back and forth and jiggled it again. The lock clicked. The screen gave way.

Sarah sped through the door, down the hall to her room and combed her hair to remove any evidence of leaves and sticks from the ivy. She sat on her bed for a few minutes before strolling to the kitchen to make lunch and cook breakfast. As Augusta stomped up the back steps, Sarah turned to greet her.

"There's cereal and milk on the table for you."

"*Humph.* 'Bout time you were useful around here." Augusta poured milk on her cereal and hunched over her bowl, her arms wrapped around it as if someone might steal her breakfast. "We're going to register at your high school this morning at nine o'clock. School starts in two weeks. Be on the porch ready to go at 8:15."

Sarah was ready for school to start. No matter how bad Broadmore High promised to be, it would let her escape Augusta for a few hours.

Seventeen

Augusta's truck bounced, backfired, and brought attention from onlookers all the way to Broadmore. Students turned to point, laughed, and raised their eyebrows at the sight of them as the truck pulled up in front of the school. Sarah and Augusta walked to the front office.

"May I help you? I'm Mrs. Brown, the school secretary."

"Need to register my niece." Augusta glowered at the woman.

Mrs. Brown's smile disappeared. "Of course. Fill out these papers. Please." She placed registration forms and a pen in front of Augusta, who filled them out and shoved them across the counter.

"Is that all?"

"Yes, Ms. Hanson. I'll make a copy of her birth certificate, then show you around the school."

"Have no interest in a tour. I'll wait in the car." Augusta marched out the door.

Mrs. Brown said nothing for a moment, then turned to Sarah. "Let me show you around, so you know the place a bit before your first day."

"Thank you. I'd appreciate that."

The hallways at Broadmore High School were dark and smelled of mold and cleaning solution. Sarah's eyes stung from the fumes.

Mrs. Brown was a short, round, middle-aged woman with rimmed glasses perched halfway down her nose; she delivered what appeared to be a well-rehearsed orientation speech as she led Sarah up wooden stairs that creaked and groaned with age. Many generations of students had polished the center of the stairs to a reddish-brown.

"Freshmen are on the third floor. A small library is on the first floor, but most students use the public library two doors down." They paused on the third-floor landing to allow Mrs. Brown to catch her breath. "Not as easy to climb as it used to be." She leaned against the wall, hand on her chest, gasping. "Take a look at the town view from the window ahead of you. It will give you a good orientation to the surrounding area." Mrs. Brown's breathing returned to normal.

From the window, Sarah noted that Main Street ended in three blocks. Two sets of railroad tracks acted as a boundary between the town and the farms beyond where tractors tilled the soil for September planting. Single-story shops separated by alleyways stood between the school and the next tallest building, probably the library. A handful of shoppers strolled in and out of the stores. Bags dangled from their hands as they hurried to their cars. Twin gas pumps near the street guarded a building labeled *GAS, PARTS, AND REPAIR*. Across the street, the town's only hamburger joint beckoned to a growing lunch crowd.

Sarah saw no movie theater, bowling alley, or place to have fun. Her orientation proved there was nothing to see in town. She turned from the window to see Mrs. Brown leaning against the wall. "Are you all right?" Sarah moved closer to the panting woman.

"I'm just fine now, dear. Let's go on, shall we? Here is your homeroom." She turned the handle on the heavy wooden door. It wobbled a little, and the hinges whined as the door swung open. "As you can see, the class size is small, which is an advantage of living in a rural town." She swept her arm as though she presented a grand piece of property for sale. "After you."

Twenty desks with seats attached, a few chipped at the edges, sat in rows facing a green chalkboard. She was five years old the last time she saw a green chalkboard in a classroom. Sarah wondered how long the damaged desks had been in the school. She ran her hand along a seat back. "Ouch." She examined her index finger.

"What is it, dear?" Mrs. Brown frowned and rushed to discern the problem.

"A splinter." She pinched her finger to coax the wood out.

"I can take care of that when we get back to the office. I'm the school nurse, too."

"Seriously?" Sarah couldn't believe her ears. She attempted to grasp the end of the sliver with her teeth.

"You probably should take that finger out of your mouth. Germs, you know." Mrs. Brown continued her tour.

Sarah surveyed the rest of her future surroundings. Paned windows set in brownish-yellow walls let in some light, but they were not tall enough for her to see outside if she were seated, a deterrent to daydreaming in class. Dark wooden floors and trim around the ceiling and windows added to the somber tone of the room. She longed for her old school, where the light shone through one wall of eight-foot windows in every room; hallways featured murals and artwork created by students, and state-of-the-art teaching tools enhanced every lesson.

The other classrooms were not much better. Spanish class had a few maps up and some vocabulary words posted above a green chalkboard. Listening stations and language labs trained Spanish students to improve their language skills. The faint odor of tacos and fajitas hung in the air.

The science room reeked of formaldehyde. Several specimens floated in large jars at the back of the room, and the usual skeleton dangled from a pole in the corner. Several sinks with faucets suggested experiments might be done, but no evidence of lab equipment was visible.

Mrs. Brown led Sarah to her first-floor nurse's office, a converted closet adjacent to the main reception area.

Between the use of a needle and tweezers, both sterilized with a lit match, Mrs. Brown removed the splinter. "There, now. Right as rain." She applied a bandage to the wound.

"Thank you. Is there anything else to see?" Sarah asked.

"No, dear. See you in a couple of weeks."

"Right." As Sarah descended the steps to the sidewalk, she grew more determined to find a way to improve any part of her life she could control. She needed to dig deep inside herself for anything positive. Even her education looked bleak. She'd always loved school. Maybe the teachers were good. They'd have to be with the meager items available.

❧❧❧❧❧❧

It took Sarah the whole weekend before school started to figure out what to do about her clothes. Augusta was always watchful, especially if Sarah's door was closed. Her aunt could move around the house without making a sound, which enhanced her ability to appear at any time.

The skirts had to come to her knees. She couldn't hem them or use scissors to make them shorter. Augusta would notice. If she folded the waistbands, the skirts would get shorter, but the layers of folded material around her waist made her look at least ten pounds heavier. It would be hard enough to be the new girl without also being the chubby one.

Sarah pulled the shirts and sweaters from the drawer and spread them on the bed. There wasn't much she could do with Peter Pan collars, but the sweaters might work, and the blue flowered dress was always there. She had some colorful chunky earrings and matching bracelets in her mattress stash that would be great with the dress and the sweaters and, in a pinch, the shirts with the Peter Pan collars.

"What are you doing in here with the door closed?"

Sarah jumped at the sound. Her aunt filled the doorway with one hand on the doorknob and the other on the door frame. She

[95]

scowled as her eyes darted around the room. Sarah thought she looked like a ferret with her thin nose and beady eyes.

"Getting my clothes ready for school, Auntie."

"Keep your door open. Don't want you messing around in here."

"Yes, ma'am." Sweet and obedient might save her more trouble, but she hated herself.

"*Humph.* Watch the time. Dinner needs to be ready at six." Augusta waved, left Sarah's bedroom, and shuffled down the hall. Sarah heard her close and lock her office door.

Sarah's duties included cooking all meals until she started school, then she would be responsible for her breakfast and bagged lunches. Augusta slept in or got up long before Sarah to work on outdoor projects. Meals together were silent except for the sound of forks and knives scraping across plates or the occasional slurping of liquids from cups of soup or morning coffee. Every meal in the dark, dreary kitchen was a necessary chore to endure.

✳

Sarah developed a plan for her wardrobe deception. She would change her clothes after she left the house. She could not put the clothing and jewelry in her backpack. Auntie always checked the contents. She needed a place between the house and the bus stop to stash the outfit she planned to wear to school. How much time did she need to leave home, retrieve and change her clothes, then get to the bus stop? She decided to begin her calculations tonight in case her plan had flaws.

"Auntie, I'm going for a walk."

"Be back before dark."

Sarah heard the kitchen door slam as Augusta left the house to do her evening chores.

She raced to her bedroom to gather her dress and black flats. She searched the slit under her mattress for a favorite blue necklace and matching bracelets retrieved from their hiding place in the brick wall, then slid the items into a plastic grocery bag. Next, she put on one of her tee shirts and pulled on her denim overalls. She slipped the bag under her shirt and tied it to her waist with a length of twine. Her overalls were loose enough to hide the bulge from Augusta if she didn't turn sideways. The grandfather clock in the living room chimed six-thirty. She had about an hour to time her walk to the bus and find a place for her bag of clothes.

If Augusta appeared without warning, Sarah's deception might be discovered. She tiptoed out of her bedroom, inched along the hall, and peered into the living room. No sign of Augusta. Sarah opened the front door to let in the evening air and surveyed the clearing that stretched from the porch to a stand of trees at the edge of the property. A squeaky screen stood between her and her goal. She pulled the handle down and pushed. The rusty hinges whined. She froze. Would Augusta be able to hear from the backyard? She waited. No sign of her aunt. Emboldened, she leaned against the frame. The bottom of the door scraped the wooden porch, then screeched and complained as Sarah gained enough room to exit. She leaned against the house and waited—no sign that Augusta heard her leave.

Sarah scampered down the front steps, across an expanse of dried grass, and waited in the bushes near the road to hear her aunt's voice shrieking threats and obscenities. Instead, the air filled with the honks and squawks of birds returning to the wetlands after a day of foraging.

She turned left on the dirt road that led to the bus stop. Ponds and clumps of marsh grasses covered the surrounding land. She needed a dry area to hide her change of clothes and give her some privacy. Sarah began to doubt the wisdom of her plan. If she had no hiding place for her outfit, she was doomed to wear what Augusta bought. A soft orange light on the horizon told her it would be dark soon. She quickened her pace. There had to be a way for her plan to work. It had to work if she wanted to avoid the stares, whispers, and ridicule of her new classmates.

She rounded a curve and spied a stand of trees set on high ground. They appeared thick enough to hide her while she dressed.

Sarah raced across the meadow to squeeze through a dense growth of trunks and underbrush. A small clearing created enough space for her change of clothes. She tied her bag to a low branch, looping the handles three times, then tying a piece of cloth to a bush within sight of the path. She continued to the bus stop, where she consulted her watch. The trip from the farm to the bus stop took almost an hour, with time added to change clothes.

Twilight gave Sarah enough light to reach the farm. She approached the fence that marked Augusta's property and hid in the bushes. A light glowed from her aunt's office window onto the front porch. Augusta sat at her desk, downing whisky straight from the bottle. Sarah knew from experience that it was only a matter of time before Augusta passed out. All she had to do was wait. She slid to the ground. Stars began to dot the sky. A warm breeze rustled the leaves overhead. She found it hard to stay awake. It had been a long day.

As soon as it was dark, she sped across the front yard, focused on her aunt, and tiptoed up the front porch steps. She crept along the wall to the window where she could get a better view of the office and peered through the glass. Her heart pounded as Augusta stood, staggered to the window, and scanned the yard. She mumbled, waved her hands, and stumbled back to her chair for another drink.

Sarah tiptoed to the screen door, grabbed the handle, and stopped. Her shoes, caked with mud, left a trail from the office window to the front door. She needed to erase the footprints and remove her shoes before entering. A broom leaned against the porch railing. She would have to pass the window to reach it. After she sank to the ground and crawled closer to her prize, she stood, reached for the handle, and missed.

Boom! Crack! Sarah and the broom handle hit the porch full force.

"Wha, what?" Augusta shouted.

She rolled over and huddled against the wall. Her knees and forehead ached.

Augusta appeared in the window. Attempting to focus as she supported her weight on the windowsill, she swayed for a moment, then disappeared. Sarah feared Augusta might be on her way to the porch.

Eighteen

Sarah crouched, every muscle tightened in case she needed to move in a hurry. Her ears strained to identify any sound in the house. *Nothing.* Curious to know how much danger she was in, she inched up the wall, slid her shoulder close to the window, and peered through the glass. Augusta lay slumped in her wingback chair, her legs akimbo, her mouth open.

Sarah grabbed the broom, swept the mud trail from the porch, and cleaned the soles of her shoes with a garden hose. A rusty screen and a poorly aligned front door posed no problems now. She strode through the entryway, shut the doors, rushed to her room, closed the bedroom door, and dropped full length on her bed with a sigh. *What an adventure.* Her plan worked. She needed at least an hour to get it done tomorrow.

Monday morning, Sarah woke earlier than planned. She had always been excited about the first school day, but this one was special. She watched the sun rise while she loaded her backpack with notebooks, pens, pencils, a dictionary, and the laptop Augusta returned to her for schoolwork only. When she was ready, she rushed to the kitchen for breakfast.

Her aunt was there waiting. "Gimme your backpack." Augusta's eyes were bloodshot, her skin drawn and pale. She winced as the rooster crowed several times. "Damned rooster." She hurried to the kitchen door, thrust it open, and shouted, "Shut up." She threw something at the poor creature.

"*Kwawk!*" It protested and was silent.

"Did you kill it, Auntie?"

"Nothin' can kill that old rooster, and don't call me Auntie."

Augusta checked every backpack pocket, looking for contraband, then rezipped them with gusto. "*Humph.*" She dropped the backpack on the floor beside Sarah's chair and stood over her as she ate. Augusta's breath reeked of alcohol and vomit.

Sarah said, "I think I have everything. All I need is my lunch, and I'm on my way." Head down, she avoided eye contact with her aunt. Her inability to lie might betray her.

"You're leavin' early. What's the rush?"

"Don't want to miss the bus on the first day." Sarah grabbed her lunch from the kitchen counter, flung one backpack strap over her right shoulder, and hastened to the front door.

"Think I'll walk to the bus stop with you. Could use the exercise." Augusta reached for a jacket and followed her niece.

Sarah stopped so quickly that she nearly stumbled over her own feet. Her mouth went dry. Her brain scrambled to form a plan of escape. She wanted to scream.

"Oh, Auntie, I need to walk fast and might meet classmates and their parents on the way. Being escorted by an adult could be a problem at my age, and you might have to talk to them." Sarah counted on Augusta's dislike of other human beings and unpredictable situations to save her plan.

"*Humph.*" Augusta shrugged into her jacket. "Well, that sounds unpleasant. Get on your way, then. I have chores to do." She stomped down the back steps.

Sarah stared after her in disbelief. *It worked.* She rushed across the living room, tugged at the door, opened the squeaky screen, dashed down the front steps, and across the yard to the safety of the bushes at the end of the driveway. She stopped, bent over, hands on her knees, until her breathing slowed. She turned left on the dirt path leading to the main road and hurried to her stand of trees.

Along the way, ponds glittered in the rising sun. Flocks of ducks bobbed on the surface of the water or took flight in pairs or small groups for their daily foraging. Wings splashed the water and vibrated in the air as the birds cleared the pond's surface—no time to stop and look today.

Sarah spied the stand of trees and the rag she tied on a bush. She glanced left and right to be sure she was alone, then dashed across the meadow to squeeze between the trees and dense underbrush. Shadows created by the rising sun darkened the clearing. She shivered.

Sarah dropped her backpack near the tree where she had tied her bag of clothing. "Where is it? Do I have the wrong tree?" A frantic search of the grove yielded nothing. Perspiration formed on her forehead. She had been so careful. Had her things fallen in the bushes? Had some animal stolen them? She pawed through the thorny undergrowth. A garter snake slithered across her path. A murder of crows in the canopy rustled the leaves, cawed their dislike of being disturbed, then rose in a black cloud, circled overhead, and returned to the treetops. A jackrabbit stood on its hind legs at the edge of the clearing. Its long ears pivoted to catch the direction of the sound before it bounded away.

"How can such a simple plan turn so wrong?" If she missed the bus, the school would call Augusta. If she went to school dressed as she was, Sarah feared she would be ridiculed or worse, shunned. Her thoughts were interrupted by the movement of a black object. Lit by the rising sun, it rippled in a sudden breeze. What now? A skunk? Curious, she edged closer. "There is the garbage bag. It must've blown down." She dashed to retrieve and inspect the contents. The ties had come apart enough to expose some of the items. Her dress was damp from the morning dew, but nothing that wouldn't dry during the bus ride. The jewelry lay on the ground, dirty but intact, and both shoes weighed the bag down to keep it from blowing away.

Relieved, she changed outfits and folded the clothes she had removed into her backpack. Her watch told her she was ten minutes behind schedule. Her plan might not work after all. She had to hurry if she wanted to catch the bus on time.

Sarah's outfit stood out at school among the other students who wore cowboy boots and jeans. During roll call in homeroom, she discovered a few of her classmates were Whitmores, descendants of the school's benefactor. They no longer went to expensive private schools but were still Broadmore royalty. She suspected that most of her classmates were descendants of Broadmore pioneers, farmers, and horse people. She would find little common ground with them as she listened to their conversations about horse shows and auctions of 4-H animals.

"Sarah Grant?" Mrs. Moore surveyed the classroom. "Where are you?"

She slumped at a desk in the corner of the room and raised her hand. "Here." All eyes turned in her direction. Whispers and muted giggles pierced her resolve to be strong, fearless, and stoic. She turned her attention to the unfinished doodles drawn in her open notebook to hide her embarrassment. She had hoped the students might save the dreary surroundings. Wrong again.

"Quiet, class. Sarah is new. Make her feel welcome."

The class went silent, but Sarah suspected the respite was temporary. Her tormentors had witnessed her discomfort at being singled out, teased, noticed. Some of her peers were bound to exploit those weaknesses. All she could hope for now was a kindred spirit to befriend her.

At lunch, Sarah found a secluded bench set among a stand of yellow-leaved aspens at the far end of campus. A gentle breeze rustled the leaves, reminding her of a rain stick Gram bought in Costa Rica. When turned end to end, it sounded like a soft spring shower.

A shrill end-of-period bell shattered her sanctuary. *Round three.* She glanced at her class schedule. Her last class was PE, the knock-out punch to a distressing day.

Physical Education in her former school had offered archery, tennis, golf, and fencing. Sarah did well with those choices. She was a disaster at team sports and was relieved that Broadmore had no pool, so no swimsuit and soaked hair. At least she didn't have to dress until she bought gym clothes. How long could she stretch that out?

Surrounded by peers who worked on farms or won awards in sports, she found it hard to keep up during the preliminary fitness test. At least the instructor had an extra pair of shorts to save her from embarrassment. Despite that, her classmates found it hilarious when she couldn't manage a somersault, ran out of strength to complete the rope climb, or failed to perch on a medicine ball without rolling over.

"Hey, weakling," one of the boys yelled.

"You're big enough to do this stuff." A group of girls giggled, then whispered behind their hands.

"Wanna' bet she can't do the last one either?" The whole class roared with laughter.

"Okay, guys and gals. That's enough. Get back to the task or end up in detention." The teacher set up mats on the gym floor for the last challenges—headstands, somersaults, and the high bar lift.

Nineteen

The sound of a dismissal bell released Sarah from her torment. She dashed to the bus stop and pounded on the driver's window. "Let me in, please."

"Whatsa matta, young lady. Somebody chasin' ya?"

"Just want to get on." Sarah pleaded as she bounced from one leg to the other.

"Thar ya go." The door hissed and opened with a thud. "Tough day, huh?"

"Something like that." Sarah sped past the driver.

"Sorry ta hear that. Kids can be really rotten sometimes."

"Yeh." She headed to the back of the bus and slumped near an open window. She tossed her backpack on the seat next to her to avoid further contact with her classmates. She leaned her face against the window frame. A lump formed in her throat. She folded her arms across her chest to comfort the ache inside.

Soon, laughter, chatter, and teasing filled the seats around her. The door hissed and then closed with a thud. Sarah grabbed a notebook from her backpack, opened it, and attempted to write. She wasn't ready to share her thoughts, even with her notebook. Instead, she began to doodle around the few phrases that crossed her mind. She wondered what Dr. Banks would say about the meaning of the scribbles that darkened with each new drawing.

The bus dropped her at its stop and drove away in a cloud of dust that choked her and left grit in her eyes.

She found the stand of trees, crossed the meadow, and entered the clearing. This time, she wouldn't have to search for her clothes. She pulled the skirt, blouse, and penny loafers from the smallest backpack pouch and replaced them with her dress and flats. Aunt Augusta would never know about her disobedience. Another ugly scene was avoided. At least she had some control over her situation.

She retraced her steps from the morning. The walk through the surrounding wetlands and her defiance of Augusta's rule began to lift her spirits. Flocks of noisy migrating birds would arrive this time of year. The wetlands would be alive with Sandhill Cranes, Canada geese, and Great Egrets. She longed to take a detour to the ponds to watch them arrive, but Augusta would be waiting on the front porch, ready to pounce if she came home late.

She slowed her pace as she entered the property and approached the farmhouse. Something was not right. The windows were dark, and Augusta was not on the porch for the usual interrogation. A sense of foreboding grew as she approached the front door, opened it, and stepped into the entry hall.

"Augusta?"

"In here." Her harsh, ragged voice came from the living room.

Sarah peered into the darkened room. Every muscle in her body tensed. Maybe she found out about the wardrobe switch. Heat rose to her neck and face. Sweat glided down the sides of her cheeks.

Augusta sat in a straight-backed chair silhouetted by the light from the window behind her. Sarah shifted her weight to the balls of her feet like a tennis player poised to move in any direction.

"Come here, Sarah. Sit." Augusta pointed to a chair across from her so she could not see her aunt's facial features. The seat was hard and had no arms to allow her to relax. She dropped her backpack on the floor next to the chair and sat, her arms folded across her chest. Her jaw tensed.

"This writing you do is a waste of time. Always believed you were doing your homework out back. You're a bigger sneak than I thought. What do you have to say for yourself?"

"Nothing." Sarah stared at the floor as her mind raced to make sense of Augusta's unexpected complaint. She noticed her aunt's hands resting on something in her lap.

"Still a disrespectful brat, then?" Augusta threw a stack of notebooks at her feet. "I found these in the barn under a pile of rusty tools."

Sarah gasped. "My notebooks. How did you find them? Have you nothing else to do but spy on me?" She bit her lip so hard that she tasted blood.

"You need to start payin' your way around here." Augusta rose from her chair and paced as she spoke. Her hands sliced the air with every word. "I only took you in 'cause your grandmother was my sister, and you came with support money. Figured it was about time I got compensated for what she did to me. Ruined my life, she did." Augusta shook her index finger. "I won't let you do the same."

Sarah shot out of her chair and lunged at her aunt. "What are you talking about? Gram wouldn't do that. You're lying."

Augusta's eyes widened as she stumbled backward to avoid colliding with her. "You're calling me a liar? You? What a crock." Recovered from the shock of Sarah's response, Augusta shoved her into her chair. "Had no need of a child to raise, but as long as you're here . . ."

She tossed two sheets of paper in Sarah's lap. "A list of chores I expect you to do, and you'll also do my errands in town. That won't leave you with as much extra time to waste. Save your writing for school. Now, pick up those notebooks and throw them in the garbage. I'll be watching you from the kitchen window to be sure you obey." Augusta rose from her chair and strode toward the kitchen.

Sarah tried to read the chore list, but her mind could not make sense of the words. They blurred and slid across the page. Her body felt heavy, and her mouth was dry.

"Hurry up. I'm watching you. Put those notebooks in the garbage, NOW!" Augusta's voice forced her out of the chair and into action. Anger replaced shock. Determination replaced weakness. Hate replaced submission.

Sarah gathered her notebooks, sauntered through the kitchen where Augusta stood waiting and opened the screen door. She stomped down the back steps, strolled across the lawn toward the garbage can, lifted the lid, turned to look at the smirking face in the kitchen window, suspended the notebooks high above her head for a few seconds, and let them drop with a thud. Sarah wouldn't let the old bat take her writing from her. The notebooks she found weren't the only ones. Her pillowcase and mattress cover hid more. *She was way ahead of Augusta.*

Sarah leaned on the edge of the garbage can. She met Augusta's eyes and held them until her aunt's face vanished from the kitchen window. She slammed the top of the can back in its place, turned on her heel, and headed into the surrounding wetlands.

Twenty

arah did not return to the house for several hours. She wandered the wetland trails, where she found comfort in the silence and beauty of the marshes. Grateful for her boots, she left the gravel path and headed across the muddy marsh to get closer to nature and farther from people. Foraging birds returned to their nests and ponds. Their calls mingled as they seemed to share the day's news. The setting sun bathed the land in a soft, hazy glow.

She spied a willow tree set on a rise above a small pond. It was sheltered on three sides by dense growth, a perfect private place to think unobserved. The grass under the tree was dry. She sat cross-legged while observing nature's evening rituals and considered her present situation.

How could two sisters be so different? Gram was a kind, generous woman who loved her deeply. They laughed and talked for hours, from lipstick colors to boys to the God Gram so loved. Gram said that they always have choices. What were Sarah's choices? She could run away, but she had no place to go. She could stay and give in to Augusta's abusive behavior until she stopped caring about anything. She hoped another choice would appear. So far, she felt stuck.

A warm breeze rustled the bushes and formed ripples on the surface of the pond. Sarah turned her attention to the birds. A few yards away, a gray and brown speckled bird with a long, slender beak probed the mud for its dinner. A mallard, the only duck she knew, glided to a landing. Its webbed feet sliced the water effortlessly. Its plain brown mate landed close behind. Overhead, a noisy flock appeared out of the clouds in "V" formation, headed for distant ponds. They banked to the left, low enough for her to see their vast, black-tipped wings and bright red-capped heads.

A Great Egret landed in the reeds near Sarah. It folded its graceful white wings, lengthened its long, slender neck, and pointed its yellow beak toward the sky. The bird turned its head toward her. Its eye seemed to study her for a moment before it lowered its head and moved forward on long, spindly legs, searching for food. A sense of awe replaced her anxiety as she was drawn to its slow, steady feeding rhythm.

A gust of wind ruffled Sarah's hair, and she tucked it behind her ears. A memory flashed, then disappeared. A steadier wind, warm and soothing, filled the space where she sat. She closed her eyes. The vision returned, and this time it remained. *She was in a bus. Her heart was heavy. She was crying.*

Someone handed her a tissue. "My name is Evie Burrows. I live a mile north of your aunt. Come and see me anytime." Sarah's eyes snapped open as the scene faded—another choice. "Ask, and it shall be given," Gram always said. Evie might help her find a way out of her circumstances.

"Thank you. Thank you. Thank you." She raised both arms to the sky. Sarah remained at the pond until the light of a full moon bathed the pathway back to the farm.

❧❧❧❧❧❧

Sarah's clothing exchange in the secluded grove worked all week. One flaw, though—she had little clothing to work with and had to repeat some of her creations. Students stared, whispered, and turned their backs on her as she passed. Her plan needed some work. That Friday afternoon after school, she needed to visit her pond to watch the migrating flocks land on the water. She had the whole weekend to revise the clothing plan.

Sarah followed the path she found yesterday. It took her through a meadow to a stand of trees and a pond surrounded by bushes thick enough to shelter her from wind and passersby. She used a fallen tree branch to support her back as she sat cross-legged on the grass with a journal from her stash.

Alarmed by the shrieks and shouts of female voices headed her way, Sarah rose from her secluded spot by the pond. She strained to understand their garbled conversation, as each voice engaged in a contest to win the loudest in the crowd. Twigs snapped, red-winged blackbirds shot from nests in the reeds, and swaths of waist-high grasses flattened in their wake. She crouched and skittered through a patch of thorny underbrush. She maneuvered her body to the ground to avoid the thorns that tore at her skin.

Voices moved closer. Bodies became more distinct as they topped the horizon of the clearing and stopped next to her hiding place.

"Did you get a good look at the new girl? That dress she was wearing is the one I took to the secondhand store in Lawson. I'd swear it."

"Sad when you must wear someone else's old clothes. The newbies are getting poorer every year."

Sarah's throat tightened. Her face grew hot, her jaw clenched. She wanted to spring from her hiding place to defend her honor and tell these mean girls her situation was only temporary.

"Hear she lives at the Hanson farm."

"Thought old, wicked Augusta died. Did you bring it?"

"Yeah, but only one. My dad won't miss one from his stash."

"Brought the lighter."

Sarah heard a click.

"Suck it in deep and hold it before you exhale."

Whoosh, silence. The unmistakable odor of marijuana seeped through the bushes. She clapped her hand over her mouth to stifle a cough.

"*Mmm*. Good weed." The smoker slurred and giggled.

"My dad buys only the best. My turn."

"Wish my parents would move to the city."

"Fed up with the Whitmore curse?"

"Got to hang on one more year. Tired of hearing, 'Our ancestors founded this town. Long history. Been here for generations.' Blah, blah, blah. Boring."

A second cloud of smoke seeped through the branches. Sarah pulled the top of her blouse over her nose to screen the fumes. She needed to stay alert to focus. Her eyes burned. She stifled a scream as a small black snake breached her space, slithered up her hand, wrapped itself around her wrist twice, and then headed back the way it came, rustling through dried underbrush.

"Did you hear that? I swear I heard something moving in the bushes." A pair of embroidered cowboy boots stepped closer to where Sarah was hiding. She had seen expensive boots like these, hand-stitched and beaded on suede, in high-end department stores.

"It's the weed playing with you. Come on. We can set up by this pond."

"Woo-hoo. Let's party. Gimme a drag." Three pairs of black leather ankle boots staggered into view as the group sank cross-legged on their blanket, their backs to Sarah. Four blondes, hair glowing in the afternoon sun, swayed as they reached for another puff and attempted, words slurred, to outshout each other.

Tears pricked Sarah's eyes as she watched her sanctuary desecrated by incessant chatter about boys, sex, gossip, and the overbearing stench of marijuana smoke—*time to escape*. Eventually, the intruders would be too high to notice her creep through the tall grasses a few yards behind her and head for the safety of the trail.

Twenty-One

Shadows lengthened as the sun reached the horizon. Sounds of senseless muttering and soft snoring encouraged Sarah to make her move. Sweat stung her eyes, trickled down her back, and blurred her vision. She stumbled over tangled undergrowth and holes burrowed by small ground-dwelling animals. Branches pricked at her skin and clothing. She reached the edge of the clearing, crouched near the ground, and focused on the trail ahead. Her arms, stretched out in front of her, cleared a path through the tall grass as twilight turned to darkness.

Free from her hideout, her feet on the solid surface of the trail, Sarah turned left on the gravel path and headed toward the farm, shivering from the cold air on her damp skin. A quarter moon shed little light, but she knew the way after so many trips to the pond.

Familiar wetland noises turned ominous in the dark. Unseen creatures skittered through bushes and rustled the tree branches that arched overhead. The scream of an animal, possibly caught by a predator, pierced the air. Every shadow, every leaf that moved, every sound enhanced her growing panic and her need to find safety.

A tree root snagged Sarah's foot. She fell face down with a thud and rolled on her back, gasping for breath. Mud oozed from her face and hands. "Sarah . . . you've done . . . it . . . now. Clum . . . ss . . . sy. Al . . . always . . . in a . . . hu . . . hurry." She lay still as she willed her breath and her fear to settle. Sarah pushed up to a sitting position to assess her possible injuries. There were none that she could see or feel. The mud had cushioned her fall. How would she explain to Augusta her dirty clothes and the absence of jeans in her closet?

"Time to get moving, girl. Come on. Get up." She rose and took a few short steps—no sprains or breaks. A breeze rustled overhead. It exposed the moon long enough to reassure her that she was headed in the right direction.

The trail surface changed from gravel to packed earth. Sarah remembered the riparian forest would give way to a meadow around the next bend and the promise of relief from the eerie darkness.

The scenery transformed from forest to open field. Mist floated close to the surface of the grass, reflecting the scant moonlight. *Freedom*. She knew the path would dead end at a paved road in a few minutes, where she would turn left to the farm.

Sarah needed a plan if she hoped to enter the farmhouse unseen. Augusta would be up. She was sure the woman never slept. She visualized her options. The front door would be the safest entrance if her aunt were in the kitchen. Once inside, she could slink down the hallway to her room, shut the door, wash her face and hands in her sink, change her clothes, and slide under her bed covers. Augusta might decide to work in her office. That would be less safe since Sarah needed to pass the office door to get to her bedroom. Usually, Auntie shut her office door and locked it for some reason. One day, she hoped to sneak a peek at what Augusta did in there, which was so secret.

Deep in thought, Sarah stubbed her toe on the slight rise of pavement on the main road. She repeated what Dr. Banks told her at the end of every session, "Always move forward one step at a time, Sarah, never backward."

"Time to take the first step, girl." Still wobbly, Sarah took one step, then another, and another. As she moved, her strength returned, and her pace increased.

She reached the dilapidated corral fence surrounding the farm and hid in the bushes to assess her options. Augusta was awake. The kitchen window glowed for a moment, then went dark. The living room ceiling light clicked on. Augusta peered out the picture window and glanced at her watch. She disappeared for a moment.

The front door flew open. A floodlight filled the yard. Sarah waited for a prison siren to wail. Augusta stormed onto the porch and paced from one end to the other. She leaned over the railing and searched the side yards with a powerful flashlight. Muttering, arms flailing, she shrieked, "Sarah, get in here. You'll pay for this."

Sarah flattened her body against the thick trunk of an oak tree beyond the light that filled the front lawn. Apparently satisfied her niece had disappeared, Augusta entered the house and slammed the door. Sarah's bedroom light snapped on and stayed on for some time. The high windows prevented any view of Augusta. Was she in the bedroom, the living room, or . . .?

As if in answer to the question, her bedroom window went dark. Minutes later, the Tiffany lamp in her aunt's office snapped on as she slumped in her chair and flipped on her computer. Augusta's head appeared bathed in a pale blue screen light, producing an eerie scene.

Her aunt spent hours browsing websites until she fell asleep, snoring in her chair. Sarah would wait a few minutes before she made her move. Auntie's head fell forward, jerked up, fell forward, jerked up, then fell forward and lolled toward her right shoulder where it remained.

She sped the few yards to the gravel driveway that bordered the property. A stand of scrub oak provided cover as she hurried to the back steps. Scant moonlight assisted her dash from the trees' safety to a dark corner under the wooden stairs leading to the kitchen. She strained to hear any sign of danger as she gathered the courage to enter the house. Sweat trickled down her forehead and stung her eyes. An owl hooted. The silhouette of a four-legged predator, prey dangling from its mouth, crossed the side road and disappeared in the tall grass. Sarah waited a few minutes. "Let's go, girl."

She dashed across the lawn, tiptoed up the well-worn wooden steps, unlaced and removed her muddy shoes, gripped the doorknob, and pushed until the warped wood scraped the floor. She squeezed through the opening, slid against the inside wall, and clicked the door shut. Sarah surveyed her surroundings. Light from the living room pooled between the kitchen and the dining room revealed a clear path forward. She stepped into the minefield of aging floorboards, ready to announce their displeasure with any misstep.

Sarah cleared the kitchen and living room with ease. She cupped her ear against the entryway wall adjacent to Augusta's office. Was she still snoring? *Silence.* She entered the hallway, edged closer to the open door, and peered in. A strong odor of whiskey assaulted her senses. An open bottle of Jack Daniels had fallen on its side; its contents stained the threadbare carpet under Augusta's heavy wooden desk.

A guttural sound ripped the air, followed by a mumble and a gasp. Augusta's eyes flew open. Sarah, her heart pounding, pivoted away from the door frame and flattened her body against the wall. "Who's there?" Augusta slurred. "Show *yoourseellff.*" Her chair squeaked. "Am comin' after ya. *Humph.* Dang it."

Sarah heard a thud. She peered around the door molding, careful to hide her body. Augusta sprawled in her chair, pounded the armrests, and spat unintelligible words. Sarah dashed to her bedroom door, stepped inside the room and eased the door shut. She removed her muddy clothes and shoved them under the bed. After lying on her mattress with her back to the door, she pulled the covers to her chin and closed her eyes.

Her heart pounded as she strained to hear sounds in the hall— a coyote howled in the distance. Tree branches, set in motion by a growing wind, tapped and scraped the roof and the window. A floorboard creaked, then another. Sarah glanced over her shoulder. A slit of light flashed under her closed bedroom door as Augusta flipped the switch in the hall.

The doorknob clicked. Sarah ducked further under her covers. Her body tensed at the scrape of wood against the floorboards. The silhouette of Augusta's head against the wall told her that her aunt had entered the room. As Augusta moved closer to the bed, an eerie shadow crawled up the wall. Heart pounding, Sarah slowed her breath to mimic sleep. A bony finger poked the soft flesh of her upper arm.

"You awake?" As Augusta leaned closer, Sarah fought her desire to gag as a strong odor of stale whiskey invaded her nostrils. Augusta poked her again so hard that it took all her concentration to avoid making a sound. "*Humph.* Never mind, girlie. Getcha tomorrow."

A shiver shot through Sarah's body. She wondered what *Getcha tomorrow* meant. Nothing good. Augusta excelled at the torture of the mind.

Augusta's shadow slid down the wall and disappeared as she left the room, closed the door, and turned out the hall light.

Sarah lay on her back. Her heart slowed to its normal beat. Evie Burrows's invitation for her to visit "any time" popped into her mind. She needed to get away from Augusta. Her aunt's next move might be dangerous, even fatal. It was some time before Sarah slept.

❧❧❧❧❧❧

"You're up, you lazy brat. It's Monday. Your bus leaves in an hour. Think you can sleep all morning just because you stayed out late last night? Your bus leaves in an hour. If you miss it, you will do extra work here." The door slammed as Augusta left the room.

It took Sarah a few minutes to clear her head and shade her aching eyes from the bright morning sun.

"Answer me." Augusta scowled. Her wiry hair stood out from her head as if she'd been electrocuted. She strode across the kitchen.

Sarah edged closer to the doorway, fearful of the blows bound to come from this crazy person looming above her. She folded her arms across her chest and could not think. Her mind floated above the scene as if she observed the action.

"Ahh!" Augusta howled like a wounded animal, spun away from Sarah, and stomped out of the kitchen.

Sarah blinked several times before she could return to reality. She scrambled to fix her lunch, grabbed a cereal box, and dashed to her bedroom. She shut the door, leaned against it, slid to the floor, and hugged her knees as she fought the terror that throbbed in her chest. "Gram, where is your God? What did I do wrong?" *Breathe in—breathe out.* Her heart slowed. She needed to catch the bus. She needed to wash her face and comb her hair. She needed to load her backpack—no time to worry about clothes. She dressed in whatever was handy—wrinkled khakis, a stained shirt, a baseball cap, and a faded denim jacket.

When ready, she left her bedroom and edged down the hall. Augusta's daily shriek at the rooster echoed through the open kitchen door. Sarah scampered to the living room, grabbed her backpack from beside the chair where she had left it the day before, fled out the front door, raced down the walk, and turned left at the gate. When she could no longer see the farmhouse, she stopped to catch her breath and glance at her watch—*fifteen minutes to go.* She resumed her frantic sprint.

She turned left as the dirt road changed to pavement. *Almost there.* She could see the bright yellow bus. Five children waited for their turn to board. As each child climbed on, she forced her aching heart and tired legs to move faster. Hope faded as the last passenger stepped up the stairs. She was close enough to hear the doors hiss shut. The bus driver would wait for everyone to be seated and settled before he turned the key in the ignition.

She called out as she saw him check the back seats. She waved. He patted a child on the shoulder in the back seat, laughed, turned his back, and disappeared down the aisle without noticing Sarah. The engine roared, the tailpipe puffed exhaust, the gears ground into place, and her hope diminished. Desperate, she veered to the driver's side in sight of his rearview mirror and pounded on the side of the bus as it edged away. Curious faces filled the windows. They shouted. Brakes squealed. Doors hissed open. Bus riders cheered Sarah on as she raced around the back of the bus to the open doors and up the steps.

"Almost left ya, Missy." The rotund driver chuckled and cocked his head. "Very dangerous to run alongside a moving vehicle."

"Thanks for stopping." At least someone noticed and helped her this morning—no shouting or threatening punishment for her late arrival.

"Here. Sit in the first seat to catch your breath." The driver pointed to a space and grinned.

Sarah slid into the window seat, grateful for the kind words and the soothing vibrations as the bus hummed toward their destination. She closed her eyes.

"Wake up, Missy."

"Whaa . . . ?" It took Sarah a few seconds to focus on the jovial bus driver standing over her. She needed to get to class.

"We're here. You need to get more sleep at night. Did you eat breakfast?"

Sarah shook her head. "No time."

The driver returned to his seat, grabbed a lunch box, and opened it. "Here. You have half of my sandwich. That should hold you 'til lunch."

"Thank you."

"See ya at three o'clock. Be on time, Missy. Don't want ya bangin' on my bus again."

"I'll be here."

Sarah waved as she hurried down the bus steps to the parking lot. The doors hissed and slammed shut. The motor roared, the exhaust pipe expelled its dark cloud, the breaks squealed, and the bus leaped forward. Hungry, she slid the sandwich out of its wrapper—tuna fish on rye, her favorite.

Students jostled each other as they filled the plaza in front of the school. Sarah elbowed her way through the crowd. She needed to hurry if she wanted a homeroom seat in the back row.

Yesterday, she ended up in the front row, an awkward place to be if you wanted to be invisible. She needed that back-row seat today and the freedom to write, draw, and form a plan to find Evie Burrows. The bus driver might know who she was and where she lived. She would ask on the way home.

To Sarah's relief, the hallways were empty. She entered home-room as the starting bell rang. She found the perfect seat in the back corner of the last row. From there, she observed her class-mates as they spilled through the door.

Boys, rowdy and loud, poked each other in the arm or pawed the air in fake fist fights before they fell into their seats in a slouch. They searched the room to discover who might be attracted to their behavior. Six blonde girls strode, giggling, to seats by the win-dows. A cloud of perfume filled the room. They eased into their seats, heads turned toward each other as they whispered their final bits of gossip. From her seat in the corner, Sarah spied the beaded suede boots from yesterday's encounter in the wetlands. She stud-ied the girl's face as she flipped her long hair behind her shoulders. Sarah planned to avoid her and her friends as much as possible.

Heat rose to her face as she remembered the ugly things they said about her. In her school in Sausalito, she was one of these girls—well-dressed, self-important, exclusive. She wondered how many people she'd hurt in the past as the careless remarks in the meadow had hurt her.

Twenty-Two

Sarah could not concentrate in any of her classes. Her notebook was covered with plans, doodles, and lists of ideas for escape. Pages of notes and observations about what happened with Augusta that morning helped ease her trauma. Dr. Banks and Gram were right about journaling. Somehow, the worst experience, when written on the page, eased her troubled thoughts and emotions. She didn't understand how it worked, but it did. Her precious journals acted as the friends she no longer had; they heard all her thoughts and feelings without judging.

She skipped her last class and found a quiet bench at the back of the campus to finish writing her thoughts. She didn't realize no one could hear the dismissal bell at the far edge of the campus. A glance at her watch told her she had lost track of time. If she missed the bus, there was no easy way home. Frantic, she jammed all her books in her backpack and dashed for the front of the school. There was no line waiting to get on. That meant the bus was about to leave.

She accelerated her speed and waved, her chest aching with the exertion. She leaped on the bottom step as the door started to close.

"Another late start, Missy? Two close calls in one day." The bus driver scowled as he started the engine. "Better sit in the front seat again. I don't have time to wait for you to find a seat before I get moving. We're late already."

"Yes, sir. Sorry." Sarah stared at the floor, grabbed the pole behind the driver, and slid into the front seat, caught in the forward motion of the bus. She heard the other riders giggling too far behind her to listen to what was said. There weren't many older students as far as she could see through the rear mirror. Lawson and the surrounding area housed few families. Most of the students at the Broadmore schools lived in town.

Sarah removed her notebooks from her backpack. She needed a distraction, so she tried to add to the notes and drawings from earlier in the day, but the bumpy back roads prevented any attempt to steady her hand. She slid the notebooks into the front pockets of her pack and allowed her thoughts to wander.

Augusta had been so angry this morning. The memory of Augusta's red face, bulging eyes, and venomous words flashed through Sarah's mind. She needed to find a way to escape if her aunt came after her again. She didn't know anyone in the area except Evie and spoke to her only once. Maybe Evie's invitation was just something to say, or maybe she was serious about the offer.

The bus lurched to a halt. Sarah, lost in thought, remained in her seat.

"Asleep again, Missy?" Half out of his seat, the bus driver turned to stare at her. "Time to get off the bus."

"Sorry. Not asleep—just thinking. Do you know a woman named Evie Burrows?"

"Can't say that I do, but I'll ask around."

"Thanks."

"Plenty of time to daydream on your walk home. Be on time tomorrow, or I'll have to leave you behind."

"Right. See you tomorrow." Sarah waved as she exited the bus, then crossed in front to avoid another onslaught of dust and gravel from the rear tires as they gained traction. She stood in the shelter of the bus stop and watched the bus disappear around the curve. She closed her eyes as she took in the rhythm of the wetlands—the steady hum of hundreds of insects punctuated by bird song and splashes of water as unseen creatures disturbed pond surfaces. The beauty of nature eased her anxiety.

She became aware of reeds rustling in the marsh across the road. A Great Egret emerged, its long white neck stretched forward in search of food. It raised its head for a moment, its beak pointed toward the sky, one eye trained in her direction. Sarah caught her breath. This was a sign, a message. Every time she was in need, the egret appeared. She waited and watched as it moved one careful step at a time through the water.

"Do you have something to show me, Great Egret? If you could speak, I bet you'd have all the answers I need right now."

Sarah eased to the ground, elbows on her knees. She waited for a sign. The bird was in no hurry. It searched the bottom of the pond, then stretched its neck full length, took a few careful steps forward on its spindly legs, and dipped its head again. After a third feeding, its beak pointed to the sky, and its wings spread to full length. With one strong beat, it took flight as it tucked its long neck close to its body.

"No, no. Wait. Don't go." She leaped to her feet and dashed across the road. The thought of losing sight of the one thing that was good about her day brought tears to her eyes.

The egret soared over a reed patch, wings beating the air in a slow, rhythmic motion. It banked to the right as it climbed above the treetops, soared without effort, then banked to the left and left again, headed toward her.

"Hooray." Sarah opened her arms to welcome her friend.

It passed overhead, circled the meadow behind her, and flew north, parallel to the road. Sarah followed the bird as it headed north again. She hurried after it, hopeful for the first time today. The appearance of the Great Egret must be a sign, a message. It seemed to appear when she needed comfort or direction. True or not, she believed she needed to follow it now.

Nausea and stomach cramps gripped Sarah as she approached the corral fence. She needed to cross from where she stood to the safety of the woods on the other side of the property. Augusta appeared on the front porch for Sarah's daily interrogation. Hands on her hips, she paced the porch, consulted her watch, and mumbled as she punched the air with her fist. She grabbed the railing to maintain her balance and whipped around to retrace her steps. Augusta appeared drunk.

The egret circled overhead and headed north. Determined to follow the bird, Sarah crouched and sped along the corral fence without another look at Augusta. She reached the stand of trees on the other side of the property, caught her breath, and peered at the porch. It was empty.

Focused on the Great Egret, Sarah headed north. What did she have to lose? Time to take a risk. Augusta behaved out of control last night and this morning. No telling what she had in store for her when she arrived home from school today. Evie might not remember her, but she needed to tell someone about the abuse. At the very least, Evie might take pity on her and help her leave Augusta. Her theory about the egret acting as a messenger could be wrong, but she was out of options.

Twenty-Three

The afternoon was clear and warm for early November. Cottonwood, thick as snow, floated and swirled across the marsh. Sarah sneezed. Her eyes itched. Her sinuses swelled. *Misery.* She searched her pockets for a tissue. Another sneeze tickled her nose. Her eyes began to tear up. "*Aachoo!*" She blew her nose, dabbed her eyes, threw her backpack over one shoulder, and moved north on the main road away from Augusta and the farm.

The Great Egret soared overhead, carried by air currents. It dipped its wings to the left and right and flew over trees beside the road. Sarah trotted and danced with renewed energy as she focused on the egret. She wished she could fly beside it, free and graceful.

As the sun moved closer to the horizon, the wetlands came alive. Sandhill Cranes, their red-capped heads visible, swooped out of formation and settled in ponds for the night. Ducks skimmed the water, then bobbed and floated on the surface. Frogs began their noisy seesaw croak. Red-winged blackbirds twittered and fluttered their wings as they swayed atop tall reeds to guard their nests. Swarms of tiny insects circled her head, flew up her nose, and threatened to enter her mouth if given the opportunity. She brushed them away with little success.

There was no judgment, bullying, or threat to her peace of mind in this world. Marsh life ran smoothly. Each creature had a territory, a predictable life, and an understanding of how to share space. Her life had been the opposite. It had been anything but predictable or peaceful. It had been chaotic, confusing, and complicated. Again, Sarah had no place to go, no one to help her.

An orange sky silhouetted the distant tree line and bled across the ponds, highlighting islands of tall reeds that dotted the marsh. Flashes of white appeared in the trees as Great Egrets returned to their nests in the branches.

It would be dark soon. A new moon was forecast tonight. Sarah began to doubt her decision to follow the egret. She glanced at her smartphone—seven o'clock. Two hours had passed since she dashed across the corral at the farm and sauntered down the road, lost in the beauty of the wetlands. Her stomach tightened as she considered her need for food and shelter.

After viewing a map that she and Maggie used to find Lawson, she knew there were other farms along this road, but she had yet to find one or see a car or any sign that other humans might be around to help. Her Great Egret had disappeared. She reached for the water bottle in her backpack. It was empty. If Evie wasn't home, she planned to wait for her to return. With no streetlights and no full moon, wandering the wetlands at night would be foolish.

There was a fork in the road ahead with two possible routes. Which one to take? Robert Frost's poem came to mind. Two paths in the road—one traveled and one not traveled. It sounded wise to take the one not traveled, but this time, she chose the one with tire tracks, lots of them, some old, some new.

"Sorry, Bobby. I need to find help." She snickered at calling Robert Frost *Bobby*. Miss Dutmeier, her sixth-grade English teacher, would have gasped.

Sarah consulted her watch again—seven-thirty. Evie's house couldn't be much farther. Evie said she lived a mile north. Sarah feared she might have missed it. Around a bend in the road and tucked in a white climbing rose bush was what she had hoped for—

a mailbox with the name Burrows printed in block letters. Deep ruts suggested heavy use by a work vehicle, a truck, or a four-by-four, but there was no sign of a house. Dense trees arched overhead and blocked what daylight was left.

"Okay, Sarah, we don't know where this leads." Her heartbeat increased. She whispered, "Reminds me of a black hole in another dimension." She plunged into the darkness with a deep breath and briefly examined her surroundings. "Here we go."

An owl hooted as it soared overhead and disappeared in the dense forest. "Great. A hooting owl. Perfect." She hesitated. She wondered if she should continue. Despite her weak knees and a lump in her throat, she needed to push forward. A faint yellow light glowed a few yards ahead. "Ah, there it is—the light of hope that pulls a traveler ever closer to her doom."

Sarah reached the edge of a white wooden fence, which horse properties used to corral animals. A white horse hung its head over the top rail, snorted, and stretched its head toward her, its nostrils flared. She gasped. *What a sudden appearance.* It snorted again, turned its head, and galloped away.

"Not very interesting, am I?" she asked.

Continuing along the perimeter, she spotted two horses in shadow at the back of the paddock. The white horse neighed, bobbed its head, and trotted before them as if reporting information about the intruder. She chuckled at the sight and continued to survey her surroundings.

On the other side of the property, yard lights shone through the branches of a sprawling oak tree. A patio with a fire pit and two padded chairs led to a house partially hidden by bushes. Light filled one window. Someone with gray hair dashed across the room, stopped momentarily, then disappeared. Sarah thought the woman might be Evie, but she was too far away from the house to tell. A floodlight snapped on as the screen door eased open, propelled by the shoulder of a woman holding a bucket. She ducked below the fence line. She heard a whistle. The horses trotted toward the fence.

"Here ya' go. Carrot time." The horses nudged each other as the woman offered a carrot to each one.

Her voice sounded familiar. Sarah skirted the fence until she had a better view. She stumbled over a water spigot and fell hard in the mud beneath it. "Ahh."

"Who's there? Show yourself." The woman strode in Sarah's direction. Her silver hair shone in the light, her lined face threatening. The closer she came, the more Sarah became confident she knew the woman. Her voice, pure white hair, and slight limp reminded her of the woman she met on the bus. Sarah grabbed the faucet and scrambled to her feet. "I'm sorry. Just someone who is lost." She brushed mud from her knees.

The woman stepped closer. "Wait, I know you. We met on the bus." A cobbler's apron, stained and faded, covered her ample body. She wore an oversized sweater and jeans underneath. Her mud-caked Wellingtons squelched across the wet ground as she moved closer.

"Yes, it's Sarah Grant. You gave me a ride to my Aunt Augusta's farm." Evie's deep blue eyes sparkled. In the light, her wrinkles softened, and the shadows disappeared. Sarah leaned forward, clasped her hands, and waited for a response.

A German Shepherd raced across the yard and circled the woman. "Sit, Deacon." The dog finished its final turn with a low growl, sat close to the woman, and trained its eyes on Sarah. Her tense muscles wanted to run, but she knew that was dangerous. She retreated a step.

"Hello there, Deacon." Her voice quivered. Deacon stood and wagged his tail at the sound of his name. Sarah's body relaxed.

"Deacon, sit." With a sigh, the dog obeyed. "Oh, yes. I remember. What are you doing here at this hour?" Evie frowned and cocked her head.

Sarah, encouraged by her reception, met Evie's eyes. "I need help."

"Sorry? I couldn't hear you. You need to speak louder."

Sarah wrung her hands and glanced at Evie. "I remember you said I could visit at any time. I can't go back to the farm."

"Ooh." Evie was silent for a moment. "Here, help me with the last of these carrots, and then we can go inside. You're not afraid of horses, are you?" Evie handed her the last of the carrots.

"No, ma'am."

All three horses moved closer, snorted, and tossed their heads. Sarah realized the horse that greeted her earlier was gray, not white. The other two shone deep brown in the floodlight. Each had a white spot on its forehead, a black mane, and black-rimmed ears. She hesitated. She'd never fed a horse before. "Do they bite?"

"Hold the carrot in your open hand, then offer it to one of them." Evie demonstrated the open hand. "You'll see how gentle they are."

Sarah stepped toward the gray horse, held out her open hand, and closed her eyes. Its soft muzzle tickled her hand as it took the carrot. She opened her eyes. The horse seemed to smile at her. "Wow. That was amazing."

"Horses are gentle creatures if you treat them well. I was about to have dinner. Will you join me?"

She glanced at Evie and then continued to feed the other horses. She considered Evie's offer. Her stomach ached—she hadn't eaten since lunch.

"Does Augusta know you are here?" Evie cocked her head and leaned against the fence.

"No." Sarah continued to avoid eye contact. Her body stiffened. She didn't want Augusta to know anything, much less her location.

"Well, then, we need to let her know where you are and ask permission for you to stay. She'll be worried."

Sarah didn't care if her aunt worried. Augusta might care about her as a cook, a housemaid, and a person she could control. Sarah took more time feeding and talking to the horses than necessary. A lump in her throat prevented her from responding to Evie.

Evie waited a few minutes for an answer. "Okay. My roast is ready. Come in if you like. It's up to you. I would enjoy the company." Evie trudged across the graveled driveway, sat on a bench beside the back door, and removed her Wellingtons. She slid her feet into house shoes and disappeared behind the screen door.

Sarah hesitated to accept Evie's offer of hospitality. She remembered how kind Evie had been to her on the bus ride to Lawson. Her gentle, deep blue eyes, soft silver curls, and ready smile reminded her of Gram. She could always keep her backpack near her if she needed to flee.

Sarah crossed the grass between the paddock and the house and stood on the patio. An odor of garlic, rosemary, and roasted meat escaped through the open door. She began to salivate. Her hunger convinced her to climb the stairs to the back porch. She opened the screen door and entered the kitchen. Its pale, yellow walls provided a warm contrast from the cold outdoors. The added fragrance of baked apples smothered with butter and cinnamon erased any doubt that she would, at least, stay for dinner.

"I'll stay. May I help?" Sarah dropped her backpack near the door.

"Good." Evie turned from the pot she was stirring. "You can set the table, and you need a change of dry clothes. The silverware is in the drawer near the table, and the dishes are in the cupboard above. I'll see if I can find you something to wear. My youngest daughter was about your size." Evie wiped her hands with her apron and hurried out of the room.

After Sarah set the table, she turned her attention to the photos and awards on the walls. Young dressage horses flew over hurdles and pranced around arenas as their perfectly groomed riders urged them on. Riders posed next to their mounts with trophies, blue ribbons, and broad smiles. Sarah wondered who they were.

"Here ya go. This should fit. You can wash up in the bathroom over there." Evie indicated a door in the kitchen corner and returned to the stove to complete dinner.

The half bath had a linoleum floor, a hand-held shower head, and a sink large enough to serve as a laundry soaking tub. Sarah guessed it had been part of the original house. It had the distinct odor of bleach and damp walls. She removed her wet, muddy clothes, put them in the sink, and ran enough water to let them soak. She sponged the dirt from her body, dried off with a towel, and slid into the jeans, underwear, and sweater that Evie had given her. They fit perfectly. The clothing, though slightly out of style, appeared new. She rinsed her clothes, wrung them out, hung them over the edges of the sink, and returned to the kitchen.

"I'm clean and ready to help." Sarah moved toward the stove.

Evie glanced at Sarah and froze. "You look so much like her."

"Who?" Sarah noticed Evie's eyes were damp.

"My youngest daughter."

"Are the pictures on the wall of her?"

Evie pointed to a photo of a young girl dressed for dressage holding a trophy. "This is one of her when she was about your age. She loved to show and was very good at it." She sighed, returned to the stove, and whipped the mashed potatoes.

Sarah thought better of asking any more questions. Gram would say it was rude and none of her business. Still, she was curious.

"Sit down. Dinner is ready." Evie carried serving plates to the table. "Before we eat, I need to do one more thing." She lifted the phone receiver. "Now. What's your aunt's phone number?"

Evie's repeated attempts to reach Augusta were unsuccessful. "Still no answer. Where could she be?" Frowning, she replaced the receiver in its cradle, shook her head, and returned to the dinner table.

"I have no idea. Augusta never goes out at night." Sarah shrugged her shoulders.

Evie and Sarah ate pot roast, mashed potatoes, honey-glazed carrots, and homemade dinner rolls oozing with butter.

"Your pot roast is amazing, just like Gram's. I am the cook at the farm. Gram always teased me about my ability to burn everything, no matter how simple the recipe. She was determined to teach me to cook. 'You have to be able to feed your family someday.'" Sarah imitated Gram's voice as her eyes softened with the memory.

Evie pushed her empty plate to the side, folded her arms on the tabletop, and leaned forward.

"Are you getting settled at school?"

"It's hard. The school isn't as nice as the one in Sausalito, and the students have their groups."

"It takes time to fit in. Living in the country is very different from living in the city." Evie cleared her throat. "And how are things with your aunt?"

"It's not the best. She scares me with demands, and she's mean. I can't go back there." Sarah could not resist the tears pooling in her eyes. She avoided Evie's gaze, hung her head, and sobbed. "I'm sorry."

Evie touched her elbow. "What are you sorry about?"

"I should go," Sarah mumbled. She reached for her backpack, held it close to her body, and headed for the kitchen door.

"It's late, and there is no moonlight tonight. I'd feel better if you rested here. I'll go see about Augusta and leave a note if she isn't home."

Sarah hesitated. She dropped her backpack near the door and whipped around to face Evie. "What if she is home?" she shouted. She clasped her hands in front of her to stop them from trembling. Her breathing slowed. She shivered. Sweat trickled down her back.

"If she's home, we can discuss whether your aunt wants to come and get you or wait 'til morning for you to walk home. I have an early appointment, so I can't drive you in time for school." Evie patted Sarah's hand, cleared the table, and loaded the dishwasher.

She placed the last dish in its slot and studied Sarah. "Why don't you lie down for a while? You look exhausted. You're welcome to use the couch in the living room."

Sarah's stomach tightened. She glanced around the kitchen. "I can find my way in the dark. No need for you to make a fuss."

"It's no fuss, my dear, but it's up to you."

Sarah's knees went weak at the thought of facing the dark night. Exhaustion weighed her down. She needed to rest. She wanted—*no, needed*—to trust Evie. So far, adults had brought her nothing but trouble. The couch was tempting. She could always leave.

"Thank you, Mrs. Burrows. The couch sounds good."

"Come on, then. I'll get you a comforter and a pillow." Evie led Sarah to a forest green velvet couch. She set a pillow and a quilt that smelled like lavender next to her. Gram loved lavender. Sarah inhaled and relished the memory of Gram as her heavy eyelids closed, opened, and closed again. "Good night, Gram. I miss you."

Twenty-Four

Sarah, a cup of coffee in her hands, relaxed in a chair in Evie's living room and considered where she was and how she ended up in a strange place wearing someone else's clothes. Yesterday started with desperation and ended with Evie Burrows's offer of sanctuary, an amazing turnaround.

An ornate antique clock above the carved fireplace mantel struck nine. Sarah perched on the edge of the green velvet couch and wriggled her toes in a sheepskin rug that covered the golden-brown wood floor between the sofa and the fireplace. Sun streamed through partially opened drapes onto a grand piano that dominated one corner of the room. Floor-to-ceiling shelves displayed books, photographs, and decorative pieces. A guitar stood upright on a stand behind two green velvet overstuffed chairs. Colorful stained glass reading lamps and books—some opened, some bookmarked—filled two oval side tables.

"Where are you, Evie?" Sarah shouted as she searched the house and yard. Evie's truck was gone.

"Did Evie leave me, too?" Sarah's heart raced. Evie had planned to go to Augusta's farm, but that was last night. The horses, still in their stalls, nickered for attention. Evie's dog barked and whined as it paced the length of its metal enclosure.

The phone in the kitchen rang. In time, Sarah dashed to the back steps to hear the answering machine beep. "Sarah, answer the phone. It's Evie. Answer the phone *now*." Evie's voice grew louder and more urgent. Sarah took the back stairs two at a time and tripped over the door frame. She grabbed the receiver and lost her grip. It slammed against the edge of the counter and ricocheted to the floor.

"What's going on there? Are you all right?" The caller shouted.

Sarah recognized Evie's voice and retrieved the phone. "Mrs. Burrows, I'm here. Where are you?"

"Your aunt had an accident. It took most of the night to get an ambulance and the information I needed from the hospital. I tried to call a couple of times after my appointment this morning. Guess you were sound asleep."

"Sorry. Will she be home soon?" Sarah plopped in a chair, closed her eyes, and caught her breath. Evie hadn't left her.

"I'll tell you what happened later. You'll be staying with me for a few days. I'll drop by your aunt's farm on the way home to pack some of your things. What do you need?"

A few days without Augusta? Another miracle. "I don't know. I don't have much. It's all in my bedroom."

"I'll figure it out. We can always go back. There are towels in the bathroom closet and food in the fridge. See you in a couple of hours."

The phone clicked. Sarah listened to the dial tone for a few seconds before she realized the conversation had ended.

At the news that she would be free of Augusta for a few days, she jumped from her seat, hands in the air, and shouted, "Thank you, God." She twirled, pranced, and danced to the refrigerator. Her stomach growled. She was hungry. A glass-covered chocolate layer cake caught her eye. Half of it was missing. She pictured Gram in her kitchen in her pajamas as she cut into a chocolate cake.

"No matter what happens, Sarah, chocolate is the answer. Best medicine ever."

Sarah cut a large slice, picked it up in her hands, and ate. Rich, gooey frosting oozed over her fingers, around her mouth, and down the front of her borrowed shirt. *Gram was right. Best medicine ever.*

What now? she wondered. She had two hours to wait, so she wandered into the living room. Heavy brocade curtains blocked most of the sunlight—time to pull them open and enjoy her morning without school and Augusta. The windows on either side of the fireplace looked out on a side yard with metal wisteria-covered arbors and more rose bushes than Sarah had ever seen outside of the Golden Gate Park Arboretum.

French doors flanked by two picture windows on the adjoining wall revealed a sloping grassy area bordered by trimmed hedges. A wrought iron gate led to a wetland pond dotted with reed islands. On one side of the pond, a stand of oak trees and a weeping willow formed a sheltered space where she could enjoy solitude. Sunlight from the windows illuminated pale green walls, a polished brown dining table, and a crystal centerpiece filled with red roses.

Evie's home was perfect. It had books, a piano, and wetlands, all things that Sarah loved and missed in Augusta's sterile environment.

She turned away from the view, ran her hand over the smooth surface of the baby grand, and lifted the top of the piano bench, hoping to find an easy piece to play. A beginner's book of Chopin, her favorite composer, lay on top of the stack of music. Gram had taught her to play when she was nine. She learned quickly and loved to play but hated practice and performance, especially in front of family and friends. She closed the bench, opened the covered keyboard, and struck middle C. The tone was rich and resonant. She opened the music book, chose Chopin's most famous *Nocturne in E Flat*, and placed it on the ledge in front of her. The meaning of the black splotches on the music staff returned, but the fingering and the key signature slowed her down. She played a few stanzas and closed the cover. "Well, I got about half the notes right."

The sound of crunching gravel in the driveway caught her attention. Evie must be home. Sarah hurried through the kitchen and out the back door. "What happened?" She grabbed the truck's door handle and yanked it open.

"Whoa. Let me get out of the truck first." Evie, with her hand on the inside door handle, started to fall sideways.

"Sorry." Sarah pushed Evie upright.

Evie pivoted out of the driver's seat and eased to the ground. "Ouch." She placed both hands on her back and leaned backward. "Hospital waiting rooms are not designed for comfort." She reached across the driver's seat and grabbed a bulging garbage bag.

"These are the things I thought you might need. I couldn't find a suitcase, so I used what I could find in the kitchen." She handed her the bag.

"Thanks." Sarah didn't move.

"Let me get in the house. I need a cup of tea."

"Sorry." Sarah ducked her head and stepped back.

"Come on. There's lots to tell you. First, I need to feed the menagerie. They must be starving by now."

Sarah's heart sank. She'd been waiting forever for the information Evie said she had. How long would it take before they could talk? "Can I help?"

"Sure. You feed the dog, and I'll feed the horses. The dog food is in the pantry."

Sarah raced up the back stairs, dropped the garbage bag by the door, rummaged in the pantry for a can of dog food, opened it with an electric can opener, and raced to the dog run. The dog barked, danced, and jumped in circles. "Get back so I can feed you, Deacon." She grew impatient and shoved the dog out of the way. "I'm in a hurry." She dumped the whole can in the dog's dish, opened and shut the gate, and headed for the kitchen.

Evie stood by the stove, a tea kettle in her hand. "Sit for a minute while I make some tea."

Sarah perched on the edge of her chair, clasped her hands, and rocked as she waited for the tea kettle to whistle. "I was worried when I woke up, and you were gone."

"So sorry. It took a long time for the ambulance to come, and then we had to wait for a doctor to see her." Evie poured boiling water into two mugs and added tea bags. "I see you had a piece of the cake." Evie glanced at Sarah's mouth and chin. "Can you eat another piece? I need one, too."

"Sure."

Sarah brought two plates, forks, and the cake to the table and cut generous slices.

Evie placed her hand on her arm. "Your aunt had a severe stroke sometime yesterday. Apparently, she fell and hit her head on the corner of a table in her office. The doctors don't hold out much hope for her complete recovery. She went too long without medical help."

Sarah struggled to make sense of what Evie said. She had often wished Augusta harm, wished someone would rescue her from a life with such a demon, wished she could leave and never see her again, but a twinge of guilt pricked her conscience. It fought with a sense of relief and fear of the future.

"Where will I end up if Augusta dies? Foster care?" Sarah bit her lip.

"Let's deal with that if the time comes. For now, Social Services has honored my request to care for you until we know if Augusta can recover. Is that okay with you?"

Sarah chewed on a fingernail and took a deep breath. The words *for now* echoed in her mind.

"Sarah?"

Sarah started at the sound. "Yes, Evie. I want to stay here with you."

"Good. I'll make the bed in the spare room, and you can settle in. We'll go to the farm for the rest of your things tomorrow."

"Okay." Sarah's jaw ached from grinding her teeth. It wasn't okay to return to Augusta's farm, Augusta's prison. It wasn't okay to end up in foster care. It wasn't okay to be at the mercy of adults and a system that left her out of the equation.

"Come on, then. Help me make your bed, and you can unpack. I put the garbage bag of clothing in your closet."

Evie led her through the living room, opened one of the closed doors on the back wall, and ushered her into a bedroom filled with light from a picture window that looked out on the wetlands. Late afternoon light transformed the soft green of the walls into a cozy, soothing retreat. On one wall was a brass double bed covered with a multi-flowered spread, matching pillow shams, and a myriad of stuffed animals.

"This was my youngest daughter's room. She loved stuffed animals, riding horses, and painting pictures of nature. Most of the art on the walls are her watercolors." Evie's eyes grew misty again.

Sarah wondered what had happened to her daughter that made her sad. Evie opened a closet and pulled out a set of flowered sheets. "Here. Help me make the bed. Put the animals on the couch."

Sarah filled her arms with lions, teddy bears, and a unicorn. She placed them side by side on the couch at the foot of the bed. It took her three trips to remove them, all except an oversized bear. Her fingers barely touched as she carried the huge stuffed animal to the couch; its floppy head bounced against her cheek. "Where did this come from?"

"My husband won it for our daughter, Wendy, at a carnival, the last one he went to before he became ill. She rubbed most of its fur off, holding it, sleeping and playing with it." Evie's eyes filled with tears again. Sarah looked away and busied herself with rearranging the animals on the couch.

"Wendy painted and won dressage trophies? You must be very proud of her." Sarah hoped Evie would reveal more about her daughter. "We were very proud. She had a riding accident. Broke her neck. She was only eighteen."

"Lunch will be ready in a few minutes; until then, you can unpack and put your things away." Evie hurried out of the room and closed the door.

Gram was right about minding your own business. She feared she had asked Evie too many questions and overstepped.

Grateful for the distraction, Sarah opened her backpack and removed her laptop. She set it on top of the built-in desk and storage cupboards that stretched the length of the picture window, sat in the swivel chair, and stared at the wetlands.

"Lunch," Evie called.

Sarah opened the bedroom door. The fragrance of leftover roast, cinnamon apples, and spiced tea filled the kitchen. Her mouth watered. She had food, a place to stay, and someone kind enough to care for her for a few days. Gram had always assured her everything would seem better after a good night's sleep. Maybe this time, she'd be right.

Twenty-Five

After all the events of the day, sleep eluded Sarah. Awakened by frightening dreams, she gave up the fight for a peaceful night. She attempted to write the visions down in her journal, but they disappeared almost immediately when she woke. Her churning stomach and clammy hands were all that remained.

She stared into the darkness as she attempted to remember her dreams. She began to write down her thoughts as they came to mind. In one dream, she was lost in a marsh and sank in a bog of quicksand. In another, an invisible presence chased her over a cliff. She landed on an outcropping surrounded by animals that growled and snapped at her. As snippets of her dreams flowed onto paper, her shoulders relaxed, and her breathing slowed. The sky changed to a lighter blue. It was dawn.

The ring of the telephone and Evie's muffled voice told her that Evie was up and in the kitchen. Sarah searched the garbage bag for something to wear. She pulled out a pair of jeans, a white tee shirt, and a pair of sneakers. "Don't have to go to school. Better day already."

The bedroom door opened. Evie's head popped in. "Oh, good. You're up. I'll fix you something to eat, then we need to go to the hospital." She disappeared before Sarah could respond.

"So, this isn't going to be a better day after all." Sarah hated hospitals. Her childhood memories of visiting Gramps before he died remained fresh. To her, hospitals meant pain, loss, odors of disinfectant, and the sound of monitors tracking the life force of bedridden human beings. She hoped the hospital didn't expect her to visit her aunt. She didn't want to see her. What would happen to her if Augusta died? Worse yet, she might have to take care of her aunt, bathe her, feed her, and always be with her. Her heartbeat increased. She found it hard to breathe. Her forehead felt cold and clammy to the touch. *Breathe in—breathe out.*

The smell of coffee pulled Sarah toward the kitchen. "Good morning, sleepyhead. Hope I put everything you need on the table."

"Who was on the phone?"

"Your aunt's doctor." Evie wore a heavy sweater, a wool hat, and work gloves tucked into her jeans' waist.

"Put some cereal out for you. Must feed the horses." Evie grabbed her jacket off a chair and waved as she rushed out the back door.

Sarah poured a cup of herbal tea and stared out the kitchen window. Hummingbirds, their red necks flashing in the early morning sun, fought for a turn at the feeder. Noisy house finches circled bird feeders full of black oil sunflower seeds and traded places as if playing musical chairs.

She slid into a chair at the table, filled a bowl with granola, and poured milk over it. The doctor had called. *Must be important.* Her chest felt wet. She glanced at her shirt that clung to her skin. *"Whaa?"* Her milk had overflowed the cereal bowl. Milk pooled on the table, ran down the front of her blouse and jeans, and splattered on the floor.

"No! What a mess." She jumped up, ran to get a roll of paper towels, and tried to rip off a sheet as she sped toward the river that edged across the floor. In her haste, she lost control of the roll. It bounced off the end of the table, flipped, and landed in the pool of liquid. Then, it slid onto the chair and landed on the floor, soaking the toweling.

Sarah was on her knees when the back door opened. "What on earth happened here?" Evie stood with her hands on her hips.

She sat back on her haunches. "*Umm.* I wasn't paying attention and—" She raised her palms and shrugged.

Evie sighed. "It's been a long time since I had to clean up after anyone but me."

Her heart beat faster as she waited for Evie's angry blast for her carelessness.

"We're going to be late for sure. Go change your clothes and hurry up about it." Evie frowned as she strode to a closet to retrieve a mop. "I'll finish up here. I need to get changed myself. I hate being late for an appointment."

Her heart sank. She fled to her room in tears. She had failed Evie, created extra work for her, and showed how much of a burden it was to have her in the house. At least Evie didn't rage or threaten her like Augusta always did. She hurried to change her clothes and return to the kitchen. This time, she wouldn't make Evie wait for her. That might make up for the mess she made.

❧❧❧❧❧❧

With the mess cleaned up and their clothes changed, they climbed into Evie's red pickup truck, slid onto the leather seats, and fastened their seat belts.

"Here we go." Evie's voice sounded higher and more jovial than usual as she gunned the engine and spun her tires in the gravel. She made a U-turn and headed along the driveway. Limbs from overarching trees slapped against the windshield, and small animals skittered across their path and disappeared in the undergrowth.

They turned left on the main wetland road and headed toward the interstate and civilization. "Sarah, we will meet with your aunt's doctor and a social worker today."

"Why? I don't understand." She felt a sudden pain in her chest. A social worker had sent her to live with Augusta.

"We are all a team, and we need to make a plan for your future if we need one."

Sweat trickled down Sarah's back and forehead. Her breathing slowed. She remembered Dr. Banks's soft voice from what seemed like a lifetime ago—*Breathe, Sarah.*

"We don't know what will happen yet. Are you listening?" Evie's voice interrupted Sarah's thoughts.

"Sure. Okay. What?"

"All I know is you can stay with me until we know about your aunt's recovery. It won't help to think any farther into the future than that."

Sarah noticed they were on the highway headed into the city. Before her life changed, entertainment, fun, and friends had been in town. She missed living there. She missed her old life. She missed family. She missed school. She lay her head against the side window. Her body seemed heavy. Aunt Augusta, a social worker, and a doctor waited inside the hospital with plans for her future. She tried to ignore her fears. *Breathe.*

❧❧❧❧❧❧❧

The squeal of brakes echoed through the hospital parking garage as Evie found an open spot large enough for the truck. "We're here," she announced as she shifted into park.

Sarah spied the name Morehouse Hospital through the concrete pillars of the parking structure.

"You need to get out of the truck to make our appointment." Evie opened the passenger door. "Let me help you." Sarah stared straight ahead for a few seconds before swinging her legs out of the truck.

She stood momentarily, confused and dizzy; her wobbly knees refused to support her. Evie closed the passenger door and linked arms with her. "We're going to be late."

Twenty-Six

Crowds of people jostled them as they entered the lobby and headed for the elevator labeled *ICU*. Everyone faced forward, packed shoulder to shoulder. No one spoke during the ride to the fourth floor, where the car stopped. Doors slid open, and the passengers dispersed.

A tall, dark-haired man with penetrating blue eyes leaned against the counter of the nurse's station. He moved toward Sarah and Evie, hand outstretched. "Mrs. Burrows, good to see you again." He shook Evie's hand. "And this must be Sarah. I'm Dr. Morris." He turned to greet her. His broad grin and kind eyes drew her in like a magnet. "Would you like to see your aunt for a few moments?"

Augusta was the last person she wanted to see, but she thought she should appear cooperative and caring. "Sure." Her stomach churned. The lie made her nauseous. Gram would have been disappointed. She taught her granddaughter not to lie. Sarah began to believe that twisting the truth might be necessary for survival.

Dr. Morris led Evie and Sarah down a corridor of glassed-in cubicles, blinking lights, and the odor of cleaning fluid. Nurses pushed computer carts from room to room as they checked patients. Three attendants scurried to respond to a red light over an ICU room.

"Here we are." Dr. Morris motioned them into the room. "This is Nurse Thomas. She cares for Augusta during the day." The nurse, petite and masked, was wearing light green scrubs that appeared to be a size too large. She was completing her final computer keyboard strokes.

"Sorry. I needed to finish recording before I forgot the numbers. Good to meet you." Nurse Thomas turned from her computer cart. "If you have any questions, please let me know. If I don't know the answer, I'll find out for you."

"Thank you," Evie replied.

Sarah was silent. Her attention turned to Augusta's body, barely a bump under the bedsheet. Her thin, gnarled hands rested on either side of her. A taped needle inserted in each veined hand pumped liquids from transparent bags suspended above her head. Her face appeared so thin and pale that Sarah could see every bone and muscle. Though unconscious, she seemed displeased with the world; her mouth pinched in perpetual bitterness.

Sarah stared at Augusta's emaciated body. *You got what you deserved. Meanness and rage finally took you down. Good riddance.* Tears spilled down Sarah's cheeks.

"Are you all right? There are tissues on top of the cabinet to your left." Nurse Thomas gestured to a glass cabinet filled with boxes of gloves, bandages, and instruments. "So sorry you're going through this."

"Thank you," Sarah muttered.

Evie opened the door and waved her hand to get her attention. "We have an appointment in Dr. Morris's office in ten minutes. Come on." She disappeared.

Sarah hurried after her, relieved.

They stepped through the open door of Dr. Morris's office. Light from a casement window brightened the oak-paneled office, desk, and crowded bookshelves that lined the walls. An overstuffed couch and three chairs upholstered in a large floral print offset the dark wood.

In his crisp white coat, Dr. Morris hurried into the room, followed by a woman who sat down in a wingback chair in the corner. He turned to Sarah and Evie. "Please be seated on the couch, won't you? Let me introduce Mrs. Morton, the social worker from Sarah's new school." Mrs. Morton stood and offered her hand to Evie.

Sarah gasped. She recognized the lady immediately and refused to shake her hand. The last time she saw Mrs. Morton, she was seated in their Sausalito living room, questioning Gram's ability to care for her granddaughter, who might need special services.

"What is she doing here?" Sarah spat out the words.

Mrs. Morton sat back in her chair, crossed her legs, folded her arms at her waist, and scowled at her.

"Mrs. Morton needs to be here since she works with students at your new school," Dr. Morris said.

Sarah noticed a man in the doorway. Deep smile lines around his eyes and a shock of pure white hair reminded her of her grandfather. He wore a minister's collar under his shirt, jeans, and a tweed sport coat with suede elbow patches like her father used to wear. "I'm Chaplain Crane. I volunteered to assist when I found out Augusta was a patient here. I grew up with your aunt and her sister, Lorraine, your grandmother, so I offered to help." He eased into the remaining chair.

Sarah trusted no one in that office except Evie. She rested her hands on her stomach, crossed her legs, and narrowed her eyes. It was three against two unless Evie sided with the others. The chaplain's collar made no difference in her trust level.

Dr. Morris sat in a leather wingback chair behind his desk, his hands folded. "My nurse set up some refreshments for us. You both must be hungry after such a trying morning. Please help yourselves."

Evie chose coffee and a muffin while Sarah remained on the couch.

"Mrs. Burrows, are you Sarah's guardian?" Mrs. Morton unfolded her arms and gestured in Evie's direction.

"No. I'm just a friend. Sarah happened to visit me on the evening I discovered Miss Hanson was injured."

Mrs. Morton wrote in a leather notebook.

"Where was Sarah at this time?" She narrowed her eyes as she focused on Evie.

"In my living room, warm and cozy. I didn't know what I might find at Miss Hanson's place, and I had no intention of leaving Sarah alone at the farm."

"*Hmm*." Mrs. Morton put her pen down. "The questions are where to place Sarah; what is best for her."

Evie's jaw tightened. She drew a deep breath. "Sarah is welcome to stay with me until we know her aunt's outcome."

"I'm afraid that will be some time, Mrs. Burrows." Dr. Morris swiveled to face his computer. "Miss Hanson has had a severe stroke as well as a head injury from her fall." A few clicks brought the screen to life. "Let's see what the latest assessments tell us." He scanned the information on the screen. "*Hmm*. Let's see." He stroked his chin and tapped his index finger on his desk. "Sarah, does your aunt drink alcohol often?"

"I don't know." She remembered empty liquor bottles in the trash every week. If she told the doctor about them in the presence of the social worker and the chaplain, decisions might go against her aunt as her legal guardian. She was at the mercy of a room full of strangers. They could decide anything. The last group of adults that made decisions for her sent her to live with Augusta. This one could send her to foster care. The thought sent a shiver through her body.

Mrs. Morton moved to the edge of her chair and leaned forward with her hands on the arms as if ready to leap. "Why do you want to know, Dr. Morris? Do you have evidence that Miss Hanson has a drinking problem?"

Dr. Morris turned his attention to Mrs. Morton. "That information is confidential. Is there another legal guardian for Sarah? She is a minor."

Mrs. Morton fumbled in her briefcase. "I need to check with legal on this. We'll need to complete a background check on Mrs. Burrows. Until then, I see no reason why her generous offer to house Sarah temporarily is a problem."

"As chaplain at this hospital and a childhood friend of Augusta's, I can check on Sarah's welfare. Would that be okay with everyone?"

Sarah wanted to run. The conversation faded into the background as her mind raced to gain control. Her throat tightened. She found it hard to breathe. A sharp pain twisted in her belly. "Where's the bathroom? I need the bathroom."

"I'll take you there." Chaplain Crane stood and motioned her to follow him. They left the office and hurried down a corridor. "Not an easy conversation. Are you okay?"

"No big deal." Sarah squared her shoulders as she struggled to keep her voice from wavering.

"Here we are. If you need help, there is an alarm button near the toilet. I'll wait for you."

"Thanks." She shoved the door open, then closed and locked it. Relieved that this was a one-person restroom, she sat on the closed toilet seat with her head between her legs. She took long, deep breaths to gain control of a room that seemed to spin around her. Immediately, her stomach lurched. Her mouth began to water.

She stood, turned, and lifted the seat just in time to lose her breakfast. Weakened, she stumbled to the sink, splashed cold water on her face, and stared in the mirror. "You're okay, Sarah. Rinse your mouth out. You mustn't let them know you are upset. Breathe in—breathe out." A knock sounded at the door.

"Are you okay? You've been in there for at least thirty minutes." Chaplain Crane's deep baritone voice reminded Sarah that she needed to return to Dr. Morris's office. Right now, all she wanted to do was sleep.

"Coming." She combed her hair, checked her breath, and blew a kiss at her reflection. "Try to behave. No more outbursts." She frowned and shook her finger at the girl in the mirror.

She stepped into the corridor.

"There you are." He smiled at her and turned his attention to the young woman beside him. "We'll talk later, Marta. Meet Sarah Grant, the young lady I wanted you to check on."

"Nice to meet you. Glad you're all right." Marta waved as she hurried to the nurse's station.

Chaplain Crane studied Sarah for a moment. "You look pale. Do you need some water?"

"I'm okay. Let's get back to the inquisition."

"*Hmm.* It does seem a bit like one, doesn't it?"

"Yup."

"They're trying to find a way forward that will be best for you."

"I just want to go back to Evie's." Sarah increased the speed of her steps.

The sign on the door read *Braydon Morris, Neurology.* "Here we are." Chaplain Crane reached across her for the door handle. "Let me go in first to check out the situation." He opened the door a crack. "I'm back with Sarah. Okay to come in?" There was a muffled response. "We're good to go." He opened the door wider. "After you, young lady."

Sarah entered and surveyed the office. Everyone in the room avoided her gaze, a sure sign that she had been the topic of conversation while she was gone. Her heart beat faster. Her face grew warm. Her jaw clenched. *Steady. Steady.* Adults needed to be handled with respect. Too bad often they didn't return the favor.

Dr. Morris raised his head, stood, and gestured toward Evie. "Sarah, please sit on the couch next to Mrs. Burrows." Evie patted the space on the cushion next to her.

The doctor swiveled in his chair, folded his hands on his desk, and cleared his throat. "We all agreed it would be best to leave you with Mrs. Burrows until we know more about your aunt's condition. Mrs. Morton will pass your case information to a different high school located in your area and assist you in your transfer there."

A new school? She didn't have to go back to Broadmore? What a relief after all that happened to make her feel rejected, out of place. Maybe the new high school would be more like her old one where she had so many friends and great teachers.

"Sarah, are you listening?" Evie brought her attention back to Dr. Morris.

"No, sorry."

"No problem, young lady. This is a lot to take in. Almost finished. Chaplain Tom Crane will help you here at the hospital and check on you regularly at home. I will inform everyone daily about Miss Hanson's progress." Dr. Morris's stony, no-nonsense face softened as he rose, walked from behind his desk, sat on the outer edge, and leaned toward Sarah. "Is this plan acceptable?"

"Sure." Staying with Mrs. Burrows and going to a new school were the two decisions that mattered to her. The rest of the conversation was a blur.

"Good," he said.

Mrs. Morton stood to leave. She smiled faintly in Sarah's direction and hurried out the door, clutching her files and a notebook. Dr. Morris shook hands with everyone as they left. "Please stay a moment, Tom. I need to catch you up on the plan."

The office door remained open a crack. Sarah overheard the conversation between the doctor and the chaplain. "I don't expect a good outcome with Miss Hanson. Stay close so that . . ." The door closed before Sarah could hear the rest. She wondered what "stay close so that" meant. She pressed her ear against the office door. No sound came through. Dr. Morris didn't expect a good outcome. Did that mean death or care, and if she needed care, then what?

Twenty-Seven

Sarah and Evie strolled out of the hospital. "I noticed an ice cream shop about two blocks away. Interested?" Evie asked.

"Perfect. I need chocolate." They turned right and focused on the huge ice cream cone sign two blocks ahead.

"A park across the street from the shop looks like a great place to sit and unwind."

They searched the tubs of ice cream for their favorite flavors. "Pistachio," Sarah shouted. "Mine, too." Evie agreed. "Three scoops in each cup and lots of whipped cream on top. This has been one of those days."

"Understood." The young woman behind the counter winked and filled the cups to the brim as ordered. "Here or to go?"

"To go." They answered in unison.

"That's ten dollars. Going to the park?"

"It's a perfect day for it," Evie replied.

"Wish I could come along."

Evie and Sarah sat on a bench in the park where a weeping willow provided shade. A small fountain bubbled behind them. Children too young for school filled the playground to their right. They shrieked in delight as they reached for the sky on swings or wobbled down the bright blue slide. Women, some with strollers, sat around the perimeter. They stared at cell phones, attempted to read a book, or tried to converse with each other. Frequent shouts of "Look at me" and the required response of "Good for you, great job" or the demand for a push on the swings disturbed any hope of personal time.

"Enjoying your ice cream? This must have been a hard morning for you." Evie seemed to remain intent on people-watching as she waited for a response.

"Yeah. What's going to happen with Augusta and me?" Sarah kept her eyes on the children.

"No one knows the answer to that. For now, we eat ice cream, then drive to the farm to pick up your things for what could be a long stay at my house."

"Good." The thought that Evie had saved her from a foster home brought tears to Sarah's eyes. Again, she realized her precarious position. She could be with Evie for an extended stay or not. Nothing was certain. She shivered at the thought.

"Here, Sarah. Take my jacket if you're cold." Evie shrugged out of her coat and placed it over Sarah's shoulders. "Is there anything you want to do in town before we head to the farm?"

"No. I just want to get my stuff."

Sarah leaned over to catch a red rubber ball headed in her direction. A child, red ringlets bouncing as she trotted after it, reminded her of Sunday afternoons spent playing in Golden Gate Park with her parents. The little girl hesitated as she stood before Sarah, who asked, "Is this your ball?" The girl nodded. Sarah continued, "I used to have a ball like this when I was about your age." Not sure what to do, the child's gaze darted from side to side. "How old are you?" The girl sighed and held up three fingers.

"My ball." She stomped, stepped forward, and glanced at Evie. "Please?"

Sarah offered the ball to the child, who snatched it and sped away.

"Good memories?" Evie glanced at Sarah.

"Yeah," she sighed. "Let's go home." She rose and hurried in the hospital's direction.

Evie jumped at the sudden change in plans. "Hey, wait for me." She leaned forward as she walked in an unsuccessful attempt to keep up. When she reached the car park, Sarah waved at her from the fourth floor.

"Show off," Evie shouted as she leaned against a ground-floor pillar, her heart pounding. "Need to catch my breath." Sarah gave a thumbs-up and disappeared.

When Evie exited the elevator, Sarah leaned against the truck with her arms folded. "What took you so long?"

"Nice talk." Evie hurried to the driver's side, unlocked the door, and plopped onto the seat. "Whew." She unlocked the passenger door. "In a hurry, are we?"

"You bet." Sarah grabbed the door handle, opened it, and entered the truck in one seamless move, secured her seatbelt, and shut the door. "Forward. Enough of this place."

Evie engaged the ignition, backed out of the parking spot, and reached the pay booth in record time.

"This reminds me of the first day I met you," Sarah mused.

"We sat next to each other then, too." Evie grinned. "Seems like a lifetime ago."

They sat in silence as commuter traffic jammed the on-ramp to the freeway. As they sped along the highway, Sarah stared out the window, lost in thought.

"Heads up. We're getting close to our exit," Evie reminded her.

"Right. The sign says thirty minutes to Broadmore." Sarah announced, "Change lanes now."

Evie exited, turned left, and then right onto Main Street. They passed familiar shops and Broadmore High School. Students rushed for buses and cars parked in the lot or lined up at the curb in front of the building. Sarah didn't miss school a bit today. She wanted her former school in Sausalito. In fact, she longed for her old life, her parents, and Gram. It was secure, predictable, filled with good memories and laughter.

"You okay? You're very quiet." Evie studied Sarah's face as they waited for the crowd to disperse.

Sarah was not okay. Dr. Banks had assured her the pain of her loss would ease. Her life would never be the same, but it could offer a new, exciting adventure when she was ready to explore her options.

"I'm fine." She sat up straight and grinned. Gram always said a smile, even a fake one, could improve anything. Why wasn't it working for her?

Evie glanced at her as they bumped over the railroad tracks and headed out of Broadmore onto the paved two-lane road that led to Augusta's farm. "Won't be far now. 'Bout twenty minutes."

A fluttery, empty feeling grew in Sarah's stomach. Her heart pounded. She found it challenging to sit still. This visit could be the last time she entered Augusta's dreary farmhouse. She began to make a list of things she needed to gather—her treasures stuffed behind a section of brick in the garden wall, her notebooks hidden in her pillowcase, her phone imprisoned on a top shelf in Augusta's office, and all the clothes from her old life that Augusta had boxed up and tossed in the attic. The list was longer than she thought. She couldn't afford to forget any of it if she intended to make this her last trip to the farm.

"Evie, do you have some paper and a pencil? I need to make a list of things to take from the farmhouse."

"Look in the glove compartment. There should be something in there." Sarah found an empty envelope and a pen. "This will do." She scribbled her list, folded it, and put it in her pocket.

"I overheard the doctor say that it looked bad for Augusta." Sarah tried to keep the sound of hope out of her voice.

"There's the sign pointing to Lawson." Evie slowed to make the turn. "Dr. Morris will keep us posted daily on her condition."

They drove by the dilapidated Lawson bus station, Sarah's first impression of her future home. She fixed her gaze on the building as they went by. A sudden chill passed through her body. Loneliness and fatigue, as strong as they had been that day, overwhelmed her. "Stop!"

Evie slammed on the brakes. The truck skidded sideways. "What is it? Did you see something?"

"I just remembered my first day here, which was not a good thought. I needed to get rid of it and make it go away. It's a tool I learned from Dr. Banks."

"I see. Well, that's a good thing, I guess. Can you warn a person before you do it again, especially when they're driving?"

"I'll try."

Twenty minutes later, Evie turned onto the gravel driveway at Augusta's farm. This time, no pinch-faced woman stood on the porch glaring at them, and no unpleasant greeting caused Sarah to feel unwelcome, uneasy, and unloved. This could be the last time she set foot on the property. Her right foot's restless tapping increased, and she could not sit still. She found it hard to believe that she might be able to leave Augusta and start over.

Before Evie stopped, Sarah opened her door, leaped out of the truck, and ascended the front steps.

Evie rounded the front of the truck. "Wait for me. I have the key." She grabbed the handrail and struggled up the steps, pausing at the top to catch her breath.

Impatient to get the job done, Sarah paced the porch and peered through windows as she passed.

"Sorry, dear. Not as young as I used to be." Evie retrieved the house key from her purse and opened the door.

Sarah bumped Evie as she hurried past her and headed for the hallway.

Evie stumbled against the door frame.

"We need to get to the attic first to get my clothes." Sarah hurried to the hallway and pulled a metal ring in the ceiling. A trap door opened, a ladder groaned, then landed with a thud on the wooden floor. A cloud of dust flew off the rungs. Dense spider webs floated through the opening. Sarah hated spiders—bug eyes, long, creepy crawly legs, and sticky web threads—but she had a job to do.

"I'll get a broom." Evie disappeared into the kitchen. She returned, loaded down with a broom, some rags, a flashlight, and a pail of water. "You might need all of these. I'll wait here to catch the boxes as you slide them down. Ladders make me nervous."

"Right. Broom first, please." Sarah climbed two rungs, swirled the bristles around the entrance, and tossed the broom into the attic. "Okay. Hand me the flashlight." She eased her head through the attic opening. "It's dark in here. Move the pail and rags a little higher so I can reach them."

"I can manage that." Evie struggled up the ladder.

"That's good." Sarah stretched her arms toward the pail and rags and hauled them into the attic.

She rolled over and clutched the flashlight as she examined the space. The roof was too low to stand upright. She would need to crawl or crouch to maneuver her boxes across the floor and down the ladder. An old, round-topped trunk, a shattered antique mirror, two rotting rattan armchairs, and a broken hat rack sat on the wall underneath the window. To her left, Sarah saw five boxes stacked close to the attic opening. She rolled on her side and sat up. "*Eww!* I have spider webs from the roof in my hair and clothes."

"Be brave. Remember your mission. Spider webs are just tiny sticky threads; they will come off when you're done."

"Right." She lifted the corners of each carton to check the contents. "Okay, I have the right boxes. These are all my clothes. Are you ready for the first box?"

"I'm here. Center the first box between the ladder rungs. Hang on to it as long as you can before you let go. That should slow it down."

Sarah inched the first box along the floor, eased it between the rungs, and lowered it. The box slid along its track. Halfway down, it tipped to one side and fell to the ground with a thud.

"Are you all right down there?"

"Don't worry about me. How do you plan to move these boxes out of the house and into the truck?"

"There is a hand trolley in the barn. That should work."

"Yeah. Send the next box."

It took an hour to finish the job. Sarah backed her web-covered body out of the attic and descended the ladder.

"Here. Let me get those off of you." Evie used a damp cloth to corral the sticky webs that clung to Sarah. "What is in these boxes anyway?"

"All the clothes I shipped ahead of me when I moved here. Augusta considered them improper for a young lady. She stored them in the attic and bought me new ones at the secondhand store."

Sarah strained to shut the trap door. It groaned and cracked as the ladder retracted toward the ceiling and locked in place.

"*Hmm.* Now what?" Evie asked.

"We collect my other treasures and leave this house for good." Sarah hurried to her bedroom, pulled two notebooks from her pillowcase, and strode out the door.

"What about these clothes from your closet?" Evie headed for the clothes rack.

"Don't want them."

"I'm headed to Augusta's office. She locked my cell phone in her closet."

Sarah found a letter opener on her aunt's desk to jimmy the lock. *Click.* The tumblers moved, the door opened, and she searched the top shelf. "It's here somewhere. I saw her put it here." Two manila envelopes fell to the floor. Sarah covered her eyes to avoid their sharp corners. "Yes. Here it is." She hugged her cell phone and sighed. "Finally. Another thing Augusta thought was unnecessary is mine," she smirked. "*Humph.* No more Auntie."

She leaned over to pick up the envelopes and noticed the writing on the front of each one. The first label read *Lorraine*, the second *Emmett*. "Gram and Daddy," she mumbled.

"What?" Evie asked.

"These envelopes must be about Gram and Daddy."

"We probably should leave those in the closet. They belong to your aunt."

"There might be something I need to see in them. They are more mine than hers."

Sarah tucked the envelopes under her arm, rushed out the back door, and headed for the garden. "I just need to get a few things hidden in the wall before we leave."

She parted ivy that grew along a brick wall that edged the property, removed a couple of the bricks, and retrieved a dozen small packages. "Ahh. At last, you're free." She opened one and inspected the glass figures inside. "Hooray. All in one piece."

"Treasure?" Evie called from the back porch.

"Treasure," Sarah confirmed. "That's it. I'm ready to load the truck. Hold these for me, please." She handed the packages to Evie. "I'll get the hand trolley and meet you in the hall."

The two of them packed the truck bed in no time and were on the paved road to Evie's house before the sun sank behind the riparian forest surrounding the wetland meadow.

Maybe it was Sarah's imagination, but the ponds, the birds, the trees, and the sky seemed brighter and more colorful than before.

"It's good to be free."

"Always." Evie glanced at Sarah but said nothing more.

<h1 style="text-align:center">Twenty-Eight</h1>

Sarah had a lot to think about on the ride home. It had been a day full of strange, unexpected events. She might finally be free of Augusta, but it was unclear what her next step would be and who would decide her fate. Everything she had left of her old life was in the back of Evie's red truck or stuffed in her backpack. She hoped the envelopes from Augusta's closet held some answers about her family.

"What could be in those envelopes?"

"Must be something meaningful to your aunt." Evie turned right onto the dirt road leading to her house. "We're nearly home. You'll know soon enough."

Evie's white corral fence came into view. Her three horses appeared, tossed their heads, and whinnied in greeting. As offspring of the same mare, the Bays had white markings from ears to nose that stood out in the waning light of dusk. The horses circled away from the railing and returned, huffing in anticipation of their usual treats.

Evie slid out of the driver's seat, crossed the patio, and leaned against the corral fence surrounding the paddock. "Easy, now. I'll be right back with your carrots." She stroked the head of each horse. They nodded and snorted as if they agreed to her terms.

Sarah dashed up the back steps and into the kitchen. She returned without her backpack and started to unload the truck bed. "Where should I put these boxes?"

"Just stack them in the spare room. I'll help as soon as I feed the herd." Evie pulled on her Wellingtons and headed to the barn.

"Okay," Sarah shouted, ascending the back steps with the first box.

She stored the box under the window. Final rays of the setting sun beamed through the picture window and pooled on the white shag carpet. Instead of the stark brown walls she was used to, these were pale green with bright white moldings.

Sarah stood in the doorway for a moment to take it all in. The double bed, centered in the middle of the north wall, was covered with a blue, yellow, and green floral spread. Its white padded headboard supported multicolored pillow shams that complemented the spread's colors.

Framed prints of wetland scenes hung on the walls. White bedside tables matched a large dresser and mirror on the opposite wall. Next to the bed, two open doors separated by floor-to-ceiling bookshelves revealed a walk-in closet and a private bathroom. She was finally in a welcoming place that belonged to her, at least for now.

She set the box under the window and hurried back to the truck for more. It didn't take her long to stack all her belongings under the window. Finally, she grabbed her backpack from the kitchen chair, carried it to her new room, and placed it on the bed. She pulled out the packages and notebooks she had hidden at the farm and Augusta's mysterious envelopes labeled *Lorraine* and *Emmet*.

"Come on. Let's go get a pizza. I'm starving," Evie called from the kitchen.

"Coming." Sarah stashed the unopened envelopes in her dresser drawer. She would deal with them later.

Evie sat in the truck, the motor running and the passenger door open.

"I love the room, Evie. Thank you," she announced as she hopped into her seat and slammed the door.

"You are very welcome, my dear. You deserve a calm place to rest after all you've been through."

Sarah wondered how long she had to enjoy her new space before she needed to return to her bleak life with Augusta. Maybe Augusta would die, and Mrs. Morton would let her live with Evie.

"Fasten your seatbelt. We're on our way. Pepperoni or sausage with extra cheese?"

"What? Oh, either one is fine."

❧

Evie turned off the road and bounced down the dirt path toward home. The fragrance of hot pepperoni, cheese, and seasoned tomato sauce filled the cab. Sarah's stomach growled in anticipation. One solar light over the kitchen door threw a pale-yellow glow on the driveway.

"Watch your step. Forgot to leave the lights on inside; we left in such a hurry."

Sarah eased out of the passenger seat as she balanced the box of pepperoni pizza and a container of pistachio ice cream in her arms.

Eager to examine the contents of the packages of treasures from the farm's brick wall, Sarah finished her share of the pizza and headed toward her room. As she unwrapped each package, she rediscovered chunky jewelry in bright colors, delicate strands of gold necklaces given on birthdays, the Mickey Mouse watch her parents gave her to help her learn how to tell time, and the miniature blown glass animal collection bought in Sausalito shops on mother-daughter outings. She arranged them on top of the dresser so she could see them until she was ready to put them away. Each one reminded her of the people she loved and those who loved her. She stacked the notebooks with her stories and thoughts on the bedside table to read later.

She had no idea what was in the attic boxes. Augusta had done the packing, she assumed, with little thought or care. At last, she would be able to dress the way she wanted, not in those horrible outfits Augusta insisted she wear.

She was right about the packing. Augusta had thrown her cashmere sweaters, silk blouses, and wool skirts together with heavy wool pants, jackets, and party dresses, none of them folded or separated. Shoes, purses, underwear, expensive lingerie, ski boots, and scarves were all tossed together in an angry jumble. Augusta had set out to do as much damage as possible.

Still, Sarah found comfort surrounded by her belongings and the knowledge that she had left Augusta's dreary clothing choices at the farm. Even if they needed laundering, ironing, and, in some cases, mending, she chose them. Part of her old life returned to normal. She sorted the contents of the boxes on her bed, including a small pile damaged beyond repair.

Evie appeared at the bedroom door. "Looks like you could use more hangers. I'll make up the couch for you tonight. Tomorrow is soon enough to deal with all this. Right now, I have a surprise for you." She had set out squares of leftover chocolate cake, walnuts, whipped cream, chocolate sauce, and cherries on the kitchen table, along with two large bowls. "This should improve your day. Come sit and begin."

"Wow. This is great medicine." Sarah's mood lifted as she filled her bowl to the brim and grabbed a piece of cake.

They sat on the patio and watched the moon rise over the treetops. Absent the city lights, the stars formed a dense, sparkling dome. Croaking frogs and chirping crickets blended with the whoosh of an owl as it swooped overhead in search of prey. The day's tension disappeared in this quiet place filled with natural beauty and the absence of chaos.

Watchful of the strange girl who invaded his territory, Deacon clicked across the concrete to sit at her feet.

Evie said, "It's okay, Deacon. Sarah will be visiting awhile." Deacon raised his head, barked, glanced at her, then back at Sarah. "I think that was *welcome*." Evie scratched him behind the ears and patted his side. He lay down at her feet, head on his crossed paws, ears searching the dark for any sign of intruders or animals to chase.

"Is it safe out here so far away from civilization, without city lights, in total darkness?"

"I feel very secure, especially with Deacon. He's a fierce protector and can hear suspicious noises before I can." At the sound of his name, Deacon slapped the concrete with his tail.

"Something or someone could sneak up on us. I've seen plenty of movies where that happened to unsuspecting victims."

"I have a shotgun, a motion detector front and back, a trusty dog, and a shortwave radio. I have lived out here for over thirty years and had no trouble. My neighbors haven't had problems either."

"It's so quiet. Spooky."

"You'll learn to enjoy the quiet soon enough."

❦❦❦❦❦❦❦

Disturbing dreams haunted Sarah all night. Visions of figures lurked in the shadows. An invisible hand pulled her underwater in a raging river. A hostile crowd pointed and laughed at her as they struck her with tree branches. She avoided sleep until exhaustion forced her to doze.

She woke to wet sniffing sounds in her ear. She turned her head and looked straight into two round black nostrils. "Deacon, that tickles." Startled, the dog jumped back a few inches and cocked his head. Sarah threw the blanket off and sat up. Deacon stood, wagged his tail, bowed his version of Downward Dog, then danced away in circles, ready to play. He dropped a squeaky toy at her feet, trotted across the room, and sat waiting. "Here ya go, boy." Deacon caught the toy in midair and raced to the kitchen; his claws clicked across the tile floor.

"Whatcha' doin', boy? Can't play now. Did you wake Sarah?"

The fragrance of bacon and coffee lured Sarah to the kitchen. Augusta considered real bacon a frivolous expense and freshly brewed coffee a luxury. Instant coffee was good enough for her. She shrugged into a robe and slippers rescued from her boxes and headed to breakfast.

In a light blue chenille robe and fuzzy slippers, Evie bent over an open oven door, removed a pan, turned around, and greeted her with muffins and a broad grin. "Did you sleep well?"

"I had scary dreams every time I tried to sleep." Sarah rubbed her eyes and stifled a yawn.

"Do you want to talk about your dreams?"

"I don't remember them this morning." She hated lying to Evie but wasn't ready to confide in her. She might have to tell the doctor, Mrs. Morton, or Chaplain Crane, and they might analyze and refer her to another shrink.

Eager to change the subject, Sarah joined Evie. "Can I help?"

"Put plates and utensils on the table. Just need to finish the scrambled eggs and bacon, and we're set." Evie placed the muffins in a basket. The bacon sizzled as she set it in a pan and whipped the eggs in a bowl. "I have an appointment in town this morning."

"Great. I want to look at what's in those envelopes while you're gone." Sarah carried the muffins and plates of finished bacon and eggs to the table.

"Those envelopes might hold painful information. Are you sure you want to look at them alone? The fact that someone hid them at the back of a high shelf might suggest that Augusta didn't want them found."

"It might also suggest they were so important that she didn't want to lose them." Sarah took a bite out of her muffin. "Yum. Banana Nut, my favorite."

"Gram was a good cook. She tried to teach me and my mom, but failed."

With the last bit of her breakfast gone, Evie cleared the table.

"I'll clean up," Sarah offered.

"I accept. It's late. I need to get dressed."

Evie returned in twenty minutes, wearing a black tailored pantsuit. Sarah followed her as she rushed out the kitchen door and down the backstairs. "See ya in a couple of hours. There's plenty of food for lunch, and my cell number is taped to the phone if you need to contact me." She slid into the driver's seat, started the engine, and sped toward town in a hail of gravel and dust.

Sarah wrapped her flannel robe a little tighter against the late October chill. The last of the fall leaves covered the ground, and the smell of wood-burning fireplaces drifted through the air, reminding her of winter days at the beach. She would sit around a stone fireplace with her parents and Gram as they sipped hot chocolate and played board games. Sarah closed her eyes and inhaled the memories of her family and their winter vacations.

Deacon greeted her as she entered the kitchen. He whined and trained his sad eyes on her. "She'll be back soon, Deacon." He tilted his head to one side. "Do you want a treat?" He seemed to understand. He stood, barked, circled her, and almost tripped her as she headed for the treat cupboard. She sprinkled some pellets on a dish and placed it on the floor. Deacon gobbled it as if he hadn't eaten in days.

A car horn and the crunch of gravel disturbed her peace. "Get dressed," Evie shouted as she burst into the kitchen and struggled to catch her breath. "Just got a call on my cell phone from the hospital. They want—to see both of us as soon—as possible." She plopped into a chair, her chest heaving.

"What now?" A chill ran through Sarah's body despite the warmth of the room.

"I don't know what they want, but you need to get dressed right now. It sounded urgent." Evie got up and poured coffee into her thermos. "I'll pack some snacks in case we need them. Chaplain Crane will meet us there."

Sarah sighed. Augusta's envelopes would have to wait. An urgent call from the hospital forced a change in plans.

Twenty-Nine

Dressed in worn jeans, a tee shirt, and a blue fleece hoodie, Sarah strolled into the kitchen. Evie was gone. She peered out the kitchen window and saw Evie sitting in the truck's driver's seat. Her fingers tapped impatiently on the steering wheel. The truck faced away from the house for a quick exit. Exhaust from the tailpipe indicated the engine was running.

She left the safety of the house, hesitated for a moment on the back porch, then meandered down the steps; she opened the passenger door, slumped in her seat, and snapped the seatbelt. As she stared out the window, she wondered where she would end up after today—with Evie, a foster family, or Augusta.

Evie put the truck in gear and stepped on the accelerator. "Here we go. Another adventure."

As they approached the hospital, Sarah glared at the enormous gray monster that lured its prey through sliding glass doors, consumed it, and spat it out in a different form. She and Evie would blindly accept the monster's invitation, be digested, spat out, and changed forever.

They parked on the garage's fourth floor, took the elevator down to the first level, crossed the street, and climbed the few concrete steps to the hospital entrance. The automatic doors whooshed open. She wanted to scream, but her fear was so strong. She didn't want to know why they were there and who they would be when the monster spat them out.

"Evie, I can't." She remained motionless, unable to enter the lobby.

"Dr. Morris is expecting us." Evie reached out to her. "Hold my hand. We can enter together."

Sarah gripped Evie's hand so hard she winced. "Hang on. Here we go."

She loosened her grip on Evie as they headed toward the elevator and pressed the button marked "4." The doors opened, and the car filled. A rotund man in a walker pushed her and Evie against the back wall. A couple and their crying children stood next to him. An older woman waited in the middle of the car. The odor of antiseptic filled the stale air. Sarah's claustrophobia made it hard for her to take a deep breath. She squeezed Evie's hand and fixed her gaze on the mirrored ceiling.

"You okay?"

"It's too crowded and hot in here. I can't breathe." Her eyes widened. She struggled to breathe. She grabbed Evie's hand.

"Hold on. Just one more floor." Evie moved to face Sarah. Her body forced a space between her and the other passengers.

Sarah glanced at the buttons on the wall panel and noticed no one would get out before the fourth floor. It seemed like an eternity before the bell sounded, the car settled, and the door slid open. "This is our floor. Let us through, please." Evie grabbed her hand and pushed her way to the exit, anxious to free her before her panic overwhelmed her.

Dr. Morris leaned on the nurse's station counter, laughing with a woman in a business suit. He redirected his attention from the nurse behind the front desk to Evie and Sarah. He shook hands with Evie. "Thank you for coming on short notice. Hello, Sarah."

She nodded and shook his outstretched hand.

"Let's go to my office."

Sarah's stomach churned. Her reservations about the hurried last-minute meeting were confirmed when Dr. Morris opened his office door. Sitting in the same flowered wingback chair as their last meeting was Mrs. Morton from Child Protective Services. She wore jeans, a turtleneck sweater, no makeup, and hair freed from its usual tight bun.

"Please sit down." Dr. Morris offered the couch. "Would you like something to drink, a snack, maybe?"

"Some water would be fine." Evie glanced at Sarah. "She could use some nourishment right now. It's been a tough day for her so far."

"I have good news that might change that. Miss Hanson seems to be out of danger now. I have a patient to check on, so I will leave you in Mrs. Morton's capable hands." Dr. Morris pressed a button on his intercom. "Hanna, please get some water and snacks for Mrs. Burrows, Sarah, and Chaplain Crane."

"Yes, sir."

"They probably need energy more than sugar. Just bring an assortment of healthy food." Dr. Morris rose and took an armful of files off his desk. "We'll see each other before you leave." He nodded and strode out the door.

Sarah's heart raced; her hands started to shake. She wanted to run, but her body felt too weak to move. Augusta might recover. She might have to go back to the farm and live with her. Wasn't her life terrible enough?

Mrs. Morton moved to the edge of her chair. "Sarah, since you are fourteen, almost fifteen, you are old enough to have some say in where you want to live. In a few months, we can discuss emancipation with your attorney. It frees you from the need for guardianship."

Mrs. Morton pulled some papers out of her briefcase. "As I said, you can let us know where you would prefer to live, pending a background check."

"What did you say?"

"Dr. Morris, Mrs. Burrows, Chaplain Crane, and I have discussed your options."

Options. She had options. Sarah chewed on the last bite of an energy bar. She slid to the edge of her seat, filled with anticipation. Evie had been right about a possible good outcome. She must have known what the meeting might be about. "Did you know about this, Evie?"

"Let Mrs. Morton finish." Evie patted Sarah's hand.

"Mrs. Burrows has offered to foster you. She seems to be the best choice since she lives near your new high school and the hospital."

Sarah became more aware that she might be unable to count on anyone long term. She no longer had a family of her own to take her in. She liked Evie. "Yes, I want to live with Mrs. Burrows." Maybe the hospital wasn't such a threatening monster after all.

Mrs. Morton opened her briefcase, pulled out a stack of papers, and placed them on the glass coffee table in front of her. She pointed to a line labeled signature. "Please sign here to accept Mrs. Burrows as your temporary guardian until Miss Hanson can care for you."

"Wait a moment, Sarah." Chaplain Crane held up his hand. "Let's read this form before you sign so you understand what you're agreeing to. Do you mind if I sit between you and Evie on the couch?"

Sarah did mind—the delay annoyed her. She wanted all this over and done. Augusta might recover. She didn't want to imagine such an outcome and needed to find a way to stop it from happening.

Mrs. Morton fidgeted as Chaplain Crane and Sarah examined the papers, and Sarah signed. It appeared to her that Mrs. Morton also wanted this to be over. "I assure you that I am not your enemy here. My job is to see that you are well taken care of until you are eighteen. Chaplain Crane, Dr. Morris, and Mrs. Burrows feel the same. You are not alone. You do need to return to school as soon as you are settled."

"I will call and make an appointment to visit your home next week." Chaplain Crane handed Evie a card. "Call me anytime if you need anything."

"Thank you. I will do that." Evie stood and gathered her purse and jacket. "Ready to go, Sarah?"

"You bet." She rushed to the door, opened it, and entered the hall. For the first time today, she took a deep breath.

She resented the time it took the adults to say polite goodbyes. They filed out of the office one by one. Ready to leave, she finally strode down the hall and waited at the elevator, arms crossed. Her left foot tapped as she observed patients and medical personnel get onboard and disappear behind the closed doors. She watched overhead panel lights blink as passengers reached their designated floors. It seemed to take forever before Evie and Chaplain Crane appeared.

"What took you so long?"

"We needed to talk to the doctor and Mrs. Morton to clear up a few things." Evie pushed the elevator call button.

Chaplain Crane held the door for Evie and Sarah when the elevator arrived. "I need to stay. I have a few patients to see. Take care, you two." He released the doors and waved goodbye.

As Evie and Sarah exited the hospital's front door, Sarah realized they had left the monster's mouth changed, this time for the better. This time, she had a place to live where she could feel safe. This time, she had hope that things might change for the better.

Thirty

Evie and Sarah retraced their steps to the parking garage, climbed into the truck, grabbed a pizza and pistachio ice cream, and headed home. The delectable fragrance of pepperoni pizza, warm cheese, and marinara sauce filled the cab. With her gaze on the pizza box top's design, Sarah could think of nothing to say. Her body was heavy with exhaustion; her empty stomach ached and gurgled.

"You're very quiet. Anything you want to share? This has been quite a day."

"*Mm.* Nope. Just tired." She cleared her throat.

"Fair enough." Evie turned off the highway and onto the main wetland road. Dusk, a dense forest canopy, and vegetation overgrowth made it challenging to see the mailbox that marked Evie's property.

"There it is. Nearly drove past it."

The truck bumped along the rutted drive that led to Evie's house. The headlights were the only illumination available on this cloudy night. As they drove closer to the house, a motion detector over the kitchen door lit up the porch. Other than that, the abandoned house was dark and seemed unwelcoming and unfriendly. It sent a shiver through her body.

Evie turned off the ignition and exited the vehicle. She hurried to open the passenger door. "Here, let me take that pizza box from you."

She handed Evie the box but remained in the truck. "The house is so dark—like no one lives here." She wrung her hands. Her breath became shallow, her mouth dry.

"Do I need to turn the lights on for you?" Evie frowned and leaned forward.

"Please." Sarah avoided eye contact. "When I first came here, the lights were on in the kitchen window. It's what attracted me to your place, that and the horses."

"No problem." Evie strode up the back steps and entered the house.

Sarah focused on the kitchen window. She chided herself for her behavior, for acting like a baby. It took a few minutes before the light filled the kitchen window where Evie stood and waved.

Relieved, she took a deep breath, stepped out of the truck, and made her way up the steps and into the kitchen.

❧❧❧❧❧❧

Evie had the pizza box open and the plates on the table before Sarah had time to sit down. "Thanks, Evie, for the light in the window. Sorry for my behavior. After this morning at the hospital, I needed to feel welcomed home." She clasped her hands at her waist.

"No problem. Our dark house bothered me a little, too. It did appear deserted." Evie served the pizza and set glasses of iced tea on the table. "Sit down. Eat."

Evie's words *our house* warmed Sarah's heart. As of this morning, it had become *our house* for both of them. Sarah ate two pieces and took two more.

"Do you mind if I eat the rest in my room? I'm anxious to look through the envelopes I sorted before we left for the hospital."

"Of course. Are you sure you don't want to talk about the arrangements made with Mrs. Morton this morning?"

"Do you?" Sarah grasped the back of the kitchen chair and leaned forward.

"We can talk later if you want."

"Thanks." With her pizza and a root beer, she hurried to her room, ready to uncover the mysteries of the envelopes hidden in Augusta's closet.

She retrieved the manila envelopes from her dresser drawer and turned them over. Both were missing part of the back fastener. She sat cross-legged in the middle of her bed and set them in front of her.

The envelope marked *Emmet* showed the most wear. The flap, torn at one corner, had been folded and unfolded many times. Drawings of broken hearts, angry faces, guns shooting bullets, and knives dripping blood covered the outside of the envelope. Stains from coffee cups, spilled drinks, and food mingled with the angry doodles.

Was this *Emmet* her father? Couldn't be. He was loving, kind, and generous. The drawings on the front confused her. She turned the envelope over to be sure she had the right one. The name was correct. Sarah ran her fingers through her hair and rubbed the back of her neck. Upsetting information could be inside, and Emmet might not be her father after all.

She set the *Emmett* envelope aside and turned to the one marked *Lorraine*. It had less wear but scattered words—*traitor, betrayed, bitch, hate you*—written in heavy black ink rimmed the front.

She did not doubt that *Lorraine* was her grandmother. How could Augusta be so bitter towards Gram? The answers to the rift between her and Augusta could be inside. She turned the envelope over, undid the clasp, and spread the contents in front of her.

One photograph caught her eye. She recognized a younger version of her grandfather, Robert. He wore bell-bottoms and a fringed vest and stood beside a young woman in a floor-length tie-dyed dress. A ring of flowers topped her waist-length hair. He had his arm around her; she had her head on his shoulder. It was a perfect picture of two people in love.

Sarah turned the picture over to see when the photo was taken. The date on the back was 1960, a year before her father's birth. However, the names shocked and confused her. She recognized her grandfather's handwriting, but the woman in the picture was *Augusta*.

She read the dates and names over and over. How could this be? It made no sense. The woman in the picture looked like Gram, but the name on the back of the photo wasn't Lorraine, her grandmother. She needed to know more.

Sarah dumped the contents of the *Emmett* envelope, shuffled through the items, and found her father's birth certificate. His father was listed as Robert Grant, his mother as Augusta Hanson, and his date of birth as July 31, 1961. Sarah wiped a cold sweat from her forehead. Dizzy, she lay on her bed, her thoughts in turmoil. *Augusta was her grandmother. That couldn't be.* Gram was her grandmother, always had been. This awful woman couldn't be her grandmother.

Next, she found an envelope from an APO in Vietnam addressed to Augusta.

January 16, 1961
Dear Augusta,

So sorry you have been ill. I know it must have been a shock about Lorraine and me. It was inexcusable of me to lead you on. I will never forgive myself, and neither should you.

Lorraine and I were married last month in Hawaii on my R and R. She knows about our short affair and has forgiven us, knowing that it happened during our breakup.

I wish you all the best. You are a good person and deserve better than I gave you.

Robert

Sarah wanted to know more about the story. Beneath the birth certificate, she found a registration form for a psychiatric facility. Augusta had been committed for depression, alcohol and drug addiction, and attempted suicide. Marge and Uriah Hanson relinquished parental rights for their seventeen-year-old daughter.

Sarah had hated Augusta for so long that she was surprised at how much compassion she felt for that unhappy teenage girl. She must have been so desperate and felt so betrayed and alone. She wanted to know more about what happened to her. Where did Augusta end up after the psychiatric facility? Who might have some answers? Her relatives were gone, and Augusta couldn't tell her anything because of her condition.

Chaplain Crane told Sarah when they first met that he grew up with Gram and Augusta. He might have some answers for her.

Sarah rushed to the kitchen. "Where is the number Chaplain Crane gave you? I need to see him."

Evie whipped around, startled. The scoop in her hand dripped pistachio ice cream on the floor. "Just in time for dessert. What is this about Chaplain Crane?"

"I need some information about Gram and Augusta. He told me he grew up with them. He might be able to clear something up."

"Clear what up?" Evie filled two dessert bowls and placed them on the kitchen table.

"Just need to know more about my family. He said I could call any time." Sarah swallowed a spoonful of ice cream.

Evie scrolled through her phone icons. "Here." She handed Sarah her phone and reached for a pencil and paper. "Write this down so you have it handy."

Sarah scribbled the number on the paper. "Thanks."

Thirty-One

At seven the next morning, Sarah was up and dressed. Restless, she devoured a piece of toast and some strawberries and took Deacon for a walk down the tree-covered driveway and back. Rays of sunlight shot through the dense branches overhead. Birds began their cacophony of morning songs as they left to find food for the day.

Sarah noticed that the dappled light appeared brighter. She glanced at her watch—nearly eight-thirty. Chaplain Crane might be in his office by now. "Come on, Deacon, let's run." Always ready for a good run, Deacon barked and pranced all the way to the house, where he sat on his haunches, whined, and slapped his tail on the kitchen floor, ready for a treat.

"Here ya go, boy." Sarah, generous with the dog treats, hoped for some peace as she picked up the kitchen phone receiver, removed the number from her pocket, and dialed. An answering machine clicked on. "We are closed now. Please leave—hello, chaplain's office." The woman on the phone sounded out of breath.

"This is Sarah Grant. I need to talk to Chaplain Tom Crane."

"He's out of the office until Friday. Maybe someone else could help."

"No, he's the only one who can help me." She paced the kitchen.

"We have other excellent counselors who can help if you are in crisis."

Her shallow breaths made it hard for her to speak. Her throat tightened. She didn't want to talk to this woman anymore. "No, I just need—Chaplain Crane."

"May I take a message?"

Frustrated, Sarah slammed the receiver in its cradle so hard that it missed and fell to the floor.

Evie rushed into the kitchen. "Are you all right?"

Sarah slumped in a chair at the kitchen table; her chest heaved—she struggled for control.

"He's—not—there."

"Who's not there?" Evie replaced the receiver in its cradle.

"Chaplain . . . Crane." Sarah lowered her head to her folded arms.

"Oh dear. Can I help?" Evie moved her chair closer to her, folded her hands, and waited for an answer.

"No. He's the only one who might have answers about what I found in one of the envelopes." She couldn't confide in Evie. She needed to keep her shocking family secrets quiet. What would Evie think about her discoveries? She might change her mind about taking her in. It was too big a risk.

Maggie was the one person she knew she could trust to listen and cheer her up. "I want to email my friend. I need to talk to Maggie."

"Of course." Evie rose, took a notepad from a slot by the phone, wrote on it, and handed it to her. "Here's the password."

"Thanks." Sarah snatched the information from her hand and headed to her room. She raced to her desk. Her computer waited to connect her to the one person who reminded her of the beach and home. She dropped into her swivel chair and swung to face her laptop. She squeezed the button that engaged her phone. The battery was dead—one more frustration. Maggie's email address was on that phone. On the verge of tears, she plugged her charger and phone into the outlet at the back of her desk—more delay.

Sarah tapped her fingers on the top of her desk and gazed out the window. Balanced on long, spindly legs, a Great Egret appeared on the back lawn; its long white neck, elegant head, and yellow beak stretched toward the sky. When the bird turned its head, one yellow eye focused on her as if watching over her. It spread its wings, tucked its legs under its body, flew over the marshland, circled back over the house, and out to the marsh again. She might be able to find the bird near her pond; Deacon needed a walk this morning. Evie expected Sarah to care for the dog.

Sarah dashed to the kitchen, grabbed a jacket and leash from the pegs by the door, stepped onto the back porch, and filled her lungs with sweet wetlands air. Deacon paced the dog run, whined, and barked when he saw her with the leash.

"Deacon. Sorry, boy. Almost forgot." She opened the gate. Deacon rushed out, bounded across the patio and back, and allowed her to attach his lead. She patted him on the head. "Okay. Let's go."

Deacon tugged at his leash as he sniffed every bush, paw print, and scat pile along the familiar path from the house to her favorite secluded pond, a fifteen-minute walk from Evie's back gate. Black coots, their bright white bills flashing in the sun, dotted the water that rippled in the cool breeze. She rested on a log under the weeping willow. Its delicate branches rustled as the tree swayed in the wind and dipped to sweep the ground. Sarah found the motion relaxing, almost hypnotizing. Her stressful morning melted away. Nothing and no one could reach her here.

Deacon paced before her, whining for his release. As she removed his leash, a flock of noisy Canada geese landed near the water. He charged toward them. The largest one must have been a male; it hissed and honked, wings extended, increasing its size and forward motion. He aimed his beak at the startled dog and charged. The dog yelped and headed for Sarah at top speed. He huddled next to her leg and lay his head on her lap, eyes trained on her as if asking for protection or forgiveness for his poor showing as a fearsome hunter.

"Look what you did, boy. Our coots and mallards fled in the chaos." She chuckled, scratched Deacon behind his ears, and offered him a treat from her jacket pocket. "That'll teach you to attack geese." He settled on the ground, crunched his dog treat, and watched the geese fly away in a "V" formation.

One by one, the coots chittered as they swooped back to the pond, bobbing on the water's surface. Green-headed mallards with brown-speckled mates quacked in unison as the flock landed and glided in circles near the reeds. A Great Blue Heron posed on its stilted legs at the far edge of the marsh. It stared at the water beneath it, waiting for its perfect prey. Sarah had always been fascinated with the bird's patience. In the end, it always flew away with a catch between its long beak.

She could stay in this spot forever, but the sun had moved. She glanced at her watch. Three o'clock, later than she realized. She reconnected Deacon's leash.

"Come on, boy. It's late. Evie will wonder where we are." She and Deacon retraced their steps home.

Relieved that Evie's truck wasn't in the driveway, she led Deacon to the dog run, removed his leash, filled his water bowl, and replenished his food. "You need to stay here until the mud dries on your coat and paws."

Deacon whined.

"Gotta go." Sarah dashed into the kitchen, removed her jacket, grabbed a water bottle and energy bar, and rushed to her room. Maggie should be out of school by now.

Settled at her desk, she hit the power button on her laptop. Her hand trembled as she typed in Evie's WIFI connection password. Would it work? Her computer chimed and displayed the menu. "Woohoo." She thrust her arms in the air. She hit email and then turned on her phone to search for Maggie's contact information. She hit the message space icon, entered the email address, and began to type.

Hey, Mags.

    Missing you. Didn't have internet at Augusta's house. Am in a new place now. Long story. Wrote you a few letters. Didn't hear back. Lots to tell you. Need to talk to a friend.

    Love, Sarah.

Sarah pressed "Send." It might be a while before she heard back. She closed her laptop, shelved the books from the boxes on her closet floor, and finished unpacking. There was nothing else to do but keep busy and check her email periodically.

Evie called to say she would be home two hours later than expected and would bring dinner. Her bookshelves filled, Sarah lay on her bed rereading one of her favorite Hermione McCray mysteries until the last rays of the sun faded.

Her bedside clock read six p.m. Evie had called three hours ago. Sarah's chest tightened. If something happened to her, would anyone know to call? She doubted it. Few people knew that she lived with Evie. Sarah shot off the bed and dashed to the kitchen. Maybe there was a message on the answering machine, a call she didn't hear while reading.

She bumped into a corner of the dining room table, slammed full force into the kitchen door frame, and nearly toppled over a kitchen chair. No light flashed on the answering machine. She flipped the switch that lit up the kitchen and the yard just as Evie's headlights rounded the corner of the driveway. Her body turned weak with relief as she stepped out on the back porch to greet her.

Evie opened the passenger door. "Come help carry dinner. Sorry it took so long."

She hurried down the steps to embrace Evie.

"Ouch! You're strong. I should stay away more often." She returned Sarah's hug.

"You're okay. You're okay. I was afraid something happened to you."

"Of course I'm okay. I just had one of those days when nothing goes as planned. I'm sorry. I should have called home again."

"What's for dinner?" Sarah released her grip.

"Nothing healthy, fried chicken, mashed potatoes, and slaw with a sinfully chocolate dessert."

"Okay!" Sarah grabbed both grocery bags and headed for the kitchen. "Come on. I'm hungry."

"You set it up while I change. I've had enough of this pantsuit. I want to hear about your day."

"Wrote an email to Maggie. Haven't heard back yet."

"Glad to hear it." Evie's voice faded as she entered her bedroom.

Sarah set the table and placed the food cartons in the center. She drew a deep breath, closed her eyes, and raised her hands. "Thank You, God." Her shoulders relaxed. Her new family, however small, lived under one roof again.

❧❧❧❧❧❧

Dressed in an oversized tracksuit, Evie rejoined Sarah in the kitchen. "Whew. Feels good to relax at last."

An open bucket of fried chicken on the table beckoned them to sit and eat. Paper plates were piled high with flaky biscuits dripping with butter and honey, mashed potatoes and gravy, and slaw drowning in its special dressing. They emptied the container in a hurry.

"Now, tell me about your day." Evie sipped a mug of tea as she waited.

"Deacon and I went for a walk and spent a few hours by the pond. A flock of Canada geese taught him not to attack them ever again." Sarah glanced at her watch.

"Do you need to check your email?"

"Please. Sorry."

"Go. I hope you have an answer from Maggie."

❧❧❧❧❧❧

Sarah rushed to her desk to check her inbox. No new messages. It was close to eight o'clock. Maggie might be angry at her. She had written letters but received no answers. Maybe their friendship faded. Could that have happened in such a short time?

Sarah found Evie in an overstuffed chair in a corner of the great room; a book lay open in her lap. Evie asked, "Any answers?"

"Nope." With a sigh, Sarah dropped into the chair across from her. "Do you think she's angry with me?"

[182]

"Mrs. Morton considered Maggie's family as a placement for you when we discussed where you might live. They couldn't take you because the father was ill. I don't know what's wrong, but it's worse than a cold. Maybe they have an emergency."

"Why didn't you tell me this before? I could have written a note to them."

"I thought you knew since you were in touch with the family."

"I never got any letters from Maggie. How would I know?"

"And how would I know it would be news to you?"

"They have always been my second family. Why didn't they tell me? Have I lost them, too?"

Evie passed a tissue box to her.

<h1 style="text-align:center">Thirty-Two</h1>

Sarah checked her inbox every hour until midnight, when exhaustion called for sleep. She woke at five a.m. The light blue sky told her it was nearly dawn. She moved to her desk and tapped her computer awake. Her inbox had a message from Maggie sent half an hour ago.

Sarah. Hi.

Where have you been? We were worried when you didn't answer my letters, and your emails were returned undelivered. Just got home from the hospital. Daddy's brain cancer is worse. I really miss you. Need to see your face. Do you Zoom? Going to sleep for a while. Can't tell you how happy I am to hear from you.

Hugs, Mags

Sarah pressed her palm against the message on the screen. Her body was heavy with loneliness and grief for the loss of her old life at the beach with her friends, Gram, her parents, and the McCanns. As she reread Maggie's message, she realized that Augusta had withheld letters when she and Maggie needed each other the most. Sarah's jaw tightened. Any empathy she had for Augusta disappeared. *What a horrible woman*. She was her grandmother and Gram's sister. Augusta made her granddaughter suffer to get revenge for what Lorraine and Robert Grant had done years before. She deserved to suffer—she needed to be punished.

After dinner, Maggie connected with Sarah on Zoom. "Perfect connection, Sarah. Our cell phones don't always work well here. Glad we have this—the split screen is great."

Maggie's familiar wiry red hair and freckles hadn't changed, but her deep blue eyes seemed tired. Her usual sparkle was gone.

"Maggie, how's your dad?"

"Not good. There's nothing more doctors can do for him. He's in hospice right now. He may come home soon."

"Wish I could be there." Sarah touched the screen. She needed to comfort Maggie, but there was so much distance between them. "Your mom and dad are like second parents to me." Someone else from her happier days would soon be gone. Losing so many loved ones was supposed to happen to older people, not teenagers.

"Your parents were the same for me. How's it going with Augusta?"

"It's awful. Her stroke saved me from her cruelty. She even withheld all the letters you wrote to me. It's scary to think I might have to leave Evie and return to the farm." Sarah placed her hand on her chest and tilted her head sideways.

"Is Evie kind to you?" Maggie leaned closer to her screen.

"She's wonderful, and I live in the most beautiful surroundings. The marsh is my refuge. There is Chaplain Crane, who knew Gram growing up, and Mrs. Morton, the social worker from my school. She scares me. She has the power to decide what happens to me if Augusta dies."

"Gotta go. Mom just got home. I'm the cook at dinner time. Mom stays with Dad at the rehab center every day. I'll connect again tomorrow if I can. Will send the time in an email."

"Say hello to your parents for me. Tell 'em I love them and am praying for them and you."

"Will do. Take care, my friend."

"You, too." Sarah pressed the *leave meeting* button. She closed her laptop and lay her head on the cold metal cover. Life had changed dramatically in one week. The family she thought she had was a lie; Augusta had withheld Maggie's letters; Maggie's father was dying, and her identity was in shambles.

She decided to hide what she found out about her family. She saw no reason to tell anyone about information she considered shameful and embarrassing, a cause for gossip and judgment. She had participated in such behavior when she attended her private school. There, she belonged to a group that ostracized scholarship students. Now that she was on the other end, she realized how hurtful and unfair she and the others had been.

A light under her bedroom door and the odor of burning wood drew her to the living room. Evie, wrapped in her flannel robe and fur-lined slippers, lounged in a wingback chair by the fireplace, and Deacon lay at her feet. The blazing fire and reading lamp behind her chair provided the only light in the room. An occasional lightning bolt struck the ground across the road, followed by pounding thunder as the storms passed overhead.

Deacon jumped as a flash of lightning flooded the room, followed by a boom of thunder that shook the house. Heavy rain pelted the windows. Evie and Sarah wrapped their robes tighter as they huddled near the fire.

"That was right overhead." Evie turned off her lamp. "Be careful not to invite lightning inside the house. Several years ago, one bolt did shoot through the window and across the room."

"Never heard of that before." Sarah slid off the couch onto the floor. "Think I'll take no chances and sit here in case it happens again."

The house shook from a second blast of thunder and lightning. It rained harder, followed by a shower, then silence and the sound of water as it ran down the gutters and eaves of the roof. The thunderclaps grew fainter as the storm moved north.

Evie turned on her reading lamp and placed her book face down on her lap. "Quite a storm." Deacon returned to his place near her, head up, ears alert. "Good, boy. It's okay."

"You all right, Sarah?"

"Yup. That was a good one. I love thunderstorms. Strange, huh?" Sarah returned to her seat on the couch.

"They are spectacular. I loved them, too, until the lightning incident reminded me how unpredictable nature can be. How are things with Maggie?"

"Not so great with her dad. Wish I could be there with her, but Zoom lets me see her face at least."

"I'm glad you two have reconnected."

Sarah sank into the soft cushions of the living room couch. She focused on the fireplace and the occasional crackle pop of burning wood. Thoughts of her life filled with chaos, confusion, and anxiety melted away. Relaxed, she put her feet up on the glass coffee table and stared into the flames as they flared, settled, and turned to glowing embers.

What she wanted most—safety, family, peace—existed here in Evie's living room. She implanted a picture in her mind of this moment: Deacon by the fire, a safe, warm room, the two of them sharing their thoughts and feelings in conversation. After Augusta's sterile, cold, unloving farmhouse, this was heaven.

At the sound of the kitchen phone, Sarah leaped to her feet, her every muscle tensed.

The antique clock on the mantle chimed ten. Who calls at ten o'clock at night with anything but bad news?

Evie rushed to the kitchen. She hesitated for a moment, then picked up the receiver. Sarah followed and positioned herself at Evie's elbow; she pressed her ear as close as possible to the receiver.

"Hello?"

"Evie? This is Tom Crane. Sorry . . ." Evie muted the speaker and turned her back to Sarah.

"No problem, Tom. We're awake."

A muffled voice on the other end prevented eavesdropping. Sarah huffed, perched in a chair, and drummed her fingers on the kitchen table.

Evie said, "Tomorrow morning is perfect. Join us for breakfast, won't you?"

The voice on the line responded.

"Good. We'll see you at nine." She hung up.

"He's coming here?" Sarah asked.

"Yes. Chaplain Crane will spend time with us tomorrow."

"Good."

"Do you want to share why you need to talk to him?"

"He grew up with Augusta and Gram. I want to know what they were like when they were young." She avoided Evie's gaze. "That's all."

"I see. Family history is important. I may be able to help with the last twenty years. Augusta was probably in her forties when I moved here. By then, she was pretty isolated from others, so there wasn't much to learn except what people said about her. Their gossip stretched the stories farther every time they told them."

"What *do* you know?"

"I tried to visit Augusta, but she didn't answer the door, even though I could see her peer through the curtains. When I asked people who had known her for a long time what she was like, their stories were pretty much the same."

"Did they tell you anything about her childhood?" Sarah brought coffee and muffins to the table.

"Their parents raised the girls in a fundamentalist Baptist church in Lawson. As a teenager, Lorraine's life was school; Augusta's life was boys. The break between them was over a boy. Augusta fell in love with him. He fell in love with Lorraine. Lorraine and the boy got married during the Vietnam War. Augusta went to live with a relative. Augusta and Lorraine came back for their parent's funeral. Augusta got very drunk and threatened Lorraine and her husband."

"Lorraine's husband was Robert, my grandfather."

"Sorry—of course, you know his name. Augusta got off a few rounds from a handgun before the sheriff intervened. Fortunately, she was too drunk to do much damage. That's all I know."

"Wow." Sarah, overwhelmed, said nothing for a few minutes. How did Gram escape such a past? *F#*!* Sorry, Gram. Sarah laughed. She realized she didn't know which grandmother would care about her saying such a word. Lorraine would be shocked. Augusta used that word all the time. Whose values counted anyway? What difference did it make anymore?

Thirty-Three

Sarah stared out her bedroom window, anxious about what Chaplain Crane might reveal from her family's past. She hoped he could fill in Gram's and Augusta's childhood information. A knock at the door startled her.

"Sarah, it's seven-thirty. The horses need attention, and Deacon needs exercise and food before Chaplain Crane arrives."

Sarah stood, squared her shoulders, and drew a deep breath. "Coming. Just need to get dressed." She pulled on a pair of old jeans and a sweater, perfect for the work ahead of her. She completed her horse-tending outfit with a wool hat, an oversized jacket, and rubber boots. The distraction of feeding horses, mucking out stalls, and playing fetch with Deacon sounded more inviting than ruminating on her situation.

She hurried to the kitchen, lured by the smell of coffee and cinnamon. "Good morning, Evie. Is that for me?"

"You bet." Evie, wrapped in her light blue chenille robe and fur-lined slippers, shuffled to the kitchen table with two steaming mugs of coffee and a plate piled high with cinnamon toast. "You looking forward to Chaplain Crane's visit?"

"I guess. Just curious about Augusta, what she was like when she was younger, why she is the way she is."

"It was a long time ago. He may not remember much."

"Maybe." Sarah drained her mug of coffee, grabbed a second piece of toast, shrugged into her jacket, and headed out the door.

Fog hugged the ground most winter mornings, especially after a storm. It clothed familiar surroundings with mystery. Sarah loved the fog. It kept her hidden from the world, wrapped in its arms. *Safe*. That's what she needed most this morning—freedom from seeing too far ahead, freedom from reality.

She opened the stalls and led the horses to the paddock. They whinnied and snorted as she filled their troughs with feed and water. Today, the hard work of mucking out the stalls in the cold air energized her. After laying down fresh straw in the stalls, she dumped the wheelbarrow of soiled material behind the barn.

Deacon trotted along the dog run fence, anxious for his turn to be fed and to enjoy a game of fetch. She latched the paddock fence and crossed the driveway to the dog run.

"Come, Deacon. Time to eat." He dropped his tennis ball at her feet, sat on his haunches, and stared at her, his tongue lolling to one side. She glanced at the patio clock. Eight-fifty. Chaplain Crane, always on time, would arrive in ten minutes and not a second more.

"Sorry, Deacon. No time to play today." He barked and whined as she filled his water bowl and food dish, then closed the dog run gate with him inside. "Later, boy."

She had just enough time to exchange her work clothes for black flannel pants, a teal blue sweater, and a pair of sneakers. She fastened her auburn hair, dampened by the fog, at her neck with a gold clip.

Chaplain Crane arrived on time dressed in his official black suit, black shirt, and white pastoral collar. Over six feet tall, wavy white hair, clean-shaven and lean, Sarah considered him the perfect example of the man she wanted to marry one day. In a recent dream, he appeared on a motorcycle to rescue her.

"Sorry about the chaplain suit. I'm on duty at noon and wanted to leave plenty of time for our conversation."

"No worries, Tom. We're happy you're here." Evie welcomed him with a mug of steaming coffee and a warm smile. "Make yourself comfortable. Breakfast is almost ready."

"Something smells very inviting. It's been a while since I've enjoyed your cooking."

"Cinnamon rolls and bacon with scrambled eggs. Simple."

Tom Crane touched Evie's upper arm and met her eyes a little longer than Sarah expected. There might be more than a friendship between them. She could use the distraction of a romance right now, even though it wasn't hers.

Tom Crane placed his coffee mug next to Sarah and slid into the seat beside her. "I'm anxious to hear why you called my office last week."

"I'll leave you two alone after we eat." Evie brought a platter of scrambled eggs and bacon. Chaplain Crane said grace. Each person filled a plate, and the room fell silent except for the scrape of forks on china and the occasional sound of appreciation for Evie's cooking.

Evie made the first move to clear the table. "I've built a fire to warm the living room. Tom, you and Sarah can talk there while I clean up."

"Sounds like a plan." Chaplain Crane stood, bowed, and swept his left hand toward the entrance to the living room. "After you, young lady."

They sat in two wingback chairs facing the fireplace. "How can I help? I noticed you seemed distracted at breakfast."

"I need to know more about Aunt Augusta and Gram. Since you grew up with them, I figured you might be able to tell me about what they were like when they were young." She folded her hands in her lap.

"That was a long time ago." Tom crossed his legs and stared at the fire. "I'll do my best." He leaned back, his elbows on the arms of the chair. "I met Lorraine and Augusta in third grade after my family moved to Broadmore. Lorraine was two years older than Augusta and me. Our fathers worked for the railroad. We all attended the same church. The girls, my older brother Stanley, and I spent every Sunday morning in Sunday school. I remember being a little scared of Mr. Hanson. He was stern and staunchly religious. His wife was the same." Tom paused and focused on the fire again.

"I didn't know you had an older brother."

"Yes. He died in Vietnam."

"Sorry." She looked away.

"Thank you. I still miss him."

"Tell me about the girls."

"Lorraine obeyed her father and mother. Augusta was another story. Rebellious and defiant, she earned a few slaps across the face when she disobeyed her father in public. In her early teens, she began smoking and drinking. In high school, she became quite the party girl." Tom grinned and raised his eyebrows.

"When Augusta met your grandfather, she stopped partying and paid more attention to her schoolwork. He and your grandmother were a couple for about a year. When they broke up, Augusta moved in to fill the gap Lorraine had left until Robert got drafted and sent to Vietnam. I joined the Navy, and all of us went our separate ways. When I came home a year later, Lorraine, Augusta, and Robert were gone. There was gossip but little real information about what happened to them."

"Did you ever find out?"

"I saw them at Uriah Hanson's funeral. I hear there was a violent argument at the house but didn't see it. I was on my way back to seminary by then."

"How did you end up back in Broadmore?"

"When my parents passed, I inherited the family property. I decided to move back here when my wife died. The wetlands seemed like a good place to heal. God's creation has a way of restoring peace and easing pain."

"I've had the same experience since I came to the wetlands, especially here at Evie's."

"She and her property have the same effect on me." Tom uncrossed his knees and turned to face Sarah. "I knew Augusta had moved back to the farm, and I tried to reconnect with her. She had no desire to see me or anyone else for that matter."

"How did you hear about my aunt's stroke?"

"I found a position at the hospital and rebuilt my life. The next time I thought about her was when I saw her name on the admittance record."

"I have a strong urge to see her. Maybe it will help reconcile some of what you told me. Will you take me to see her?"

"Are you sure?" Tom leaned closer. His eyes widened.

"I want to see her today. I need to see her, please. If Evie can take me, can we meet at the hospital during your shift?" Sarah didn't know why she needed to see Augusta, but now that she knew some of her past, she might be able to see her differently.

"All right. If it's that important, but I'm concerned that a visit could be traumatic for you. Augusta may not be able to talk or even open her eyes."

"I can handle it."

"If it's okay with Evie, I will get permission for you to see your aunt."

"Thank you." She leaped out of her chair, hugged Chaplain Crane, and dashed toward the kitchen. "Evie. We have something important to ask you."

"What is it?" Evie appeared at the kitchen door, a towel in her hands. Sarah rushed to her side. "Chaplain Crane can get me in to see Augusta today."

Evie arched her right eyebrow. "Oh, he can, can he? I'm not so sure that's the best idea Chaplain Crane has ever had." She cleared her throat.

The tall chaplain spread out his arms and turned his hands upward as if begging for mercy. "I told her it was up to you to decide what to do. You are her guardian. Your word is law, literally."

"Great. It's up to me. Just great." She threw up her hands and returned to the kitchen. Sarah followed her.

"Please, Evie. I need to see her."

"I don't like the idea of a fourteen-year-old experiencing such a sight. Hospitals don't allow minors to visit the *ICU* anyway, do they?" Evie frowned, raised her right eyebrow, and stared at Tom Crane.

"I can arrange it since Augusta is her only family, and you and I will be present." He squared his shoulders and clasped his hands at his waist as if about to give a sermon. "I can meet you there before my shift starts, and we can go together."

"Fine." She removed her apron, strode to the back door, grabbed her purse and jacket from the peg on the wall, and turned to Sarah. "Okay. If it's that important to you, get your coat and meet me at the truck." She glanced at Chaplain Crane, shook her head, and hurried out the door. "Be sure the door is locked on your way out." Evie did not wait for an answer.

Tom followed close behind. "See you at the hospital." He waved, climbed in his SUV, and drove down the driveway and out of sight.

⚜

"There's not much traffic today. We'll arrive at the hospital in record time." Evie gripped the steering wheel. Her body leaned forward as she pressed the accelerator to the floor. The truck tires spun from the sudden forward motion. With gravel spewing behind, she sped out of the driveway, down the rutted dirt path along her corral fence, and turned left on the paved wetland road to the highway.

"Lucky us." Sarah bit her nails, a habit she thought she had ended long ago.

"Almost there. Last curve ahead." Evie often announced street signs, exit signs, and billboard information. It could be annoying on longer trips, but her habit reassured Sarah as they approached the gray concrete monster again. She hoped it would make a difference that she chose to go this time rather than having someone else make her go inside. She was on guard, watchful.

Chaplain Crane met them at the front entrance. "Are you sure you want to do this?"

"I'm fine." She strode to the elevator with Evie and Chaplain Crane close behind.

She pushed the *up* button. Steel doors opened. She hesitated for a few seconds, entered the car, and faced forward, ready to press a button on the panel. "Which floor?"

Evie stepped to the back of the car. Chaplain Crane reached in front of Sarah and pushed the button marked 10.

The elevator whirred upward until it bumped and settled to a stop on level ten. They exited at the nurse's station. A woman, dressed in green scrubs with a stethoscope around her neck, greeted them. "So glad to see you again, Tom. We got your message. Miss Hanson can be seen now."

"Thank you, Anita, for making an exception for Sarah."

"I understand. All three of you may go in under the circumstances." Marjorie led them to room 16 and peeked through the *ICU* windows to see if the nurses were ready for visitors. Three women in surgical masks nodded and left the room.

Sarah edged closer to Augusta. Even in a coma, Augusta appeared angry. Canyons of bitterness remained etched on her face, between her eyes and down her cheeks. An atmosphere of despair, decay, and impending death filled the room. Sarah stared at Augusta but felt nothing for her—no anger, hatred, or compassion.

Augusta's body, thin and wasted, seemed lost under her bedclothes. Her clawlike hands and skeletal arms rested on the covers, needles inserted in veins barely visible under her translucent skin.

The constant beep of life-sustaining machines pinged off darkened walls. Their soft blue and green lights threw eerie shadows on the ceiling. Oxygen sucked and whooshed through the tube in Augusta's mouth. Sarah wondered how the nurses could insert it in a mouth so pinched, rigid, and rancor filled.

"Sarah?" Chaplain Crane's voice interrupted her thoughts.

"Sorry. What?" She jumped at the sound.

"Do you still want us to stay?"

"No. I'm done. Nothing more to see here. Let's go." Sarah turned away from the bed, strode out of the room, and fled to the elevator. Once inside, she punched the button labeled *Lobby*. The elevator lurched and sank. Lights on the panel to the right blinked 10, 9, 8—the count seemed endless.

Her heart raced when a stop at the sixth floor added seven passengers to her escape pod. They shouted and gestured to each other in a foreign language Sarah didn't recognize. Elbows, fingers, feet, and bodies invaded her space. She huddled in a back corner for safety. It took time for them to pass through the elevator doors, time that robbed her of her goal. Again, she stared at the panel ticking off the floors—5, 4, 3.

One of the ladies directly in front of her wore heavy perfume. The scent made Sarah's eyes water. She sneezed despite every effort to hold back. The woman whipped her head around and glared, her brown eyes outlined in black. She said something in a guttural tone. Sarah pressed her body farther against the wall.

The doors slid open. Three more people entered. Sarah thought she might suffocate as the crowd pushed closer. Someone's pungent body odor added to her discomfort. Perspiration trickled down her back and face. She must not have a panic attack again. Her *breathe-in, breathe-out* exercise wasn't an option this time. Attempts to focus on the mirrored ceiling made her dizzy. The crowd blocked the wall panel. It seemed an eternity before the doors opened, and the car began to empty.

Sarah sped across the hospital lobby. She needed to escape the monster. Doors marked EXIT slid open. A nurse stepped forward with a wheelchair. Sarah did not slow down. She dashed through the partially open sliding door as the nurse struggled to step out of the way.

Safe on the sidewalk, she bent over and planted her hands on her knees as she gulped cold air. It was the first deep breath she had taken since they entered the hospital.

Chaplain Crane's words to the charge nurse echoed in her head. "She's the only family she has."

"No!" Sarah collapsed on the concrete sidewalk.

"Oh, dear." A woman gasped.

"Chaplain. Good thing you're here. I'll find another wheelchair."

Two sets of arms helped her stand. Two familiar voices whispered in her ears.

"It's all right." Evie crooned.

"We gotcha." Chaplain Crane assured her. "Let's get you up and into this wheelchair."

Sarah opened her eyes. What she saw horrified her. She was headed for a sliding door marked EMERGENCY. *Back into the monster.* It wouldn't let her escape. The beast provided medical help and medication to calm her down, but she wanted out.

"We should probably keep her for observation." A male voice spoke, ready to hold her prisoner.

"Wanna go home. Don't wanna stay." She found it hard to focus. *The room was tilting.*

"Let's take her home. It will do her good to be around the animals. Doctor, I'll take responsibility as her guardian." Evie pushed a wheelchair next to Sarah's bed.

Her sight in focus, she recognized Evie through a guardrail attached to the bed. A computer at her right beeped to tighten her blood pressure cuff. "Ouch." She raised her hand to ease the pain. The needle in her arm, attached to a suspended bag of clear liquid, stung with every movement. "What is this?" She raised her hand. The needle, fastened to her arm with tape, sent more pain up her arm. "Ahh. Take it out."

A young woman in green scrubs glanced at a man in a white coat at the foot of her bed. "Her numbers have returned to normal, Doctor."

"Let's disconnect her and get her ready to go home."

"Evie is right. Nature is a great healer. We can both keep an eye on her," Tom Crane assured the doctor.

"I'm okay with that. I'll send some relaxants home and information on aftercare. I understand she collapsed on the sidewalk. Look for signs of concussion. Bring her back here for that."

For a moment, with Evie and Tom, Sarah felt safe. Still, without a family, her future was tenuous.

Thirty-Four

Sarah remembered little of the ride from the hospital to Evie's house. The medicine the doctor gave her made her drowsy and unable to focus. Cars on the freeway blended into red, blue, and chrome streaks. Letters and graphics on signs shimmered and blurred together, distorting any attempt to decipher their meaning.

The truck slowed, tilted forward, and turned left. She guessed they were on the two-way road that cut through the wetlands. She rolled down her window to breathe in the musty scents of fertile earth and decaying vegetation. A symphony of warbling red-winged blackbirds, croaking frogs, and honking geese added to the joy of her return. She heard the familiar crunch of gravel under the tires and the whinny of the horses; their heads hung over the corral fence to greet them.

Evie's truck rolled to a stop. Sarah opened the cab door, slid out of her seat, and fell to her knees. "Oomph."

"Are you alright?" Evie ran toward her. "I couldn't grab you in time to stop you. Those meds they gave you are powerful."

"Can't see well, or stand, or walk. Weird."

"Here. Grab my hand." Evie lifted Sarah to a standing position. She steadied her, one arm around her waist, the other under her elbow. They trudged up the steps and into the kitchen. Evie eased her into a chair. "Are you hungry?"

"No, just tired; I need to sleep."

"Rest is probably the best thing for you. The meds should wear off in an hour or two. Plenty of food in the fridge if you get hungry." Evie helped her stagger to her room. "Here, sit on the bed. I'll get your pajamas."

Sarah attempted to focus. Walls rippled and shifted. Her stomach lurched. She slipped under the bed covers and closed her eyes.

"Already in bed, I see." Evie lifted the sheets and removed her shoes. "Never mind. You can put your pajamas on later." She pulled a comforter over the sheets and closed the blinds.

"Thanks." Sarah relaxed into her soft mattress and slept.

❦❦❦❦❦❦

Sarah woke with a start. Diaphanous ochre curtains billowed at the windows. Odd. A yard light must be on. She sat up. Someone outside whispered her name. "Sarah. Tap, tap, tap." A single line of shadowy figures marched across the yard as they whispered her name and tapped on the glass.

"Who are you? What do you want?" The procession continued. The taps grew louder as they shouted her name.

"Go away. Go away." Fear skittered up her spine.

"Shame, knock, knock, knock . . ."

Sarah shivered as the shadows' anger intensified. *Would they break the windows? Where could she hide if they decided to attack?*

"What do you want? Answer me!"

"Wake up." Evie switched on the overhead light and rushed to sit next to her. "You had a nightmare."

Dazed, Sarah gasped for air. The thin curtains and tapping shadows vanished, replaced by the pale rays of the rising sun. Her clothes and hair were damp. She shivered and wiped sweat from her forehead and tears from her cheeks. "Oh, I was so scared. They kept calling my name, tapping on the windows. They wouldn't stop." She covered her face with her hands and sobbed as she leaned against Evie's shoulder.

She placed her arm around Sarah. "You're safe now. You're fine." Evie crooned as she rocked her. "Could you take a shower while I change your sheets?"

"I think so." Sarah's voice was thin and childlike. She wiped her eyes, blew her nose, and stood. Cautious, she took a few steps toward the bathroom. "No more dizziness." She signaled a thumbs up.

"Come out to the kitchen when you're done. You need to eat something." Evie grabbed the sheets and pillowcases off the bed and left the room.

Hot water and steam from the shower restored her. Life seemed more normal again. Her hair and body were clean; she wrapped a bath sheet around her, wiped the steam off the mirror over the sink, and stared at her image. Dark circles under her eyes, sallow skin, and adhesive marks left from her heart monitor attachments reminded her that she needed food and rest.

She slipped into a pair of gray running pants, a loose black turtleneck, and a pair of slippers and headed for the kitchen. Her empty stomach growled at the aroma of pork sausage, coffee, and cinnamon rolls.

❧❧❧❧❧❧❧

Sarah loaded her plate with pork sausage patties, French toast, scrambled eggs, and a cinnamon roll coated with cream cheese frosting. Sprawled in the corner, Deacon thumped his tail and whimpered for attention. She patted him on his head. "Good boy." He panted and started to get up.

"Sit, Deacon. Not Now. Good boy." Evie gave him one of his dog treats.

"So, how are you? Your dream must have been frightening, the way you yelled out."

"Yeah. Spooky." Sarah took a deep breath and then blew it out with force. She took a bite out of her cinnamon roll to prevent more conversation. Wanting to move on, she needed to forget as much of yesterday and last night as possible. Frosting dotted her chin and smeared her upper lip; she dabbed the corners of her mouth. "*Mmm.* You sure can bake, Evie."

"Thought I'd go for a walk after breakfast. Look for a tree to sit under." Sarah finished her meal and took her dishes to the sink. "Let me help clean up before I go."

"I'll get it this time. Be sure to take your phone in case you need to call."

"Thanks. I will. I won't go far. Probably down to the pond."

Sarah returned to her room for a jacket and loaded her backpack with notebooks, pens, pencils, and a cell phone. About to leave, she stopped, turned around, and headed for her dresser. After opening the top drawer, she slid out the manila envelope marked *Lorraine* and sat on her bed. The unopened letters piqued her curiosity; she turned them over, tempted to read them. How much did she want to know after yesterday? Would the letters help her complete the revised picture of her family? She removed her jacket and changed her plans for the day.

She sat cross-legged on her bed. The return addresses on both letters were from Sausalito. Gram and Gramps had settled in their house by the time they wrote them to Augusta. She opened the one with the earliest postmark. A black and white photo of a young child fluttered and landed in her lap. She had seen the picture before. On the back, she read *Emmett, three years old.* A larger framed version of this photo of her father had rested on Gram's bookshelf ever since she could remember.

Sarah removed the letter from its envelope. She recognized Gram's handwriting and the faint aroma of lilacs, her favorite scent.

Dear Augusta,

Thank you for letting us know about Daddy's funeral. We were glad to hear from you after all this time. We tried to contact you after we found out from CPS that Emmett is Robert's son, but your doctors would not allow it. After they told us Emmett was in foster care, and you had relinquished your parental rights, we filed papers to adopt him.

It took a long time for me to forgive both of you, but Emmett needed a family. As it turned out, I am unable to have children. God was gracious to all of us—Emmett had a family, Rob could raise his son, I had a child, you were free to rebuild your life.

We plan to be at the funeral. Emmett will stay with Robert's parents in Chester. Let us know how you are doing. You are welcome to visit us, but that is up to you.

See you next week,

Lorraine

Sarah wished she had Augusta's return letter if one existed. At least Gram tried to reconcile with her sister. Now that she knew the circumstances of her father's birth and that Augusta's parents abandoned their daughter, her aunt's addictions made sense. She needed to get rid of her emotional pain. Sarah wondered if she would decide to do the same without a family.

She opened the second letter in Gram's handwriting.

March 20, 1968

Augusta,

You're lucky you're a bad shot. Robert spent a week in the hospital recovering from his wounds. Mine were superficial, easily patched up.

What were you thinking? Hopefully, you will be sentenced to years in jail, given your criminal history with drugs.

Do not attempt to contact us or visit Emmett. It is clear you are mentally unstable, not someone we want in our son's life. Glad Mom and Dad were not alive to witness the gruesome scene and your drunken rant. You're lucky you didn't kill us, which was clearly your intent.

We'll see you at the trial as witnesses for the prosecution.

Robert and Lorraine

Its tone answered Sarah's question about the family estrangement.

Saddened and shocked by what she found, she returned the letters and the picture of her father as a boy to the manila envelope and placed them in her dresser drawer. Heavy with regret, sadness, and pity for her aunt, Gram, and the broken family, she realized how choices, even the good ones, could affect future generations. Right now, adults made all the decisions for her. In four years, she would turn eighteen and become a legal adult. The consequences of her actions would be on her and those she chose to have in her life.

She needed her wetland pond, a quiet place to think and write under the willow tree. Animals, plants, and birds operated on instinct, not fear of consequences. They knew how to behave and where to live. She envied the rhythm of their uncomplicated lives. Gram used to quote scripture about birds that God provided for, and lilies that did not need clothing because they were more lovely than any garment. Scripture cautioned believers to avoid worry. They would be all right. There was a time when all of this had been true for her. She had everything she needed or wanted. That time seemed over for her. Life wasn't predictable for humans.

She took a deep breath, shrugged into her jacket, swung her backpack over one shoulder, and left the house. Hands in her pockets and head lowered in thought, she crunched along the graveled driveway, passed through the side yard, and turned left on the path that led to her pond and the willow tree.

Sarah spent hours at the pond, filling the pages of her notebook, sitting quietly to watch the birds, and napping in the late afternoon sun. Honking geese startled her awake as they flew overhead, finished with their daily foraging. Mottled light threw shadows across the pond and the marsh as the sun sank behind the trees. In less than an hour, the setting sun would paint the sky with brilliant shades of yellow to orange, pink to purple to gray, and then black studded with millions of stars. She lingered to watch the spectacle. Even with a new moon, the well-worn path home would be short and easy to navigate.

When the last rays of light disappeared below the horizon, Sarah trudged up the dirt path, down the side yard, and onto the gravel driveway. A warm, welcoming glow shone through the kitchen windows. Motion detector lights flared as she stepped on the patio. Deacon began to sound the alarm from the kitchen, saying that everything was not as it should be. Snorting horses trotted to the fence to investigate the situation, then lost interest when they recognized Sarah. She bounded up the back steps and opened the kitchen door. Deacon circled her. The scent of pot roast filled the room. Welcomed by horses, Deacon, and a pot roast, she was glad to be home.

"There you are. Was about to send Deacon to find you." Evie served her a mug of hot chocolate from a pan on the stove.

"Lost track of time. Sorry."

"Did the marsh do its healing?"

"Yup." Sarah removed her jacket and backpack, hung them on a hook by the door, and settled in a chair with her elbows on the table. Deacon wriggled under her arm to rest his head on her lap. "Never fails."

Evie opened the oven door, removed the sizzling roast, and placed it on the stove. "Time to set the table."

The dinner conversation centered around Evie's talk with Sarah's high school principal. "You have a few alternatives, but you need to attend your new school after the Christmas holidays if you want to move on with the Freshman Class next year."

"What are my choices?" Sarah moaned. "Repeating freshman year is not acceptable."

"You could return in person, continue to work on assignments at home, or be homeschooled with the understanding that you must pass all the skills tests for your grade level. We need to let them know what you decide before winter break."

Sarah slumped in her chair; her joy from the afternoon disappeared. "Reality just vaporized my good mood."

"It has a habit of doing that. After you clear the dishes, I'll meet you in the living room for dessert." Evie removed her apron, made some tea, and left the kitchen.

Sarah finished her chores, fixed two dishes of ice cream, and joined Evie in the living room. Logs crackled and snapped in the fireplace. Their conversation, interspersed with companionable silences, continued until their eyes grew heavy, and the antique clock on the mantel struck twelve.

"How did it get to be so late? I'll douse the fire unless you want to stay up." Evie grasped the fire iron.

"No. I'm ready for bed. Hope the nightmares will leave me alone."

"I hope so, too. Good night." Evie poked the fire and doused it with sprays of water.

Sarah entered her room. She removed her clothes, threw them on a chair, put on her pajamas, and fell into bed. It had been quite a day. She turned on her side and slept.

❦

"Sarah, honey, wake up." Evie pulled the chain of the lamp on the bedside table. "I have news." Sarah placed an arm across her forehead to avoid the glare. Afraid this might be another bad dream, she shot up to a sitting position. Her computer clock blinked five-thirty. "What? Where am I?"

"You're in your bedroom, and this is not a dream. Your Aunt Augusta passed an hour ago. The hospital asked if you wanted to say goodbye."

"What? Isn't she dead? Why would I want to see her now?" She grasped Evie's hand.

"Ouch. You have quite a grip there."

"She's really gone. I won't have to live with her again?"

"Tom told me that Augusta's attorney and the funeral home have been notified. Is it all right if Tom comes to see you later today?"

"Of course. Always good to see him, yes. I need to tell Maggie. Must talk to her." Sarah's breathing became shallow. Her voice grew shrill as she activated her laptop to email Maggie.

Thirty-Five

Sarah paced her bedroom, unable to decide what to do next. She had no desire to contact the funeral home or Augusta's attorneys. Chaplain Crane was responsible for necessary notifications and arrangements; phone messages and emails sent to Maggie two hours before produced no responses.

"Sarah?" Evie stood at the door.

"What?" Sarah spun around, annoyed.

"Final Rest Funeral Home wants to speak with you."

"What do THEY want?" She clenched her jaw. Every muscle in her body tightened. Every breath was shallow and rapid.

"I don't know. As your guardian, I'll need to be on the extension."

"Right." Sarah strode to the kitchen and grabbed the receiver on the counter. "Hello?"

"Miss Hanson, I'm Cedric Garner from the Final Rest Funeral home. We are very sorry for your loss."

"My name is Sarah Grant." Her last name would never be Hanson. *Never in a million years would she carry that name.*

"So sorry, Miss Grant."

"What is it that you want, Mr. Gardener?" Sarah smirked at the mispronunciation.

"It's Garner, not Gardener."

"Right." Sarah drummed her fingers on the counter.

"Miss Hanson was transported here according to her contract with us. As her next of kin, you and your guardian must stop by to sign papers to release her for cremation, as she requested. Do you want to view your aunt to say goodbye? We can arrange that when you come in to sign the papers." His deep, measured voice oozed sympathy.

Sarah's eyes were fixed on a Ruby-throated Hummingbird outside the window; she had nothing to say.

"We could arrange a public viewing and a funeral service if you would prefer." His voice gained momentum and a few decibels. She wondered how many upgrades he hoped for on Augusta's contract.

"No. I don't want to see her ever again."

"Miss Grant, you are very emotional right now. You might want to wait a few days to make a final decision. Perhaps her friends would like to say goodbye."

"She has no friends."

"Mr. Garner." Evie's voice interrupted the conversation. "This is Evie Burrows, Sarah's legal guardian. Miss Hanson's contract is clear. Follow it. When do you want us there to sign the papers?"

"We close for the Christmas holidays on the twentieth."

Sarah's jaw ached. Her head throbbed. She needed to be done with Augusta. All she wanted was to move on.

"Can you come in tomorrow?" Sarah detected a judgmental, dismissive tone in Mr. Garner's voice. "We will let you know when the cremation is completed."

"No need." Sarah's hand shook as she hung up the phone. Her weak knees forced her to drop into a chair at the kitchen table with a thud, fold her arms on the surface, and rest her spinning head. They just kept coming, people who wanted decisions and asked her questions she didn't know how to answer.

The following morning, another phone call interrupted Sarah's breakfast. "Hello?" She swallowed her last spoonful of cereal.

"Miss Grant?" A woman's voice this time, clipped, resonant, precise.

Sarah froze. She wanted to escape, hang up, and lie about her identity. "Yes. I'm Sarah Grant."

"I am Marion Wentworth, Augusta Hanson's attorney. Our office has handled the Hanson family's affairs for years. Miss Hanson died without a will. The search to identify family members revealed that you are Augusta's only living relative and heir to the Hanson family home, property, and any personal items Miss Hanson left behind. Since you are a minor, we notified your family trust attorney. He agreed to meet with all of us at your convenience to discuss legal matters and sign papers."

She stared at the receiver as if it were an unfamiliar object. Above her, a spider crawled across the ceiling. She followed its path, fascinated with its determination. It seemed to know where it was going. *Lucky spider.*

"Hello? Are you still there?"

"Yes. Sorry."

"Chaplain Crane has the numbers—ours, your trust attorney, and the funeral home. He offered to help with legal matters and coordinate the meeting."

"Thank you. My guardian isn't home right now. She's the one you should call." Sarah reached for the notepad and pencil next to the phone. "May I take your number?"

The woman ignored her request. *Was she an answering machine with a script?* "We'll be closed the week of December twentieth for the holidays. We want to start the transfer before the new year. We are very sorry for your loss."

The phone went dead. Sarah wondered why people always said they were "sorry for your loss," another one of those empty phrases to fill an awkward silence. People assumed everyone was sorry about the loss. She wasn't sad at all, but relieved, ecstatic, grateful for the death of that horrible woman, her aunt. She would never have acknowledged her biological relationship to Augusta.

She noticed the spider had reached the corner moldings above the kitchen table. In less than an hour, she had created the intricate design of the web. The huntress, planted in the center, waited for prey. *Impressive.*

The squeal of the screen door hinges and a thud against the kitchen door distracted her.

"Sarah, are you there?" Evie shouted, "I need you to open the door for me. I have quite a harvest in this basket."

"Coming." Sarah hurried to open the door. Evie wouldn't be happy about another business call.

"Oh, good. You're here. I thought you might be in the wetlands. Look what I have this time." She held a wicker basket loaded with produce, and a satisfied smile covered her dirt-smeared face. A certified Master Gardener, she grew enough quality fruit and vegetables for her use and the local food closet.

"Oh, Evie. More than last time."

"Whew. This is heavy." Evie set the basket on the table, sank into a chair, and wiped the perspiration from her forehead with the back of her gardening gloves. Her attention moved to the muddy trail her Wellingtons left on the kitchen floor. "Help me get these boots off, will you? I'm a little stiff today. Cold, damp weather is not my friend." She removed her gloves and flexed her fingers. "*Sss, ah, mm, ow.*" She rubbed her hands together to warm them.

Sarah knelt to remove Evie's boots. "Augusta's lawyer called. They need us to come in for some paperwork. According to them, I am her only living relative. I get the house, property, and belongings. At least something good came from all the torture."

"You need to have me on the line when lawyers call—you are only fourteen. I thought you went to the meadow."

"I changed my mind at the last minute. Just wanted to sit around in my pajamas."

"Getting everyone together for a meeting this time of year could be a problem." Evie turned to look at her wall calendar. "Did you get her phone number?"

"She hung up before I could. Mrs. Wentworth said their office would be closed for the holidays the week of the twentieth."

Evie groaned. "Great." She picked up the phone receiver and dialed a number. "Yes, hello. This is Evie Burrows calling for Chaplain Crane." There was a short pause. "Thank you." Evie tapped her foot and sighed. "Tom has all the numbers we need."

"Tom? This is Evie. The funeral home called today. We have business to take care of before the twentieth. I need to contact Sarah's attorney. Mm. I see—sure. Okay—let me see." Evie glanced at her calendar. "Actually, any time between now and the fifteenth is perfect. Are you sure you want to take that on?"

Sarah noticed that Tom Crane's response made Evie blush as she leaned against the wall. Her voice was soft and throaty.

"That's very generous of you, Tom. I'll wait for your call."

Sarah had noticed girls acted this way when they wanted to attract a boy. Evie and Tom were old. Evie had pure white hair, and she was retired. It had been a while since Evie called Tom "Chaplain Crane." Sarah's heart began to race. If they were flirting, they could get serious. Evie and Tom might not want her around anymore if they decided to marry.

"Sarah, are you okay?" Evie frowned. "You look like you're going to cry. It's been such a tough week for you. Let's have some tea and a chat." She plugged in the kettle and reached for two yellow mugs from the cupboard.

Sarah nodded. "Sure." She wanted to talk to her, but needed to be cautious about sharing too much. She must not cry. She must stay strong, tough, self-reliant.

"Tom offered to take care of the meeting with Augusta's lawyer and your trust attorney." Evie placed her hands on Sarah's shoulders and locked eyes with her. "It will be fine, I promise. We can trust Tom."

Sarah's throat tightened. Her jaws ached from her effort to gain control of her emotions.

"In the meantime, we need to wash and store my harvest from this morning." Evie moved to the sink to sort the bounty in her wicker basket. "Peel damaged leaves off the cabbage, lettuce, chard, and Brussels sprouts. I'll wash the carrots and shell the peas for dinner. The oranges and grapes can go in the bowl on the counter. My garden is done for the season. This is the last of it."

Grateful for the distraction, Sarah inspected leaves on her assigned produce as if it were the most important task of her life.

Tom called around four that afternoon, and Evie answered. "Oh good, Tom." Evie motioned to her. "Sarah is right here." She covered the mouthpiece. "Tom needs to talk to both of us. I'll pick up the extension in my room." Evie passed her the receiver.

"Okay. I think I found a good dinner recipe." Sarah placed a bookmark in the cookbook in front of her and picked up the phone. "Hello."

"Ah. There she is." Tom's deep baritone voice reassured her. A click on the line told them that Evie had joined. "You know, Tom, I am very concerned that the funeral home called Sarah without adult notification. They must know that it is illegal to speak to a minor without a guardian present."

"I reminded them of that. Apparently, they neglected to read the whole message and assumed Sarah was of age. I called to let you both know that Sarah's trust attorney, Ian McCleary, plans to contact you around seven tonight. He wants to discuss a time for a meeting between Augusta's attorney and us. Does that work for you?"

"That's fine. Sorry I was so short with you this afternoon." Evie sighed. "I'm so grateful that you are handling things. Don't know what I would do without you."

"No worries. These matters are always stressful."

Though Sarah couldn't see Tom, she imagined his broad, compassionate smile, gentle blue eyes, and the slight tilt of his head as he calmed their fears.

"I'm on my way to see a patient. Talk to you later. Hopefully, we can all find a date to meet soon."

"Thanks, Tom."

"Talk to ya later, Chaplain Crane." Sarah hung up the phone.

"Goodbye, you two. God bless."

Sarah placed the receiver in its cradle and returned to her recipe book. Dinner was one task she could accomplish. Legal matters, living arrangements, and her life remained in the hands of adults for three years and four months until she turned eighteen, the age of consent.

Ian McCleary called at seven, as promised.

"I'll answer it, Sarah." Evie dried her hands, wet from washing dinner dishes. "Hello. Yes, Mr. McCleary, we expected your call. Let me get on the other line while you talk to Sarah."

"Hello, Mr. McCleary. So much has happened here. Can't wait to see you again. Will you come here?"

"Sarah, slow down. Take a breath. Wasn't certain you'd remember me. We met at such stressful times in your life."

How could she forget? She and Gram sat in his office after her parents died. She pictured the floral armchairs they sat in, the rectangular polished wood desk stacked with case files, the forest green walls and ceiling trimmed with white molding, and the kind green eyes of the man behind the desk. The only difference was that when Gram died, Maggie's father sat where Gram had been.

"Yes, I remember you very well." A click on the line interrupted their conversation.

"This is Evie on the line, Mr. McCleary."

"So glad to meet you. Tom Crane tells me you are an excellent guardian for Sarah. So glad to hear that. I've been their family attorney for three generations. She's had quite a rough start in life."

"Yes, she has. Your long relationship with the family reassures Sarah that she's not in this alone. What procedures do we need to follow to help her move on?"

"I'll be brief. We'll need to meet with Augusta Hanson's attorney to sign papers to transfer Sarah's inheritance to her trust. If there are no stipulations on how the assets are distributed, I will meet with you and Sarah to discuss the management of her trust. There is a separate fund for her education. The rest remains in the trust until she is twenty-one. Under the circumstances, we must negotiate an allowance, extra expenses, and spending money for her. How does your calendar look for the next couple of days?"

"Clear."

"Let's shoot for Friday. I'll let you know where and when."

Sarah lost interest in the conversation—she felt left out as adults took over her life *again*. If she had a say in the workings of God and the universe, she would trade her three houses and piles of money to have her family back. She glanced at the spider web. Five sacks of prey, trapped to feed her family, dotted the web. *Even the spider had a family*. She sat at the kitchen table, head in her hands. Her body shook as tears rose from the depth of her stored pain. *Weakness. It had to be tamed.*

Thirty-Six

Sarah gazed out her bedroom window as dawn broke over the trees that surrounded the marsh. A rising sun turned the fields and grasslands orange, then yellow as it topped the trees. After yesterday's constant barrage of legal chaos, her sleep had been fitful. She had tried to reach Maggie by phone and email for two days, but there was no response. She began to worry.

She headed to the kitchen. Food soothed her anxiety. The last few weeks had tightened her waistbands. Maybe a walk instead. She needed to escape the demands placed on her by the hoard of adults clawing at her from every direction.

She longed to be young, to giggle and gossip again with friends about boys, clothes, and the new girl in homeroom. It was hard to remember the last time she attended school or had a group of friends.

Half a chocolate cake from last night's dinner rested on a covered plate on the counter. She cut a chunk, thick with frosting, and stuffed it in her mouth.

"Leave some for me."

She dropped a glop of frosting in her lap as she whipped around to face Evie.

"Guess you had a hard night. Bad dreams again?"

"Yup." Sarah wiped frosting from her mouth and lap with a napkin.

Evie grabbed a fork from the dish drainer and sat next to her. "Want to talk about what happened yesterday? It upset me. Must have been very hard for you, too."

"It's all so confusing, scary. I still don't know where I will end up. These people tell me I have money and property, but what does that matter if I have no family?"

"I had that same feeling when my parents died before I met my husband. In time, I formed my family of dear friends, then married and had my children. It takes time. In my case, it took about twelve years."

"And, now you have Tom. You two seem happy together." Sarah wanted to know how happy.

"He's been a great support for both of us." Evie peered at the kitchen clock. "Time to get dressed." She took the dishes to the sink.

"Right now? What about my pajama day?"

"Sorry to say, my dear, we have more to do today. Tom texted me that the funeral home needs to finish Augusta's paperwork. He is free to go with us at ten o'clock. I said yes. No sense in putting it off."

"Right." Sarah checked the time. Nine thirty. What did one wear to a funeral parlor? Maybe her farm work clothes smeared with manure or jeans or, God forbid, a dress.

❦❦❦❦❦❦

Sarah heard the crunch of Tom Crane's SUV on the gravel driveway at ten o'clock. Right on time, as always. She threw a black knee-length wool jacket over her teal turtleneck and dark blue jeans. She pulled knee-high leather boots over her pant legs. Good enough for now. She headed for the kitchen.

The kitchen door slammed. "Good morning, all. Ready for another adventure?" Tom sounded upbeat as usual. "Where's Sarah?"

"Oh, Tom. So glad you're here. Sarah doesn't seem okay this morning. I'm worried."

Sarah stopped short of the kitchen door to listen. Gram used to warn her about the consequences of eavesdropping, but this time, she realized Tom and Evie were talking about her.

She moved closer to the kitchen door. What she saw stopped her from entering. Evie and Tom stood with arms wrapped around each other. Tom kissed Evie on the top of her head as he stroked her hair.

Sarah's heart sank. She was right about them. Her future seemed more tenuous than ever.

"Hi, you two. I'm ready to go." She strode into the kitchen as if she had just arrived at the scene.

Tom and Evie separated as if they were guilty teenagers caught by a parent. Sarah wanted to laugh, but the ease between them told her that it wasn't the first time they had embraced.

"Sarah!" Tom's face flushed. Evie stood behind him, her eyes fixed on the floor.

"It's almost ten. We need to hurry." Sarah scuttled out the back door. The cold December air revived her as she headed for the SUV, hopped in the back seat, and slouched until her eyes were even with the bottom of the window. Tom and Evie slid into the front seats, glanced at her, and then at each other. She enjoyed their discomfort—two adults caught and speechless. As they headed for the main road, Evie stared out the passenger window, and Tom focused more than was necessary on his driving. No one spoke until they reached the funeral home forty-five minutes later.

❧❧❧❧❧❧

"Here we are. The funeral director is expecting us, and Augusta's attorney is across the street, close enough to walk. We could get our business finished in one day." Tom opened the passenger doors for Evie and Sarah. They walked along the portico to an ornate front door, where Tom pressed a button. A deep three-note chime echoed inside and clicked to release the lock and allow entry. The colonial-style front door led to a somber hallway carpeted in deep red to match upholstered benches set outside, where wood doors were spaced evenly along the wall. Light fixtures in the shape of candles produced a soft golden glow on rose-beige walls. At the end of the hall, a floor-to-ceiling stained-glass window depicted a lush garden with a fountain.

A tall, gray-haired man strode toward them. "I'm Cedric Garner, and you must be Sarah." He gazed at her with gentle cobalt eyes and offered his hand in greeting. His deep, resonant voice reminded her of her grandfather, and his warm hands encompassed her own.

"And you are Mrs. Burrows and Reverend Crane." He greeted them with the same warm handshake. "Follow me. I have Augusta's papers ready for you." He led them through a door at the end of the hallway. An oval polished wood table with pale blue upholstered chairs filled a room looking out on a manicured lawn surrounded by trees stripped for winter.

"Please take a seat at the table. We don't have much to do today. Miss Hanson bought and outlined specific arrangements. Unless you have changed your mind, we will follow your aunt's plan as written. We need signed confirmation that that is what you want."

"Sarah, are you satisfied with the plan as written?" Evie held Sarah's hand and leaned toward her for an answer.

"Yes, the plan is fine." She and Evie signed several pages.

"Is that all?" Sarah moved to the edge of her seat.

"That's it." Mr. Garner tapped the stack of papers on the table and placed them in a file folder. He stood and escorted them out of the building.

Sarah took a deep breath. The air smelled like rain. Clouds grew darker as a storm approached. She wrapped her jacket tighter as the wind swirled around them.

Tom cleared his throat. "Well, that was easy. Augusta's attorney is across the street, and her calendar is flexible all day. Sarah, do you feel up to more business?"

"Okay. Might as well get this over with."

"We're headed to that single-story structure close to those railroad tracks." Tom pointed the way. The three of them ran across the street as rain turned to hail.

Gold letters on the office door read WENTWORTH, WENTWORTH, AND COLLINS. A bell rang as they entered the office waiting area. The receptionist's desk occupied the front portion of the space. Behind that stretched two rows of cubicles, desks piled high with folders, and employees in conversation or clients seated across from them.

"May I help you?" A young, energetic receptionist flashed a smile and stepped from behind her desk.

"We're here to see Marion Wentworth about Augusta Hanson's will."

"Are you Tom Crane?" A voice from the corner of the room interrupted the conversation.

"Yes." Tom turned to face a sandy-haired man with his hand offered in greeting. Backlight from the rear window made it difficult to discern his features. "Do I know you?"

"I'm Ian McCleary, Sarah's attorney."

"Mr. McCleary? Is that you?" Sarah, delighted to see Gram's attorney again, hurried toward him.

"The same, my dear."

Without hesitation, she wrapped her arms around the waist of the man who had advised three generations of Grants and was about to serve a fourth.

"I didn't expect to see you today, Mr. McCleary." Tom turned to Evie. "This is Sarah's family attorney and trustee."

"I did have another appointment today, but Sarah is family, so I changed plans."

"I'm Marion Wentworth. My receptionist tells me you are here about Augusta Hanson's will."

Mrs. Wentworth filled the room with her height, voice, and personality. Sarah guessed she would be a formidable presence in any negotiation or trial. She made up her mind to be like this well-dressed, confident woman someday.

"Please come with me. Anita, bring us a couple more chairs. We'll be in the conference room. Coffee, water, and pastries are on the sideboard. Help yourselves. We'll get started as soon as Anita brings the chairs."

The oval, polished wood table filled the whole room. Straight-backed chairs, designed to force their occupants to sit up and pay attention, and windows set above eye level to prevent daydreaming signaled that this was a place of business, not a place to linger or socialize.

When the extra chairs arrived, Marion Wentworth settled in a white leather wingback chair at the head of the table and opened a thick file and her laptop. "As soon as you have your coffee, I want Sarah and Mrs. Burrows to sit on either side of me, Mr. McCleary next to Sarah, and Mr. Crane next to Mrs. Burrows." Anita returned with a laptop and sat at the opposite end of the table, facing Mrs. Wentworth. "Anita will take notes of the meeting."

"This firm has handled the Hanson family's legal affairs for generations. I understand Mr. McCleary has done the same for your family, Sarah. Since Miss Hanson died intestate, we will work together to close probate and transfer Miss Hanson's estate to your trust.

"Here is a copy of the list of items Sarah will inherit as her aunt's only living relative." Anita passed copies of the list around the table. "They include the farmhouse, its goods, and surrounding property worth three million dollars in today's market, as well as five hundred thousand dollars in cash and bonds."

"I don't want her stuff," Sarah declared.

"Let's not be hasty. Take your time with this news." Mr. McCleary rose halfway out of his chair.

Evie reached across the table to touch her hand. "I'm sure you don't mean that. Your inheritance will set you up for life."

"We can discuss this with Sarah privately, and Mr. McCleary and Mrs. Wentworth can hammer out the details at their meeting." Tom searched the faces around the table. "This news has been a shock for everyone here. Best to calm down."

"Of course. We make no decisions today. This legal matter will resolve itself in time. I'll get back to you on our costs, probate, and the meeting you and I need to have, Mr. McCleary." Marion Wentworth closed the file and pushed her chair back from the table to signal the end of the meeting.

"Thank you all for coming. We'll be in touch as things progress. It's a long process." She rose from her chair, crossed the room, and opened the door. "Show these clients out, will you, Anita?"

The group went out the door and onto the sidewalk in record time.

"What just happened in there, Ian?"

"Strange meeting, cold, matter-of-fact, dismissive. Marion and I will have another face-to-face soon, I assure you. There is a lot to discuss."

Sarah plopped on a wrought iron bench. "I'm hungry."

Evie said, "Right. So am I. How about we pick up a couple of pizzas, some beer, and a half gallon of Baskin Robbins to take home? Will you join us, Ian?"

"You bet. Can't resist that menu, Evie."

"Tom, are you with us?"

"I'm off duty. You can count on me where there's pizza."

During dinner, Ian McCleary answered Sarah's questions about the family and the information she had found in the envelopes in Augusta's closet. He shared about the days surrounding her father's adoption and the struggle Gram and Gramps endured to form a family despite their life decisions that caused so much trouble and confusion.

Sarah's family had been broken for at least three generations before her birth. If the people she so admired, believed in, and treasured made so many mistakes and carried so many secrets, she might do the same.

She tried to comprehend her situation. She would own three houses—the family home in Sausalito, the vacation cottage at the beach, and Augusta's farm, plus about two million dollars in her trust. But she had no family and an uncertain future. For now, she was blessed with three supporting and caring adults. Maybe "for now" was what her life would be about from now on, the most she could expect.

Thirty-Seven

en days ago, Sarah had experienced the legal end of her life
with Augusta. She wondered how much longer her emotions, memories, and disturbing dreams would haunt her.
Her journal lay open on her desk, filled with detailed thoughts
from the last two weeks, memories of Christmases past, and anxiety
about the one to come with Evie's family. In the last hour, she
poured words onto fifteen pages. It was eight o'clock; Evie would
fix breakfast soon.

With five days left before Christmas and the arrival of Evie's
children and grandchildren, she hoped the family could add a
stranger to their celebration. She needed to buy gifts. Evie told her
it wasn't important to do that. In her mind, this made her an outsider—a guest, a stranger, a girl forced to sit in a corner and watch.

Christmas shopping had been a joyful event in her family—a
trip to San Francisco, where store windows displayed tableaus of
lifelike animated figures. In one window, elves built toys in Santa's
workshop; in another, carolers dressed in Victorian costumes sang
in snow-filled streets. In toy store windows, excited papier mâché
children opened presents under glittering Christmas trees, and
families, bundled in colorful blankets, enjoyed sleigh rides through

a snow-covered forest. The family ended their morning at Thompson's department store, where Santa welcomed excited children to sit on his lap and share their hopes and dreams for Christmas morning.

Gramps and Dad disappeared in the afternoon while she, Mom, and Gram rode the trolley car to Ghirardelli Square for ice cream. Later, the whole family met at Fisherman's Wharf for clam chowder served in a bowl of hollowed-out sourdough bread as they watched fishermen return with their catch of the day.

Just before sunset, they took the trolley back to Union Square to pick up their car for the trip across the Golden Gate Bridge, turned orange by the setting sun. Thousands of lights strung from tower to tower and along the walkway railings reflected on the rolling water of the bay beneath. *Magical.*

This would be her first Christmas without any family. Maggie came to mind. She was almost family. Sarah wrapped a wool blanket around her shoulders and opened her computer. A message alert popped up. It was Maggie.

Sarah,

Sorry to take so long to answer. Sad to say, Daddy died. He didn't suffer; he just fell asleep. He was home with us when it happened.

Went back to Denver to stay with Gramma for a while. She has no computer. Imagine that? We're home now. Would love to have you come for Christmas if you can. You could take the bus to Monterey. Mom is also willing to pick you up at Evie's. Think about it.

Love, Mags

Sarah didn't have to think about Maggie's invitation. What would she need to pack? A wetsuit for surfboarding, sweats, and a down jacket for cold nights on the beach, and flannel pajamas. A book to read in case of a storm, wool socks, hiking boots. Christmas might not be so dreary after all.

Mags,

So sorry about your father. Such a good person. I'll miss him very much. I'll ask Evie about the visit. She'll call to make plans.

Gotta go. Phone's ringing again. What now?

Hugs, Sarah

Curious about the call, Sarah dashed to the kitchen door, where she hesitated. The speaker phone was on, and an unfamiliar male voice lectured Evie.

"Mom, we're all coming on Christmas Eve. Made hotel reservations in town this year since your spare room is full. Why you're taking in a foster child at your age is beyond me. Is she stable? Some of those older kids are damaged beyond help. We worry about your safety."

"Steven, she's a lovely girl from a good family. She's just had a few traumatic years."

Sarah peeked around the kitchen door. Evie, her phone propped on the windowsill, frosted cinnamon rolls as she talked to her son. She remembered from the family portrait in the living room that Steven was Evie's youngest child.

"Well, that may be so, but you should enjoy retirement instead of raising someone else's child. Mavis and Joy agree with me on this one."

"Honey, you and your sisters have never agreed on anything. The fights you used to have were fierce."

"We'll see what she's like when we get a look at her. Of course, Mare and I are concerned about exposing our children to her."

Evie pointed a frosting-filled knife at the phone to punctuate her lecture. "Now, I expect all of you to be civil and give this poor girl the respect she deserves, you hear me?"

"Yes, Mommy," Steven grunted. "When will the rest arrive? Nice that they live so close to you."

"They'll be here for lunch and Christmas Eve dinner. This year your brother will spend Christmas with the in-laws." Evie picked up the phone and turned off the speaker. Steven remained on the line.

Evie rolled her eyes. "Yes, dear. You have had your say. See you soon. Love to Mare and the children." She turned off the phone, put it in her apron pocket, and mumbled something Sarah could not hear.

With her best fake smile and a yawn, Sarah strolled into the kitchen and headed straight for the pot of coffee on the counter. "Evie, I'm up. Breakfast smells great. What can I do to help?"

With her stomach in knots, Sarah forced herself to finish breakfast. She realized her unfair "foster child" stereotype might be hard to overcome. Neither she nor her family had caused her plight. Fate, a cruel God, or a series of unpredictable circumstances had created the situation. One day, she hoped to understand which. Right now, she needed to pretend the phone conversation between Evie and her son meant nothing.

She took a deep breath and waited for the lump in her throat to disappear. So what if Steven disapproved of her? Above all things, Sarah must not cry or show any emotion. Animals in the wetlands knew that any show of weakness left them open to attack. That also seemed to be true of humans.

"I heard from Maggie." Sarah finished her last bite of scrambled eggs.

"Wonderful. What did she have to say?" Evie began to clear the table.

"Her father died."

"Oh, so sorry. He seemed a lovely man."

"Mr. McCann was a second father to me." Sarah's voice wavered as tears filled her eyes. Sarah tensed at what she was about to ask. If Evie agreed, Christmas might be saved. If she said no, she would spend the holiday with people who disliked her before they even met her. "Maggie wants me to spend Christmas with them."

Evie hesitated for a moment. "How would we do that? Christmas is at the end of this week. I'm not even sure you could go without permission from Mrs. Morton."

"Maggie said they could send a bus ticket or come to get me." Sarah's voice grew louder. Its pace increased as if volume and speed could prove her trip was a good idea.

"You are certainly due for a break, but there is no way anyone can make arrangements for you this close to Christmas." Evie placed the last dish in the dishwasher, slammed the door, and turned to face Sarah. "Maybe after Christmas?"

"But Maggie said her mother could come get me." The timbre of Sarah's voice turned into a high-pitched whine. She clasped her hands together as if begging might work.

Evie crossed the kitchen, sat at the table, and covered Sarah's hands. "Let me see if it's legal for you to go. I don't know how that works."

Sarah lowered her head and whispered, "Okay, I guess."

"Let me try to get hold of Mrs. Morton." Evie drew a cell phone from her apron pocket. After finding the phone number, she dialed and turned on the speaker.

The phone rang three times before an answering machine responded. "We're sorry. Our office is closed for the holidays. Leave a message. Mrs. Morton will return your call after we reopen on December twenty-seventh. If this is an emergency, press one."

Evie left a message.

Unable to tolerate one more disappointment, Sarah slumped forward, her head on her arms. Christmas with Maggie's family appeared impossible. Mrs. Morton stood in her way. The law stood in her way. Her age kept her at the mercy of strangers again.

"I'm so sorry, Sarah. I'll happily call Maggie's mother to discuss plans to visit the beach next week." Evie scrolled down her contact list and tapped Mrs. McCann's number.

Mrs. McCann listened to Evie's plan. "Oh, the girls will be so happy to see each other, and I welcome something positive right now." The speaker's voice caught and wavered.

"I heard about the passing of your husband. So very sorry. I know how hard that is for everyone."

"Thank you. We expected it, but the reality is tough."

"I agree. No way to prepare for such a loss."

"Is the twenty-eighth convenient? Maggie and I will come to you. We could use the trip."

"The twenty-eighth works for me. Would you like to talk to Sarah?"

"Of course. Maggie wants to talk as well."

Evie turned off the speaker and handed the phone to Sarah. "I'll be outside if you need me."

"Mags, are you there?" Sarah bounced from one foot to the other as she waited for a response.

"Oh, Sarah. This is amazing." Maggie shouted. "Can't wait to see you."

"Is my surfboard waxed and ready to go as promised? We can go surfing right away, have a cookout on the beach, go shopping, go to the boardwalk with friends, and ride the Ferris wheel, and—" Sarah took a breath as she paced the kitchen.

"Slow down. We can do all those things. Told the gang you will be here in a couple of days. They're already planning stuff." Maggie giggled.

Sarah could hear Mrs. McCann talking in the background.

"Gotta' go. Soon, we won't have to worry about a long-distance phone bill."

"Right. See ya next week." Sarah hung up the phone, cheered, and danced around the kitchen.

✤✤✤✤✤

Baking, cleaning, and shopping for the grandchildren filled the five days before Christmas. Christmas Eve and Evie's family visit came faster than Sarah hoped.

Mavis, the oldest, arrived first with five-year-old twin boys who shot out of the car before it came to a complete stop, sped up the back steps, and burst into the kitchen. They threw themselves at Evie, who struggled to keep her balance.

"Whoa, you two. You'll knock Grammie down." Mavis hugged Evie. "Merry Christmas, Mom. She placed several grocery bags on the table. "Here are the side dishes you ordered for tonight. Where is the girl?"

"You mean Sarah?" Evie glanced toward the kitchen door where Sarah stood to avoid all the chaos.

"Uh, yes, Sarah." Mavis followed Evie's gaze. She eyed Sarah from head to toe. "*Hm.*"

Sarah took a step back to avoid her stare. Mavis shrugged, turned her back, and began unloading the grocery bags.

Sarah took an instant dislike to the tall, angular woman. She was attractive enough with her wavy black hair and almost black eyes that seemed to pierce deep into anyone she needed to put in their place.

Mavis redirected her attention as her boys, still in constant motion, pinged off every surface in the kitchen and poked each other in any convenient body part. "Stop it, you two. Sit."

The boys froze in place and strode to the kitchen table, their heads low to avoid their mother's angry stare. She might have been talking to Deacon rather than two energetic children. The fear in their eyes made Sarah's heart ache.

Evie's middle child, Joy, arrived next with a diaper bag slung across her body and a baby carrier filled with a screaming child. "Sorry about the noise. Can't get her to settle down even with a ride in the car." Despite the chaos, Joy's eyes sparkled. Her name suited her. She set her burdens on the kitchen table, hugged her mother and sister, and spied Sarah.

"Oh, you must be Sarah." She crossed the distance between them and opened her arms for a hug. "What a lovely girl you are with that gorgeous red hair. I'm so glad to meet you finally." Her sky-blue eyes, kind and welcoming, lifted Sarah's spirits.

Joy's nephews lit up when they saw her, but they dared not move from their chairs for a hug, so Joy joined them at the table and wrapped her arms around both boys as she kissed them on the head. "You two are getting so big. Love you, love you, love you."

Mavis glowered at her sister, crossed her arms, and clenched her jaw. Joy picked up her now quiet baby and bounced her a couple of times. "You boys must have quieted her down. Good job."

"Where's Steven and Rob?"

"Steven is on his way. He left work late and had to pick up Eloise and the children before heading this way. Rob is with the in-laws for Christmas."

Evie, a baster in her hand, opened the oven door. The tantalizing aroma of a twenty-five-pound turkey stuffed with sage dressing filled the room. Homemade pumpkin, pecan, and apple pies cooled on the windowsill, and spiced apple cider simmered on the stove. Sarah's mouth watered.

"Hullo, everyone," Tom Crane shouted as he backed through the kitchen door, arms full of shopping bags. "Brought wine and champagne." He headed for the refrigerator, placed the bottles inside to chill, closed the door, and kissed Evie long and hard on the mouth.

Mavis, Joy, and Sarah gasped. The twins giggled.

"Merry Christmas." Evie and Tom gazed at each other as if they had a secret. "The gifts are in the car. Be back in a second."

Mavis and Joy, eyebrows raised, busied themselves with the baby. Sarah's stomach churned with dread that tonight might hold unexpected announcements from Evie and Tom. Champagne, a passionate kiss, a family gathering at Christmas—all signs that her life might change again.

Tom returned, arms loaded chin high with packages wrapped in bright red and green designs. Glittery ribbons and tinsel trailed across his arms and shoulders. Sarah thought it was a miracle he opened the screen door without spilling his load. "Better get these gifts under the tree before I drop them."

Mavis and Joy, their children settled, hustled out the kitchen door, and returned with an equal number of brilliantly wrapped offerings to place under the tree.

Sarah bought gift cards for each family, a sweater for Evie, and slippers for Tom. It embarrassed her that she had so little to offer. Only Evie and Tom knew how wealthy she was on paper. She hoped that remained their secret. A red luxury sedan and a silver town car were parked in the driveway, and numerous gift packages in elegant wrapping piled under the Christmas tree told her Evie's daughters had money. She wondered what Steven would add to the overflow and how many hours of chaos it would take to open everything. This could be a long night.

By the time Steven arrived, the boys had been fed; the adults slurred their words a bit and laughed louder with every drink served. Their mother's attention distracted, the twins seized the opportunity to race outside, greet their twelve-year-old cousins, and disappear with them around the side of the house. Sarah grinned from her seat in the dining room as she watched them leave. Their mother hadn't stunted the boys' sense of adventure.

Steven roared into the house, barking orders; his bulging hazel eyes and powerful six-foot frame electrified the room. According to him, everyone had conspired to cause a late start—the girls spent more time than expected at a neighborhood Christmas party, Eloise packed their suitcases incorrectly, his boss made him stay to address a baseless error in a report, and the gas tank was close to empty.

Tom disappeared in the direction of the living room and returned empty-handed. "I'll help Eloise and you unpack, Steven."

"Not necessary," Steven growled. "I'm sure Eloise has a plan to get the job done by now."

Eloise stared at the floor and mumbled. "I'm fine, Tom. Thank you for offering."

Eloise unpacked the car alone. She seemed exhausted, her hair straggling out of a bun. One puffy eye was rimmed in a healing injury's pale purple and yellow, suggesting she had been crying. Petite, bony, and pallid to the point Sarah thought she might pass out, the woman refused all offers of help.

"Where are the girls?" Steven whirled around to face Eloise, who jumped at the sound of his voice. The packages she carried tumbled out of her arms.

"I thought they were behind me." She avoided his angry eyes.

"They should be here. They need to eat." He grunted, "Get someone to help you with those gifts. Hope they're not ruined." Steven flung a dismissive hand at Eloise. "I need a drink."

He poured three fingers of whiskey into a glass and drained it without taking a breath.

"Here, let me help you, Eloise." Joy hugged her sister-in-law. "I'm sure everything is fine." She glared at her brother.

Sarah fled to her room, glad she had eaten with Mavis's twins. Dinner with the adults would be tense. What would happen when Steven discovered his girls and the twins wandered away, out of his control?

"Hey, not so fast, Sarah. I haven't had a chance to wish you Merry Christmas." Cross-legged on the living room floor, Tom sorted through a stack of vinyl records.

"Whatcha' doin' there?" Sarah bent over Tom to get a better look.

"Evie asked me to find Christmas music to calm people down during dinner."

"Stereo? Vinyl? I didn't know anyone had those things any-more."

"They're coming back, you know. Evie and I kept ours. We have quite a collection." He rose with effort. "*Uhm, mm, ow.*"

"You okay?"

"I will be. Hey. Grab a jacket and meet me on the patio. I'll turn on the heaters out there, and we can talk for a while. I can eat left-overs."

"Sure. Meet you there." Sarah hurried outside, grateful for a chance to talk to someone she knew.

Tom had blankets and mugs of mulled cider on each side table. With the outside lights off and the kitchen lights dimmed, they eased into lounge chairs and stared at the sky.

"Look at those stars. Sirius, the Dog Star, is brightest in De-cember. Historians believe it shone over Bethlehem when Jesus was born. I saw it at Point Reyes a few years ago, and it was mag-nificent. No city lights or traffic interfered with its brilliance."

"Tom, I have a question that bothers me."

"What is it? I'll answer if I can."

"Does God give some of his children *things* instead of people?" Sarah stared at her lap. "I mean, I have more money and property than most people, but—" She cleared her throat. "Can anyone live without a family and close friends? They all seem to leave one way or another, and I need to start over with strangers, people who don't know me." Sarah wrung her hands and turned her attention away from Tom.

"Sarah, look at me." Tom swung to a sitting position and covered her hand with his. "I know how that feels to lose those you love. It seems senseless and cruel and leaves you questioning the existence of a loving God. But I can tell you, Sarah, that God loves you. He has a plan for your best life."

"This can't be my best life." She pulled her hand from Tom's grasp.

"In time, it will be. You'll see."

"I'm miserable. Maggie wants me to visit her at the beach, and I must get permission from Mrs. Morton. They're the only people I consider family and have known most of my life."

"Sarah. Tom." Evie appeared at the kitchen door. "It's time for dessert."

"Okay. We'll be there in a minute." He turned to Sarah. "Evie and I need you to join the family now. We have news we want to share with those we care about."

"You're getting married, aren't you?"

"We are. This is our gift from God. I lost my whole family many years ago in a plane crash, and Evie had a marriage that brought her very low. Maybe she'll tell you about it. It's not my story to tell."

"Ooh, I'm so sorry about your family. How awful." This time, Sarah reached for his hand.

"Evie and I were close friends once, but we lost touch during my two years in Vietnam. She married. I married. You and Augusta brought us together again. Coincidence? Maybe, but I doubt it."

"*Hmm.* Maybe." Sarah returned to her stargazing as she considered Tom's beliefs about coincidence. No wonder he understood her loss so well. He had lost a family, too.

Tom said, "Please join us. Evie and I are very fond of you."

Thirty-Eight

ecember twenty-sixth, a new day. Christmas Eve, Christmas Day, Evie and Tom's engagement, endless gift exchanges, screaming children, and rude remarks from Steven's pre-teen twins were all behind her. The house was empty and quiet.

Evie and Tom left early to go into town with the family. They invited her, but she feigned a headache and an upset stomach from all the holiday food. In truth, she did feel ill. As soon as she saw the taillights of their cars leave the driveway, her health improved.

Sarah hurried to her bedroom, grabbed her backpack, and filled it with notebooks, pencils, and pens. She added a yoga mat and blanket. The fog remained near the ground in the winter until the sun burned it off. She expected cold and damp. She needed time in a safe space to sort out her experience with Evie's family, Tom's conversation on the patio, and the engagement announcement.

She grabbed her parka off the hook by the kitchen door, then pocketed a handful of energy bars from the jar on the counter. After descending the back stairs two at a time, she strode out the gate to the side yard. She relaxed the minute she reached the well-worn path that led to her willow tree and solitude.

The azure sky, filled with slow-moving cumulus clouds, showed no sign of rain. A line of fog hugged the ground in the distance. Sarah loved to watch the clouds form and reform to create ever-changing shapes that challenged her imagination. At this hour, few birds bobbed on the pond's surface except for a dozen coots on the far side of the water. She spread her mat on the ground, sat cross-legged, wrapped the blanket around her, and closed her eyes. She drew three deep breaths and allowed the sighing of the surrounding trees, the gentle slap of pond water against the grassy shore, and the calls of distant unseen creatures to fill her with peace. Her body felt light, her mind clear of anxiety, her worries nonexistent.

Dr. Banks, her first and only counselor, taught her to meditate. Sarah pictured her in her long flowing skirts, patient and understanding. Next flashed a memory of Isabelle, the kind gray-haired clerk at the secondhand store, who recognized her discomfort at being there with her aunt. Then, the jolly round school bus driver who cheered her up, shared his lunch with her, and watched out for her. Sarah realized that someone had appeared to help her when needed—doctors, attorneys, teachers, and, most of all, her Great Egret. Maybe Tom was right about God's caring for her.

❦

Evie arrived home at five o'clock without the rest of the family.

"Where is everybody?" Sarah stood on the back porch to greet her.

"In town for a movie and dinner." Evie headed for the corral. An unexpected icy drizzle meant she would have to feed the horses in their stalls.

When Evie reentered the house, thunder, lightning, and hail raged overhead.

"I thought Mrs. McCann and Maggie were due to pick me up on the twenty-eighth.

That's day after tomorrow. What's the plan?"

"I need a hot shower. Tom and Mrs. Morton need to talk with you."

As Evie crossed the kitchen, she increased her pace. Her boots tracked mud across the floor and the carpet that led to her bedroom. "Patience, dear." She closed the door behind her.

Sarah knew that meant the conversation was over. She stood at the closed door for a few minutes, confused. Evie had worn boots in the house, spread mud on the floor and carpet, and trailed water from the kitchen door to her bedroom. None of these behaviors followed Evie's house rules.

Mrs. Morton and Tom wanted to talk with her. *It could be bad news.* Was that why Evie avoided her? A cold sweat formed on her forehead. Her heart began to race. Evie's family hadn't warmed to her. Maybe Evie decided it would be best if she lived somewhere else. Her head throbbed. She fled to the safety of her bedroom, closed the door, lay on her bed, and repeated her mantra. "Breathe in—breathe out."

Sarah dozed, plagued by the return of disturbing dreams. Cardboard figures pointed at her this time, chanting "guilty, guilty, guilty."

"Guilty of what?" she shouted. No answer.

The sound of her voice woke her. It was dark outside. Snarled in bedsheets, her blouse damp with sweat, she glanced at her bedside clock—seven o'clock. Evie might be waiting to serve dinner. A quick shower and a change of clothes revived her.

She headed for the kitchen but smelled no odor of cooking food. A note on the table read: *Help yourself to food if you're hungry. I'm in my room preparing for tomorrow. See you in the morning. Hugs, Evie.*

Another strange behavior from Evie made it obvious that Sarah needed to worry. *More secrets, more changes, and more loss must be coming.* She fixed a tuna sandwich and a glass of milk, took them to her room, and watched a movie on her laptop.

❦

The next day, the house was silent when Sarah opened her bedroom door to join Evie for breakfast. She wandered into the kitchen. *No Evie.* Where was she? She peered out the window over the sink. Her truck was gone. A sense of foreboding slid down her spine and swirled around in her stomach. Had there been news, an emergency? This time, there was no note or explanation.

The shrill ring of the phone startled her. Part of her wanted to know who was calling and why. Another voice inside urged caution. She placed her hand on the receiver. It felt heavier than usual as she withdrew it from its cradle and held it to her ear.

"Hullo?"

"Oh, Sarah, you're up." Evie sounded cheerful, a good sign.

"Where are you?" Sarah wasn't sure she wanted to know the answer.

"I'm at the hospital to pick up Tom and Mrs. Morton. A couple of friends will follow us home. We should be there in an hour or so. I thought I'd let you sleep. There's some quiche in the fridge."

"Thanks. See you soon." Sarah replaced the receiver.

A couple of friends? Who could they be? Was it another foster placement, another change, another problem to face? Sarah tried to eat the quiche, but the lump in her throat made it hard to swallow. She decided to go for a walk with Deacon. It could be her last chance to enjoy his company and her precious wetlands.

The minute she passed through the back gate and headed down the well-worn path toward the pond and her willow tree, her tension eased. Deacon ran ahead. He loved to harass any creature he found along the way. When she approached the pond, Deacon discovered his first prey. He danced in circles around something in the grass, barking and pouncing in its direction.

"Whatcha got there?"

Deacon dashed to her side, away from her, and back again.

"I'm coming. Hold on."

In his best Downward Dog position, Deacon pointed his nose at his victim, red tongue lolling, and glanced at her as if to say, "See what a great creature I have found for you?"

"Let's see what you have this time." Sarah peered in the grass and started to laugh.

Deacon dropped to the ground and lowered his head on crossed paws with a growl and a sigh.

"Sorry, sweet boy, to make fun of you. That's a fine specimen of a turtle shell. The rest of him is hiding inside."

Sarah picked up Deacon's prize and carried it to the pond's edge. Deacon trotted beside her. She scratched him behind the ears as they watched the turtle scuttle to the safety of a log. The dog whined as he turned sad eyes in her direction.

"Good boy." She kissed him on the top of his head. He wagged his tail and trotted along the shore, his eye on the turtle. She sat cross-legged under the willow tree to enjoy the quiet. Deacon joined her, his head in her lap.

The day was warm for December. Broad strokes of wispy clouds painted the pale blue winter sky. A red-tailed hawk dipped and soared on thermal breezes as it hunted for food, then dove to earth to capture its prey. Sarah marveled that many winged carnivores could spy on their victims from such a height.

A Great Egret circled the pond and landed legs first in the water a few yards away. While standing, it stretched its slender neck, pointed its yellow beak upward, and trained one eye toward her. The egret had always been a hopeful sign when it crossed her path. It assured her that all was well.

Deacon's urgent bark interrupted her thoughts. He dashed away and back as he begged her to follow him.

"What is it, Deacon?" In the distance, she heard it, too. Someone called her name. She got up and focused on the sound. It was Evie.

"Okay, boy. Time to see what's up." She was in no hurry to face Evie after last night. Deacon raced ahead, then back, convincing her to move faster.

Sarah rounded the house and stopped to take in the sight. Tom's black SUV, Evie's red truck, and a maroon SUV crowded the drive-way. Satisfied he had done his job herding Sarah home, the dog raced to Evie and circled her legs in greeting.

All three vehicles were empty. "Where is everybody?" Sarah asked.

"They're all inside. We need you to get started with the party." Evie slid her arm through Sarah's elbow and led her up the back steps.

"She's here." Evie stepped back to allow her to enter first. Tom and Mrs. Morton sat at the kitchen table, clapping.

"Hooray. You're here." Maggie dashed across the room and embraced Sarah, who stood frozen with surprise.

"Mags, why are YOU here?" Sarah frowned.

Maggie stepped back. "To see my friend."

"Oh." Numb and uncertain, she searched the faces.

"Sarah, we need you to join us at the table. We need to talk."

Wary of the phrase, *we need to talk*, Sarah lowered her body into the nearest chair.

Evie served a rich chocolate cake and drinks, but Sarah refused to eat. In her mind, the cake represented comfort food. It suggested the meeting required "medicine." Gram always called chocolate cake medicine.

The lively conversation around the table seemed odd. What were these people planning to do?

Tom interrupted the party. "Guess we better get started. Mrs. Morton should go first. She is the one that came up with the plan."

Sarah had learned to be skeptical of the word "plan." No matter what they had decided, she feared the details. Until she turned eighteen, she planned to keep her mouth shut and obey.

"Evie and Tom came to see me about your future. I found a solution for you that might be a good fit." Mrs. Morton pulled a file folder from her briefcase.

Sarah folded her hands on the table. She needed to remain calm, control her emotions, and hide the fear that gripped her. Mrs. Morton had opened file folders before with dire consequences.

She attempted to read the body language of the adults at the table. Evie rested her arms on the table, tented her fingers, and lowered her eyes. Tom sat next to Evie; his shoulders tensed, fingers entwined, knuckles white. He angled his head toward Mrs. Morton as she spoke. Mrs. McCann's eyes darted from person to person; a slight tick flickered on her left eyelid. Maggie grasped Sarah's hand under the table so hard that she flinched.

The sight alarmed her. Why were they so tense? *The news must be worse than she imagined.*

Mrs. Morton continued. "When Augusta died, the McCanns wanted to take care of you, but Mr. McCann was ill, so Mrs. Burrows stepped in to help temporarily. Their situation has changed."

Sarah held her breath. *Now what?* The situation could mean anything.

"Chaplain Crane, Evie, and Mrs. McCann met with me about moving to the beach while you finish high school with Maggie and the friends you knew growing up. What do you think, Sarah? You're old enough to decide where you want to live."

Evie raised her head and gazed intently at Sarah. "I have loved your company, but Tom brought it to my attention that you miss being around people who have known you most of your life. You are welcome to stay here if you want, though. Tom and I are very fond of you."

Sarah was sure she had heard wrong. A few days ago, she begged for a visit with Maggie. It seemed Mrs. Morton offered more.

"Maggie and I have plenty of room, and the high school has agreed to accept you for the second half of the year. You would have to pass a test for the first semester, but we're sure you can ace that."

More words. Sarah could hear what was said, but the meaning was unclear.

"I don't understand what you want." The room began to spin. She stared at the people seated around the table, one by one, as she tried to gain control of her body. Sweat dripped down her forehead. She wiped it with her napkin. She needed to be calm, strong, and in charge of her emotions. *Breathe in—breathe out.* She fought to drive each breath into her abdomen to clear her mind and relax. No luck. Her body went limp.

"Sarah, wake up." Hands patted her face. She sensed cold tile beneath her. *Where was she?* Tom's face appeared above her. "Hey there. Welcome back. You fainted."

She stared at the kitchen ceiling. A spider waited at the center of an intricate web for the hunt to begin. Same spider, but in a different corner. Lucky spider, simple expectations, same job.

Tom helped her to stand. "Here. Sit in this chair for a minute." She eased onto the chair with his help. "What happened? I couldn't understand what was going on."

"Mrs. McCann and Maggie have offered their home to you permanently. It's up to you if you want to stay here with Evie or move to the beach and live with the McCanns."

"I don't believe it. All I asked for was a visit." The room was empty. "Where is everyone?"

"They're in the living room. We felt only one person should stay with you after you came around."

"Maggie was here, right?" Sarah straightened her body, leaned forward, and grabbed Tom's hand.

"She sure was, but she was so upset that her mom decided she needed to leave the room."

Her face warmed. How embarrassing to faint, show weakness, and make such a scene. Maggie would be disappointed. Sarah had always been the rock and the strong one in their friendship. Maggie depended on her.

"Oh, no. I hurt and worried everyone." She slumped in her chair and covered her face with her hands. "I can't face them."

"Yes, we were worried, but we all love you. I know they want to see that you're okay." Tom held his hand out. "Come on. Hold my hand if you need to."

Sarah removed her hands from her face and straightened her back. No way would she hold Tom's hand like a child. "No thanks. I can do this." She stood, wobbled for a second, lifted her chin, and strode into the washroom off the kitchen. She splashed cold water on her face, ran her fingers through her messy hair, and reappeared.

"Let's go. I'm good."

"Atta girl." Tom stood aside to let her pass.

Tom and Sarah strolled into the living room, where the others spoke in muted tones as they waited for news.

"We're here, folks. She's good as new." Tom stood behind Evie and placed his hands on her shoulders.

"Sarah," a chorus of voices greeted her. Everyone on the sofa stood to make room for her to lie down.

"We'll come back tomorrow. Gives you time to decide." Mrs. Morton collected her things and stood to leave.

"Wait. I've decided. I love you, Tom and Evie, but I want to live at the beach. Always have."

"Are you sure? I'll call your attorney. He can be here tomorrow." Mrs. Morton moved to stand beside her.

"For once, I get to decide about my life. Call Mr. McCleary. I'm sure."

On December thirtieth, Sarah left Evie's.

A rain shower tapped on her bedroom window as she finished packing. She slid the window open a couple of inches to breathe in the earthy fragrance of damp wetland vegetation for the last time. She would miss the marsh. It had helped her through many hard times.

"Are your bags ready?" Tom stood at the bedroom door. His offer to drive her and Evie to the beach relieved their concerns about Evie returning home alone, and Tom would keep the conversation positive.

"That's everything." She pointed to suitcases and a few boxes at the end of her bed.

"Whew. That's a lot of stuff, there." Tom grabbed the two largest suitcases and disappeared. He returned with a dolly for the boxes. "Can you handle the rest?"

"Sure." She closed the window and took one last look around the private sanctuary that had rescued her from Augusta's cruelty.

She closed the door with a sigh and headed for the kitchen. Duffle bags hung off both shoulders, and a huge crossbody bag bounced off her hip.

"Morning, kiddo. Your bags and boxes are in the car, ready to go."

She joined Tom and Evie for breakfast. Tom stared at his coffee as he swirled the dark liquid. "Will miss you, Sarah."

"We'll both miss you terribly." Evie poured coffee into all three mugs. "Are you still happy with your decision to leave? You could change your mind, you know, right up until we get to the beach."

It pained Sarah to know that her move caused Tom and Evie discomfort. "It hurts me to leave you, too, but the beach and Maggie always remind me of my parents and Gram. I'll be back to visit you this summer for your wedding."

Evie glanced at the clock. "We better get started, then. Tom and I agree that your decision is best for you, but I hate seeing you go."

All three stood at once, took their plates to the sink, and headed out the door. Deacon greeted them at the bottom of the steps. Sarah knelt and hugged him so tightly that he fought to escape her grasp.

"Come on, Deacon. Let's go." She led him to the dog yard, kissed his head, and locked him behind the gate. Her throat ached from the effort to hold back her tears as he whined, barked, and rattled the gate.

She stared out the back window of Tom's SUV at Deacon, Evie's cottage, and the horses lined up at the white corral fence until Tom turned left on the dirt road and headed for the highway.

"You okay back there?" Evie glanced at her in the rearview mirror.

"Yeah. I'm good." Sarah turned her attention away from the back window to face the direction she was going, forward.

Thirty-Nine

Sarah closes her laptop and reviews her story timeline taped to the walls around her work area. Tom Crane's assurance that helpers appear when we need them proves true. She marvels at the unbroken line of people who pulled her through her childhood. Tom, a widower at the age of ninety-five, still insists there are no coincidences. In transposing her journals, she has to admit he had a point.

Twenty-eight years ago, Sarah left Evie's house to live with Maggie and Marcie McCann. Her team of saviors. Dr. Morris, Mrs. Morton, Tom Crane, and Evie Burrows weave in and out of her story with Augusta. Her definition of family is altered because of them.

As she revisits her childhood, she realizes how thankful she is that Dr. Banks and Gram encouraged her to record her life in journals. Many details of her past had been forgotten or buried. Reflecting on her journey causes great pain but reveals a pattern. Helpers appeared in the difficult chapters of her life to comfort and move her forward. She believes they still do.

"Good morning, my friend. I've been standing in the doorway for a while. Lost in your work again?" Maggie pads across the living room and looks over her shoulder. "Your front door is unlocked."

Sarah swivels around. "Guess I better keep it locked. No telling who will wander in." She stands and hugs her friend. "I thought you were in Monterey today."

"I was at the Monterey Bay Aquarium by invitation of the Director of Marine Biology Research." Maggie takes her hands in hers. "I got the research job. I start on Monday. I'm in the game again."

"Fabulous. I spoke with my publisher today. She loves my book idea so much that she offered me ten thousand dollars to develop it as a memoir. Who knew my public panic attack would interest anyone?"

"I knew it wouldn't hurt your career. Shared experiences make you human. Your fans will buy it in bulk." Maggie pulls a bottle of expensive champagne from her bag.

"What's this?" Sarah removes two flutes from the china cabinet.

"Time to celebrate two resilient middle-aged women starting their next forty-plus years, hopefully wiser than they were in their first half." Maggie pops the cork and fills the glasses.

"We'd better be wiser after all we've been through—marriages, divorces, illness, and much loss. Let's sit on the porch swing and enjoy the view."

"You know, we are back at White Sands Beach, neighbors again. It's as if we never left." Maggie settles on the swing.

"Don't ask me to build sandcastles, though."

"If I ever sat cross-legged on the beach now, I'd never get up. I would have to go out with the tide."

Sarah grabs her jacket, steps onto the porch, and opens her arms to embrace the salty, sweet air and the powerful rhythm of the waves that pound the rocks along the shore.

"Life is good." Sarah raises her glass and joins Maggie on the swing. "Amen to that."

Author's Notes

Special thanks to my editor, teacher, and mentor, Gini Grossenbacher, who taught me the craft of writing, guided my writing through her expert critiques, and shepherded me through the many stages of the publication process. Her tenacious encouragement kept me headed toward my goal of publication.

To the many fellow writers, critique groups and teachers who provided input on my writing through the years, my gratitude for my growth in and expanded knowledge of the craft we all share.

To the many friends who took interest in my goals even when I faltered, who expressed excitement when they saw the cover of *Full Circle* for the first time, your contribution to my life and to this achievement enriches me every day.

About the Author

Sandra Heaton lives in Northern California with her husband and an aging ginger cat named Baby. Though her creative nonfiction pieces have been published in *Caregiver* and Inspire Christian Writers anthologies, this is her first novel. The characters are based on a combination of people she has met and spent time with throughout her life. Sarah's panic attacks, search for community, and personal resilience represent the author's true-life experiences.